29/11

# Murder at
# Ashton Steeple

## Karen Baugh
## MENUHIN

Image by Shutterstock, Mo Wu,
Hidcote Manor Garden, Cotswolds

First paperback and ebook edition.

ISBN 979-8-8525960-1-7

*For*
*Michael and Eve Williams-Jones*
*Dear friends*

# CHAPTER 1

**May 1923**

'And it went right into his heart.' Constable Fossett nodded earnestly.

Swift leaned on the battered oak table for a better look at the long, slim shaft of an arrow, then moved it carefully into a ray of bright sunshine. The light played across the blond wood and dark-red stain reaching four inches down to the steel head. 'Any fingerprints?'

'I tried brushing powder on it, but it wouldn't stick, so I don't know, sir,' Constable Fossett admitted; a young lad with thick brown hair and brows, a long thin face and ready smile. He spoke with the local Cotswolds accent, which was hardly a surprise as he'd grown up in the area.

'It's designed for target practice,' I said, having used them at school.

'Aye, you're right, Major Lennox.' Fossett sounded impressed. 'I found a load of them in a shed near some big round targets in the grounds.'

We were sitting around the reading table in the library

at my home, the Manor at Ashton Steeple, which Swift had designated our 'incident room'. We'd returned late the previous evening from Lancashire after uncovering a particularly vicious murderer.

Swift had been itching to spring into action after hearing about the death in the village, and first thing this morning he'd telephoned DCI Billings at Scotland Yard. Billings had barked 'get on with it', which was his usual response, and Swift had summoned Ashton Steeple's local bobby for his report. Constable Fossett had arrived almost on the instant.

'Coffee, sirs.' Greggs entered with a tray laden with silver coffee pot, the usual cups and whatnots, and a freshly baked chocolate cake smothered with burnt butter icing. 'Lady Persi and Lady Florence helped Cook make the cake.'

Persi was my lovely wife and Florence had wedded Swift a few years ago at her family castle in the Scottish highlands.

Constable Fossett's face lit up. 'Now that's a proper cake, that is!'

Swift looked less pleased at the interruption. He was keen to continue and had already opened a brand new notebook in preparation.

'Large slice for me, old chap.' I gave my butler a grin. I'd missed the comforts of home, even though we'd only been away a few days.

Greggs placed the tray on my cluttered desk near the unlit fireplace, then picked up the silver coffee pot. He was about to pour when a very small Jack Russell puppy raced in to run rapid circles around us, yapping in excitement, then dashed over to the butler and began snapping at his ankles.

'Sir, sir!' Greggs was almost dancing on tiptoe, the puppy at his heels.

'No,' Swift shouted and grabbed the fly swat lying on the table, raising it in the air. 'Nicky, stop that.' The pup stopped to stare at him for a second, then turned tail and dashed out. 'I'm sorry, Greggs.' Swift put the fly swat down. 'We're trying to teach him some manners.'

'I cannot and will not wear boots, sir.' Greggs' colour had heightened, his chins wobbling in indignation. 'Nor am I able to wield a fly swat at any given moment.'

'You could try leather gaiters.' I'd already suggested this as a perfectly sensible solution, which he'd completely ignored.

The puppy had been found as a stray, and Swift's two-year-old son, Angus, had become besotted with the little tyke. The pup was a typical Jack Russell: white with black and tan patches, a tendency to over-excitement, and a determined ankle biter. The household had taken to wearing boots at all times, but Greggs had resolutely refused. Greggs and I had been through the war together. He was a stalwart old soldier, fond of Irish whiskey and amateur dramatics, with an eye for the ladies. Neither boots nor gaiters were his style.

'Right, can we get on?' Swift turned back to the arrow on the table, his dark eyes fixed in concentration.

'I'll have two sugars in my coffee, please,' Constable Fossett told Greggs as he began pouring.

'Fossett,' Swift reminded him, 'carry on with your report.'

'Aye, all right, sir.' The constable shifted in his chair to face the former inspector. 'Now, that arrow was what killed Mr Devlin Saunders the day before last at Ashton Hall.' Fossett pulled a small notebook from the top pocket of his police uniform, and flicked through the curled pages. 'He was found at twenty-five minutes past nine in the morning, lying on the balcony outside of his bedroom. It was the gardener who found him...well, he didn't actually *find* him, he *saw* him.'

'Wait...' Swift was jotting down notes. 'Where was the gardener?'

'In the garden, sir.' Fossett's eyes were on Greggs as he cut the cake into large slices and carefully placed three pieces onto china plates.

'So the gardener was standing below the balcony?' Swift continued.

'I'll have that one, Greggs,' I said and pointed to the biggest slice.

'Very well, sir,' he intoned and placed the plate in front of me. The scent of rich, dark chocolate filled the air.

Swift turned to the young constable. 'Fossett?'

'Oh, sorry, sir.' He peered at his notebook. 'The gardener was walking past the house and saw Mr Saunders lying next to the fancy railings round the balcony. He went and knocked at the back door. The gentry were having breakfast, and the servants were serving, and no-one but Cook

4

could hear, and she were out of sorts, so she didn't come right away.' Fossett launched into a stream of explanation which set Swift writing furiously.

Greggs placed cups of steaming coffee in front of us, then took a yellow cloth from his tailcoat pocket and began dusting leather-bound books on the shelves. I knew why he was doing it, he wanted to listen to the tale; the whole district was agog to hear of the appalling murder at the big house in the centre of the village.

I cut a forkful of cake as Swift sipped coffee.

He put his cup down. 'Name?'

'Fossett, sir.'

'Not your name. The gardener's.'

'Oh, aye.' Fossett grinned ruefully. 'He's called Mr Bent, an' he is bent too, his back's gone, poor old codger.'

'Were the household eating breakfast upstairs or downstairs?' Swift asked.

'They've got a dining room and a breakfast room, sir. Both of them are on the ground floor, and so's the drawing room,' Fossett replied. 'But it's not a proper big house. Not like this.' He indicated the Manor.

Swift turned a fresh page. I suppose I should have taken notes too, but I was eating cake, so I didn't.

'How did the gardener see the body on the balcony if he's bent?' I asked.

Fossett's eyes widened. 'Oooh, I never thought of that. I suppose I'll have t'go and talk to him again.'

'We'll do that.' Swift made a note.

'What was Saunders wearing?' I asked.

Fossett flicked back through his pocket book. 'A green velvet dressing gown over his pyjamas, which were also green and had his initials on them, in gold. The arrow didn't go through the dressing gown, just his pyjama top, because his dressing gown was open,' he explained in convoluted manner. 'I dunno where they are, now. At the morgue I suppose.'

Swift made another note.

'Where exactly had the arrow entered the body?' Swift glanced up.

'Just here.' Fossett pointed to a spot on his blue police jacket between the fourth and fifth buttons.

'Below the sternum,' I said. 'Which direction was the arrow pointing?'

'Going up, sir, as though he'd been shot from the ground,' Fossett said then took a big bite of cake.

I finished mine, wiped my hands on the napkin, and then my tweed trousers before reaching for the arrow. 'There are tiny spots of blood all the way along the shaft and on the feathers.' I pointed to them.

'I know,' Swift replied. 'It's an anomaly.'

'Is it?' Fossett's brown eyes rounded. 'You can hardly see them.'

I rolled the arrow between finger and thumb to better observe it. Although of a standard design, it was beautifully made, with a simple head of steel shaped like a sharpened bullet. 'The arrow would have passed through the fabric, pierced Saunders' body, and the flesh would have sealed around it,' I said.

Greggs had inched closer, duster in hand, to peer over my shoulder. I pretended not to notice.

Fossett leaned in for a closer look. 'It can't have sealed up because loads of blood had come out of the wound. Why are you bothered by them little spots?'

'It's an anomaly,' I repeated Swift's scant explanation, which only confused the lad further.

He wasn't ready to give in. 'But it might have happened when it was pulled out by the bloke who did the post mortem.'

'That would have been some hours later. The blood would have pooled in the lower part of the body by then. It wouldn't spatter out,' Swift explained.

Fossett remained bemused.

I switched tack. 'When's Dr Fletcher due?'

'Any moment now, sir,' Greggs replied, then *harrumphed* because he'd given himself away.

'Perhaps you could go and let him in,' I suggested dryly. 'If you're finished in here.'

'I was about to do so, sir,' he remarked, then puffed up his paunch and left the room in a dignified huff.

'What happened when the gardener alerted the household?' Swift finished his cake and returned to questioning.

Fossett was still staring at the arrow, but raised his eyes. 'Erm…well he said that Cook shouted at him to go away, but then he told her that Mr Saunders was dead up on the balcony, and there was blood dripping off onto the… Oooh wait a minute!' Fossett's eyes opened wide. 'That's how Mr Bent knew there was something wrong. It was the blood dripping onto the terrace below the balcony.' He gave a grin.

'Obviously. Carry on.' Swift leaned over his notebook, a furrow between dark brows, the angles of his face sharply accentuated by sunlight and shadows.

'Well, according to Mr Bent, it got all frantic. The cook ran shrieking into the breakfast room and Mrs Saunders began shouting, and that got them all a'clamouring. The butler ran upstairs to the balcony, but he was overcome and had to go and lie down. Bent said Lady Clementine was the only one with any sense, she telephoned the doctor, and then she called the station, which I answered, because there's only me there, now. All the rest are retired or sent to the bigger stations. Anyway, I jumped on my bike and pedalled fast as I could and arrived the same time as Dr Fletcher.' He paused to drain his coffee cup. 'Dr Fletcher told me to telephone you, Major Lennox, because he said you're a proper detective now, but Lady Persi said you was busy detecting in Lancashire, so I called up the main station in Oxford.' He rattled on.

'Did a detective inspector come and visit the scene?' Swift had turned a page and was filling it with neat notes.

'Aye, one of them came.' Fossett nodded. 'But it was almost an hour before he arrived. He had a flat tyre on the way, so it was just me and Dr Fletcher to start with.'

'What did the Inspector say?' Swift continued.

'Well, things had calmed down by the time he turned up,' Fossett continued. 'I'd gone and bought a box of chalk from the post office so I could draw a line around Mr

Saunders' body.' He looked earnestly at Swift. 'I couldn't do it all the way around because the blood would have ruined the chalk. Anyway, Dr Fletcher declared he was dead – which anyone could have told him. Then he said I should question the folk in the house and take their fingerprints, but they was mostly toffs and they just shouted at me.' He sounded aggrieved. 'Even after I told them I was the law! Then Dr Fletcher ordered them to sit down and write out statements. In the end they did, but it wasn't much use, because, like I said, they were all eating breakfast when Mr Saunders was found.'

'Statements,' Swift demanded and held out his hand.

Fossett opened the battered leather satchel he'd brought with him and extracted some crumpled papers. 'Here they are, sir, and there's a big sheet of paper in there with all their fingerprints and their names on. And you should have heard the fuss they made about doing that!'

'Did you use fingerprint powder on the balcony?' Swift took the sheaf of papers and began leafing through them.

'Yes, sir.' Fossett nodded. 'But I only found Mr Saunders' prints, there weren't any others.'

'Didn't you think that odd?' Swift glanced up.

'I did, sir, and I asked the maid about it, and she said Mr Saunders liked everything neat and tidy and she'd been made to clean it when the family arrived from London.'

'Hmm.' Swift returned to the statements he was reading. 'Well done, Constable.'

Fossett beamed in response.

'The Oxford inspector didn't want to keep the papers?'

I was surprised because Swift was an ex-inspector of Scotland Yard, and obsessive about procedure and paperwork.

'I think he did, sir, but he'd called Scotland Yard because Mr Saunders was rich and came from London, and the Yard said Inspector Swift and you would be doing the investigation, so he just asked a lot of questions and went off when they took the body away.'

Swift had been reading through the statements and stopped at one written in large, untidy writing. 'This one is the gardener's, and he says he had already passed the terrace shortly before nine and there was no sign of blood on the terrace at that time.'

'I know, sir, and the gentry had all been together for breakfast from nine o'clock,' Fossett explained.

Swift shook his head, crossed a sentence out in his notebook and wrote a lengthy paragraph below it.

'Have you secured the scene of death and searched the victim's room?' Swift continued questioning.

'I did, sir, and went back again yesterday to do more fingerprint powdering. And they were even more annoyed with me!' Fossett said in exasperation. 'Demanding I should let them go back to London. I said they couldn't because they had to wait until you and Major Lennox came and interviewed them.'

'Good.' Swift nodded. 'Have any of them actually left?'

'Don't think so, sir.' Fossett frowned in seriousness. 'I told them I'd have to arrest them if they tried.'

My chubby black cat, Mr Tubbs, jumped onto the table

and sat down in a patch of sunlight. I watched him, waiting for mischief. He shut his eyes, feigning innocence.

Sounds of car tyres crunching on the gravel were heard outside, then dogs barking somewhere in the house, followed by voices in the hallway.

A few moments later, Greggs ushered in Dr Cyril Fletcher, nattily dressed as usual in plus fours, mustard-coloured waistcoat, and spotted dickie bow.

'Heathcliff, old chap, heard you'd returned. This is a rum do! Who'd have thought it, and in Ashton Steeple too.' He shook my hand, grinning with affection. Cyril Fletcher had been our family doctor since before my birth almost thirty-two years ago, and despite his age, remained trim and energetic.

Fossett had leapt to his feet as the doctor arrived, and Swift stood too, smoothing down his grey city suit.

'Dr Fletcher,' Swift introduced himself, holding out his hand to shake the doctor's.

'Ah, so you're the blighter who tried to have Heathcliff hanged!' Fletcher grinned behind his trim moustache. 'Haha, that was a near miss, and now you're working together to hunt down villains. Bet you didn't think that would be the outcome, did you!'

'I didn't anticipate it at the time, sir, no.' Swift was genial in reply.

It was true Swift had tried to convict me of murder at Melrose Court, and he'd have seen me hang if I hadn't uncovered the culprit myself.

Fletcher eyed the remains of the cake.

Greggs was quick to notice. 'May I cut you a slice, sir?'

'You certainly may, old chap.' Fletcher pulled out a vacant chair and sat down. 'And a cup of strong black coffee to go with it.'

We decided we'd take more of everything, and Greggs served the cake and topped up our cups before going off with the empty coffee pot. I poured Tubbs a saucer of cream, which he insisted on dipping his sooty black paw into rather than lapping it, like proper cats.

'Dr Fletcher, sir,' Fossett began. 'You saw the arrow sticking out of Mr Saunders, but the Major and Inspector says there's an amanoly.'

'Anomaly,' I corrected him.

'Is there, by Jove?' Fletcher said. 'Well, I suppose that's why you're detectives and I'm a mere country doctor.'

# CHAPTER 2

We asked Cyril Fletcher to tell us what he'd seen and listened over coffee and cake.

'Saunders was lying on his side close to the iron railings, facing out towards the garden,' the doctor explained. 'The body was still warm when I reached him.'

'What time was that?' Swift was determined to extract every detail.

Fletcher pulled a large gold watch from his waistcoat and stared at it, for some reason. 'It would have been around quarter to ten. What do you think, young man, was that about it?' He turned to Fossett, who was mid-cake.

'Mmmm.' He nodded agreement.

Fletcher slipped the fob watch back in his waistcoat pocket. 'I assumed Saunders had been leaning over the railing and someone shot the arrow straight up at him. Strange sort of thing to do, but there you are. Anyway, I made the necessary examinations, and young Fossett did his best to questions the inhabitants, although they were a bolshy lot, apart from the divine Lady Clementine, of course.' A twinkle gleamed in his eye as he spoke her name. 'The inspector from Oxford turned up eventually, and around midday the ambulance took Saunders off to the mortuary.'

'The Oxford mortuary?' Swift checked.

'It was, and I had to go all the way there myself yesterday at the inspector's request and attend the post mortem,' Fletcher said, then sighed. 'I'd really rather see patients while there is some flicker of life left in them, but it had to be endured. There was little of note about the man, other than the arrow through his chest, of course.'

'What were the contents of his stomach?' Swift continued writing, the frown of concentration more pronounced.

'Just coffee. His bloods were clear of poison and what have you,' Fletcher replied. 'The medical examiner has requested more tests from the laboratory. It may be a day or two, as yesterday was Sunday and they weren't working. It's quite a science now – pathology. Everything's changing, and rather too quickly for my liking.'

My mind was on the murder, because something wasn't adding up. 'Were there any cuts in the flesh around the shaft?' I asked.

'Yes, there was a small nick which had allowed the blood to leak out.' Fletcher took a meditative moment. 'I suppose one would expect the skin to close around the shaft as it went in, although it was a first for me.' He brightened. 'We don't have many murders around here, do we Heathcliff?'

'One is more than enough excitement.' I gave him a

grin because I was fond of the fellow, even if he did insist on calling me Heathcliff – the ridiculous name I'd been saddled with by my romantically minded mother.

Swift made another note. 'What was Saunders like?'

'Heathcliff can tell you.' Fletcher nodded toward me. 'You encountered him at that dreadful dinner last month, didn't you old chap?'

'So did you,' I countered.

'I was ensconced among the ladies,' he chipped back.

I frowned. 'Saunders was exceptionally loud, braying with laughter, and made himself the centre of attention – the sort of blaggard best avoided whenever possible.'

'I meant what did he look like,' Swift replied with a touch of exasperation.

'Ah, well, you should have said,' Cyril Fletcher bounced back. 'Silver hair, overweight, aged sixty-three and in reasonably good health, apart from being dead, of course.'

'Everyone said he liked to flash money about,' Fossett added.

'He did,' Cyril Fletcher agreed, then raised a brow. 'The very antithesis of the country squire.'

'Eeeeeeuuuummmm!' A loud screeching noise preceded a small boy who came running in, holding his arms outstretched in aeroplane mode.

He was immediately followed by our boot boy, Tommy. 'Sorry, sirs, he's the Red Baron, he's been looking at the pictures in my comic book…'

Angus raced around behind our chairs, continuing the racket.

Tommy chased after him, but came to a sudden halt as he spotted the arrow. 'Oooh, is that the one what killed Mr Saunders, sir? Can I touch it, can I? Everyone's wanting to hear about it. When I get back to school, I can tell them I touched the actual arrow!' He stood staring, eyes wide in a freckled face, his school tie adrift, spots of egg on his grey jumper, his trousers too short and socks rucked around his ankles.

'Why aren't you at school?' I demanded.

'Forgot my lunch, sir. Teacher told me to fetch it during break.' He reached a hand toward the arrow as Swift made a grab for Angus.

'Oh, Angus!' Florence came in, arms outstretched. 'I said you must be quiet while Daddy's working. I'm so sorry, my love, he's full of beans today.' She took him from Swift, who gave her a soppy grin as he let the boy loose. She'd tied a green apron over her white broderie anglaise frock.

Dr Fletcher leapt to his feet. 'Lady Florence.'

'Oh, goodness, how do you do?' She clasped Angus with one hand and held out the other. Fletcher kissed it with a gallant bow.

'Lennox.' Persi came in. 'Greggs is trying to catch a wasp in the kitchen and Cook is in a flap. She's frightened there's a nest.'

I stood up, pleased to see her despite the interruption, and went to kiss her on the cheek. 'Hello, Kitsy.'

She smiled. 'Are you going to insist on calling me that?'

'I might.' I grinned. After Swift and I had returned last

evening, we'd all shared a bottle of champagne. Persi had told us that she'd been telling Angus a story about a clever cat called Kitsy, and I'd teased her about it. 'You can be my Kitsy.' I gazed at her, still astonished that this lovely woman was now my wife. She looked beautiful in a blue dress the colour of her eyes, and a matching band to hold back blonde hair.

That made her laugh. 'I may have to call you Heathcliff then.' She turned to place her hand on Tommy's shoulder. 'We've come to shepherd the miscreants out.'

'Oh, m'lady, can't I stay?' he protested. 'I'll be ever so quiet, I can stand here and no-one will even notice...'

'Back to school, Tommy,' I ordered, suspecting he'd forgotten his lunch deliberately. 'Or PC Fossett will have to take your name down.'

'He already knows my name. He knows everyone. His Mum teaches the little'uns at school.'

'I'll come and see the headmaster if you don't get back to class smartish.' Fossett wagged a warning finger and tried to look stern.

'Off you go.' Persi steered Tommy towards the door, then called back over her shoulder, 'Lennox, we're planning a picnic lunch to eat in the garden later.'

Florence still held the squirming Angus in her arms. 'Dr Fletcher, would you like to join us in the parlour when you have finished here?' She spoke in a soft Scottish accent.

Fletcher had remained on his feet. 'I'd be absolutely delighted, Lady Florence.' He beamed and turned to us. 'I believe we're done, gentlemen?'

17

'For the moment,' Swift agreed, the smile still lingering on his lips as he gazed after his wife and child.

'Excellent.' Fletcher straightened his bow tie. 'Now, do give Lady Clementine my best regards,' he instructed. 'Toodle-pip!' He followed Florence out with a jaunty step.

Swift straightened up and reverted to stern police mode. 'Right, we'll go and examine the scene.'

Fossett jumped to his feet, scattering cake crumbs from his uniform. 'Righto, sir.'

'I meant Major Lennox.' The lad's face fell, and Swift added, 'But I suppose you could be useful.'

Fossett nodded eagerly. 'I can show you where the body was, and the shed and targets...'

'Come on.' I rose to my feet.

Mr Fogg, my little golden spaniel, came rushing in, tail wagging frantically; he gave a woof for no reason, then dashed out again. Tubbs decided to go with him and bounded out, black tail in the air.

'Can I ride with you, sir?' Fossett hurried to catch up. 'I've never been in a Bentley.'

'You have a police bicycle, Fossett,' Swift reminded him.

'Yes, sir,' the lad muttered and slowed his pace.

The car was where I'd left it on the turning circle in front of the house. I paused on the doorstep, the long driveway bordering the flower-filled garden opening ahead of me. I felt the sun on my face, breathed in the scent of rich earth and fresh-cut grass, and let out a long sigh.

The Manor had been built back in Queen Anne's time; red brick, stone porch, sash windows on three storeys, all under a slate roof. It had been our family home since its construction, but despite my best efforts, the house was suffering from creeping decrepitude. Funds were required to keep it upright and watertight, funds I didn't have, and the situation was playing on my mind – so were the warnings from my financial adviser.

'Come on, Lennox, I'll crank her up.' Swift cut into my brooding.

I shook the thoughts from my mind and climbed into the driver's seat. Swift turned the engine until it caught, then hopped in and we raced off in a blast of exhaust fumes. The village was further by road than along the old cart track up on the ridge, but I preferred the smooth tarmac winding between high hedgerows of hawthorn and rowan.

Spring had brought its own enchantment; trees freshly verdant and dappled with fragrant sprigs of white blossom, fields flushed vibrant green, and birds trilling from every shrub and thicket.

We found the gates to Ashton Hall closed. I slowed to a halt and sounded my horn. Nobody came. I contemplated the fine scroll work the blacksmith had wrought into the design and tipped with gold leaf, then hooted again. Fossett arrived on his bicycle, pink-faced under his police helmet, having sped down the hill to brake to a stop beside us.

'Took the track, sirs,' he panted as he climbed off his bike to lean it against the high stone wall. 'I see they've shut the gates, an' I can't say I blame them.' He pulled off his bicycle clips. 'Every man and his wife has been stopping to stare into the garden, and you can't even see the balcony from here, so they're wasting their time.' He continued chattering as he pushed the gates open. 'Now you just go along and I'll shut them behind…'

He may have said more but I'd put my foot down and accelerated away up the long drive, spraying gravel in my wake.

Ashton Hall was situated in the centre of Ashton Steeple village, but set far back from the road in its own walled grounds. It had been built a little over twenty years ago in a neo-Georgian style, with an imposing portal fronting a three-storeyed facade and large windows. It was a handsome house, showy rather than homely, and in rigidly proportioned style. Owners had come and gone, mostly city types, who barely skimmed the surface of local life before flitting off again.

'What do you know of the family, Lennox?' Swift asked, as we approached the mahogany front door.

'Nothing.'

'You had dinner with them last month,' he reminded me.

'Yes, and I'm not doing it again.'

He threw me a sideways glance as he rapped the brass knocker.

A plump man with thinning dark hair, oiled and cut in a sleek style above a smooth face, opened the door. 'Yes?'

'Police.' Swift didn't prevaricate.

The man's brows drew together. 'Oh, not again.' He was

around forty, dressed in a red blazer, cream flannels, and pink shirt with a flamboyant cravat in ivory silk.

'This is a murder enquiry.' Swift stepped forward.

The man backed away as we entered. 'Well, I daresay it is but...' He took a closer look at me. 'I say, aren't you the chap from the Manor?'

'Yes. Where's the butler?' I replied.

'You may well ask.' He sounded indignant; I recalled the popinjay, he was some sort of business associate of the dead man. 'He's packing. It's ridiculous. What the devil is the world coming to when servants are able to just pack up and leave of their own accord.'

'They're servants not slaves.' Swift's lean features sharpened. We walked into the grand hallway, black and white marble tiles on the floor, a sweeping staircase to the right and a grandiose fireplace opposite. Mahogany doors led off, the ubiquitous umbrella stand in the corner and an oval table with a huge vase of flowers in the centre.

'Well, obviously I'm perfectly aware they aren't slaves, but they should at least work their notice,' he argued, 'and—'

'Who are you?' Swift cut in, fixing dark eyes on the man.

'Cardhew. The Honourable Sebastian Cardhew, actually.' Cardhew stretched his neck, trying to appear haughty. He failed.

'Why must people keep knocking on the door?' A woman marched down the stairs, middle-aged, coiffed chestnut hair, subtly maquillaged and dressed entirely in black. 'Who is it, Sebastian?'

'Police,' Swift repeated. 'We've been sent to investigate—'

'About time,' she cut across him. 'I hope you are from Scotland Yard, because my husband was a very wealthy man and I have been expecting someone with authority to take charge.' She spoke in loud, plummy tones and advanced on high heels clicking across the tiles. I recognised her as Mrs Margaret Saunders.

'We've been authorised by Scotland Yard...' Swift tried again.

'He's not police.' Sebastian Cardhew was listening to Swift, but pointed to me. 'He lives at the Manor. He came to your "launch party" last month, don't you remember?'

I frowned at him. He took a step backwards.

'Oh, tush, Sebastian. That's our neighbour, Sir Heathcliff.' Mrs Saunders' tone suddenly warmed as she turned her gaze to me. 'Someone mentioned you were a consultant detective to the Yard. Well, at least we can be assured this ghastly episode will be treated with discretion.' She advanced with hand held out for me to peck.

I did the honours. 'This isn't a social call, Mrs Saunders.' I spoke coolly. 'And it's Lennox.'

'Ah, you are on duty, dear Major Lennox, and I have not forgotten that you are our gallant war hero.' She simpered unconvincingly. 'But really there's no need to stand on ceremony. We are neighbours, and friends, after all. Now, may I offer you coffee, or perhaps something stronger?' She arched her thin brows and forced a smile to her painted lips.

'We'd like to see the balcony, please.' Swift remained professionally polite.

'Oh, yes, I'm sure you would.' She raised a hand to her forehead. 'Dear Sebastian, would you take them to...' her voice trailed off as she adopted a stricken pose.

'I suppose I must,' Cardhew replied.

Mrs Saunders had pulled a lace handkerchief from somewhere and wafted it in our direction. 'I shall be in the drawing room.'

# CHAPTER 3

We followed the Honourable Sebastian Cardhew upstairs, the thick beige carpet dulling our footsteps. Swift glanced back at the hallway, probably wondering where Fossett was.

'We've no idea who killed him.' Cardhew continued along a wide corridor with gilded furniture, and wallpaper in shades of pastel peach. 'It's becoming intolerable. The kitchen staff are quite unruly and the butler is doing nothing about it.'

'What's his name?' Swift demanded.

'Ackroyd. He simply announced he was going without so much as a by-your-leave. Why should he be allowed to go? We were ordered to stay until your arrival,' Cardhew complained.

'Has Ackroyd been employed here long?' I asked.

'No, and Margaret said he was supplied by an agency, which I suppose is why he thinks he can go whenever he pleases.' Cardhew came to a door set in a grand portal.

A sign had been pinned to it: *"Police don't go in. PC Fossett."* It obviously wasn't secured, as Cardhew opened it without hesitation. He led us into a large, luxurious room filled with sunlight.

'Why isn't this door locked?' Swift demanded.

'Oh, Margaret wanted the maid to clean it. The constable had left powder everywhere,' Cardhew replied in bored tones.

Swift looked furious. 'Where's the key?'

'In the door.' Cardhew pointed to where it was sticking out of the lock.

'She seems to be taking her husband's death stoically,' I remarked.

'That's the way she is,' Cardhew agreed, entirely missing the irony in my voice. 'An admirable woman, perfectly poised, even in the face of disaster.'

'Which disaster?' I asked.

'Well, any disaster.' He sounded rattled.

Swift had stopped to survey the room. The bed was made, a green silk quilt smoothed across its width, matching silk pillows propped against the burr walnut headboard. Despite the size of the bed, it appeared small in the room, where everything had been designed to complement in colour and style, including the thick rugs covering the floor.

'Has anything been moved since Saunders was killed?' Swift went to a gleaming walnut dressing table under a window and gazed at a range of lotions and aftershave in cut-glass bottles.

'I don't think so. Ask the constable,' Cardhew replied. 'Can I go now?'

'No,' Swift said. 'Tell us what happened the morning Saunders was killed.'

Cardhew puffed out his smooth cheeks, but complied. 'The butler served Devlin coffee on the balcony at eight o'clock, which was his usual morning routine. I'd come along shortly afterwards, just to have a quick chat with him. I hadn't dressed or completed the ablutions, you know...' He wafted a plump hand aimlessly. 'Devlin wasn't in a particularly receptive mood, so I left after a few minutes. The butler had already made the bed. Devlin liked everything in orderly fashion.'

'What time did you leave him?' I beat Swift to the question.

'About ten past eight, something like that.' He assumed a nonchalant air. 'Not that it matters, it was obviously done by an outsider.'

'Why do you think that?' I eyed the blighter.

'Well, it wasn't one of us.' He spoke with assurance, which faltered under my gaze. 'We were all together at breakfast, you can't possibly think—'

'Did Mrs Saunders share this bedroom with her husband?' Swift interrupted his protestations.

'No, no – not that it's any of my business.' Cardhew's voice rose an octave.

Swift strode over to a pair of French windows, opened them wide and stepped out onto the balcony beyond. I strolled out behind him, feeling the warmth almost sultry in the sunshine. The aspect was south-facing with fine views over impeccably cut lawns, trimmed yew hedges, and bordered by majestic trees.

Saunders' bedroom dominated the east wing, the balcony jutted out from the house supported on stone pillars above a large terrace. There were no furnishings other than a large wicker chair and low table next to it. It obviously hadn't rained in the last couple of days because the chalk outline drawn on the quarry tiles was still evident, as was the blood stain, which had dried and turned a tarry reddish colour. Residue of grey fingerprint powder was still visible on some of the ironwork surrounding the balcony.

Swift turned to Cardhew. 'Inform the other guests we want to speak to them in the drawing room, and that nobody is to leave the property until we've completed our enquiries.'

'What? We've already been held up here for two days since Devlin died, and I have to return to London.' Cardhew looked outraged. 'You can't just incarcerate us for no reason, you have no authority—'

'Yes we do, and you can call Scotland Yard if you have any doubts,' Swift was quick to retaliate.

The popinjay turned red in the face. 'Well really, I don't believe you can order me about—'

'And send the butler here,' I cut across his wittering. He stalked off, muttering to himself.

Swift threw me a wry eye. 'Tetchy today.'

I sighed. I knew I'd been short-tempered. 'There was another letter waiting for me when we arrived home; it was about the loan.'

'Lennox, whatever the amount is, I'll find it and lend

it to you.' He was insistent. 'You saved my neck last year when Montague Morgan stole the Braeburn funds...'

'Swift, I'm not going to borrow money from you.'

He looked exasperated, then sighed. 'If you really won't accept my help, Mrs Saunders has offered a reward of two thousand pounds.'

'That's hardly reliable, is it.' I was dismissive. 'These people aren't the sort to keep their word.'

'Perhaps, but she's made the offer and she's legally obliged to keep it. And I'll make damn sure she does,' he added, then glanced at me. 'All we have to do is solve this murder and convict the killer, Lennox,' he said lightly, then gave me a grin. 'You're actually quite good when you put your erratic mind to it.' Swift may have been a hardened policeman, but I'd found him to be the best friend you could have when the chips were down. 'Come on, let's get on with it.' He went to study the chalk outline.

Fossett had done a reasonable job of drawing the shape of a body lying on its side. One arm was thrown up, the other presumably under him; one leg extended, the other bent at the knee. The head was egg shaped and where you'd expect to find it. The blood stain had covered quite a large area in the middle, having pooled against a raised metal lip below the rail. There'd been sufficient blood to form a pool before overflowing and trickling down the front of the balcony and onto the terrace.

'It was set up to appear as if he was called to the railing by someone in the garden and shot from below.' Swift leaned over the balustrade and looked down. I peered over too. Dark droplets of blood on the sandstone paving were quite obvious.

'It was daylight, who the hell walks around someone's garden with a bow and arrow in hand – anyone could have seen them,' I said.

'Exactly, and given the angle from the ground, they couldn't have hit Saunders below the sternum. Not unless he was taller than you, Lennox.'

I was six foot three. 'No, he was shorter, and turning to fat.'

I had brought my magnifying glass, and extracted it from my jacket, feeling rather like Sherlock Holmes, or at least a proper detective. I squatted on my haunches. 'No blood spattered on the iron work.' I followed the scrolls and squirls carefully, then rubbed a finger around the underside and held it out to show a film of greyish grime and the residue left by Fossett's fingerprint powder. 'No trace of blood.'

Swift nodded.

'The chair.' I went over to where it stood in the corner. Nothing was visible on the wickerwork, which gave me pause, so I picked it up and turned it upside down. 'There.' I grinned and pointed to a small area of tiny spots on the woven strands of willow the killer had failed to wipe clean.

Swift nodded. 'This is where he was murdered.'

'And not by an arrow,' I said and righted the chair to sit on it – it was actually very comfortable. 'Cyril Fletcher said there was a nick in the skin, so probably a long, thin blade.'

'A stiletto.' He considered. 'An assassin's weapon and easy to hide. The murderer stabbed him, waited for him to die...'

'Which wouldn't take long,' I added.

'No, the blade must have pierced the heart,' Swift agreed. 'The knife was then extracted, causing blood to spatter, and then they pushed the arrow into the wound.'

'Why?' I asked the obvious question.

He pulled his lip. 'A subterfuge? According to the statements, everyone was at breakfast at nine o'clock onwards. The gardener passed the terrace shortly before nine, and there was no sign of blood, but twenty-five minutes later he saw the drops.'

'So somebody devised all this just to establish an alibi.'

'And make it look like it was someone from outside,' he agreed.

'Wouldn't the killer need to be sure of the gardener's movements...' I began but was interrupted.

'Good day...Hello...' A man's voice reached us from the bedroom. 'May I enquire as to Sir Heathcliff Lennox?'

'Wait there a moment, would you,' I called out.

'We must be thorough, Lennox,' Swift said, and then took out his own magnifying glass.

'Fine.' I left him examining the wall behind the wicker chair and went inside to find the caller.

'I'm Major Lennox,' I told the chap, who was evidently a butler by his smart black tails, starched shirtfront, white gloves and starched dickie.

'My compliments, sir.' He bowed. 'I am Ackroyd. I

assume you will recall me from Mrs Saunders' "launch party" last month—'

'Yes,' I cut in.

'Indeed.' Ackroyd flared his nostrils. 'I believe you would like to see me, sir?'

'Yes. You can't leave.'

His pale face paled further. 'But, sir, I cannot remain. The events of the past few days have been absolutely ghastly, and there are barely any staff. Really this establishment is not to my usual standard. You must understand that my reputation is at stake.'

That gave me pause. Did butlers have reputations? 'What?'

'I am a butler of quality, to the quality, sir.' He stiffened his already stiff spine and raised his pointed chin. I guessed him to be in his mid-thirties, dark hair parted precisely in the centre above a pinched face, flaring nostrils, thin lips and a prominent Adam's apple. He spoke with a nasal tone.

'I understand you work for an agency?'

'I do indeed, sir. The Golden Star Service to the Gentry, and it is most particular.'

I gave him a closer look. He seemed quite serious.

Swift walked in. 'You're the butler?'

'Indeed, sir, and I was trying to explain that I cannot remain—'

'Nobody is leaving until we say so.' Swift didn't beat about the bush.

'But...' Ackroyd tried to object.

'What time did you last see Saunders alive?' Swift advanced on the man.

'I... Oh, this is really very irregular.' Ackroyd looked as though he were about to burst into tears. 'He was quite awful. They're all awful, apart from Lady Clementine.' He sniffed. 'She is simply divine.'

Swift turned hawkish. 'I asked you a question.'

Ackroyd pulled himself together. 'Very well, sir, if you insist. I removed Mr Saunders' morning tray from the small table on the balcony at eight fifteen precisely. I am very particular about punctuality and order. Precision promotes perfection.'

I grinned as Swift stared.

He recovered quickly. 'Did you see Mr Saunders alive again that morning?'

'I did not.' Ackroyd's nasal voice quivered. 'It was I who entered this room first, after Cook had raised the alarm. The time was twenty-five minutes past nine, which I had observed by the hall clock. Mr Saunders was lying beside the railings, and there was blood. I was almost overcome, it was the most appalling sight.' He sniffed again. 'I can assure you, Mr Saunders was most certainly deceased.'

'Who had been in here between eight fifteen and nine twenty-five?' Swift continued.

'I have no idea, sir. After I removed Mr Saunders' tray, I went to the breakfast room to make necessary preparations, and from nine o'clock onwards I was occupied in serving.'

'Did anyone see you during the period?' Swift tugged out his notebook.

'Indeed. The maid helped me throughout the morning, sir.'

'How long had Mr Saunders been staying here?' Swift added.

'He arrived with Mrs Saunders and all their guests on Friday evening from London. I had preceded them two days before, to prepare the house, which was last Wednesday,' Ackroyd replied in precise terms. 'I had begun working for Mr and Mrs Saunders shortly before Christmas at their London abode in Grosvenor Square. Their last butler had left rather precipitously. Apparently there has been quite a turnover of staff, which was not communicated to me at the time of my interview.' He closed his eyes momentarily as though pained. 'My first visit to Ashton Hall had taken place last month. The visit was intended to conduct Mrs Saunders' launch party and devised to introduce the family to the district.' His eyes flicked over to me, but I refrained from comment. 'The day after that the household returned to London. Then last weekend Mrs Saunders informed me we were returning here again, along with their business associates. These were the same associates who attended the launch party. I am sure you recall the house guests, Major Lennox.'

'No,' I replied.

Swift had been making rapid notes as Ackroyd rabbited on. 'Could you list these 'house guests' please?'

Ackroyd flared his nostrils in readiness. 'I can, sir. In

addition to Mrs Saunders, there is the Honourable Sebastian Cardhew…'

'We've just met him,' Swift said as he wrote.

'Indeed, sir,' Ackroyd said. 'There is also Mr and Mrs Alfred Palgrave, Mr and Mrs Marcus Marriott, and Mr Cedric Smedley the third.'

'The third what?' I asked.

'I suppose him to be the third Cedric Smedley, sir, although I do not believe his family is in any way distinguished,' Ackroyd replied snootily.

'Did you bring Saunders a newspaper with his coffee?' I switched tack.

'Naturally, sir. Mr Saunders took the *Financial Times*. I pressed the paper before conveying it to him on the tray, along with his morning coffee.'

'What happened to the paper?' I asked.

'I…I…' he stuttered then got a grip. 'I believe it may have been left on the floor next to the chair, sir. I'm afraid I had to lie down after the encounter and could not assist the authorities until later. The doctor took charge and he expressly forbade anyone from entering this room. The young PC insisted I sat at the kitchen table to write a statement, along with Cook and the housemaid.' He sighed in exaggerated manner. 'Really, to expect me to sit at a kitchen table…'

'Are there only three staff in the house?' Swift wasn't interested in the butler's complaints.

'There are, sir. There had been two more maids from the village, but they left last month, after the launch party.'

'Why?' Swift made a note.

'I am not at liberty to say, sir.' He puffed up, then noticed the frown between Swift's brows. 'Ahem, I believe they took offence at Mrs Saunders' complaints. She told them they should learn to speak properly because her guests could barely understand a word they said.'

Swift shook his head and wrote another note.

'What about the garden staff?' I asked.

'Ah, that would be Mr Bent, sir. He is here at all times and lives in the stable-yard cottage. There is also a young man who comes twice a week to trim the hedges and cut the lawns. He does not have a uniform, he wears overalls, and uses an exceedingly noisy machine—'

I interrupted him. 'Does Bent regularly pass the terrace at the same time each day?'

He sighed. 'I cannot contest to his habits when the "house" are away, sir, but when they are in residence I can confirm that he collects a cup of tea from the kitchen just before nine each morning. He conveys this to his shed and returns the cup half an hour later. This consists of his morning break,' Ackroyd explained.

Swift stopped writing, having worn his pencil down.

'Inspector!' Fossett arrived, red-faced and out of breath. 'Sorry sirs, Lady Clementine caught me. She had this huge old lion skin in a chest and wanted it carrying to her bedroom and she said no-one would help. So she asked me and I couldn't say no.' He plonked his helmet down on a side table.

'Fossett where is the newspaper that Saunders had been reading on the balcony?' I asked.

He drew a breath. 'I've got it, sir, here in my satchel. I thought I'd best hang on to it.' He undid the buckles of the battered leather bag slung from his shoulder, rooted about, found the folded pink newspaper and held it out.

Swift took it. 'Well done, Fossett.'

The young bobby broke into a grin.

'But this room was unlocked when we arrived,' Swift added the accusation.

The lad's face fell. 'I made sure to lock it, sir, so someone here must have done it.' He aimed a glare at Ackroyd.

'I was instructed to open it yesterday, sir,' Ackroyd said in his defence. 'I believe the guests wanted to search for any documents left in here by the late Mr Saunders. The maid subsequently cleaned up. Mrs Saunders made us do it.'

'Did they find any documents?' I asked.

'I believe not, sir,' Ackroyd replied.

'Let's take a look at this.' Swift took the newspaper to a large writing table in the area leading to the French windows and balcony beyond. We all followed.

'Clear it off, Fossett,' Swift instructed.

It took the lad only a moment to remove the blotting pad, ink stand, and the usual whatnots. 'There you go, sir.'

'Right.' Swift unfolded the pink paper and placed it on the gleaming walnut surface.

'Sir, that could be blood!' Fossett pointed to a minute dot in the margin of the front page.

Swift drew out his magnifying glass and aimed it.

'No, it's just ink.'

We scrutinised the broadsheet, bending over the long

columns of black typed articles, extravagant advertisements and occasional bleary photographs. Examination completed, he straightened up, turned a page and we repeated the same. By the third turn it was becoming tedious, so I gazed out of the window to watch a buzzard drift across the blue sky, its outstretched wings barely moving.

'Sirs,' Ackroyd spoke up. 'Please observe the page numbers.'

We did.

'Some of the pages are missing,' I said. We'd been too absorbed with minutiae to notice.

Swift flicked back through the entire newspaper. 'Two centre pages are missing,' he concluded. 'Were they there when you gave it to Saunders, Ackroyd?'

'I can assure you they were, sir. I ironed each one myself.'

'Has anyone lit a fire since Mr Saunders' death?' I asked.

He hesitated, then admitted, 'Only Lady Clementine, sir.'

# CHAPTER 4

'Ask Lady Clementine to come to the drawing room and join the others there, please,' Swift ordered Ackroyd.

'I shall make the request, sir, although she may not comply. M'lady can be rather unconventional,' he intoned, then went off, nostrils flaring.

'What does he mean by "unconventional"?' Swift asked Fossett.

'Nuts, sir, but nice with it.' He grinned.

'Did Saunders have an office in the house?' I asked, because he must have put his papers somewhere.

'Mrs Saunders said he's got a proper office in London, sir,' Fossett explained. 'But there's a vault next to this room, and after he died they were all running round trying to find the combination for it.'

That caught our attention.

'Show us,' Swift demanded.

He led us from the room and a short distance along the corridor, then stopped in front of a door much like the others. 'I heard one of them call it the "silver vault" sir.' He turned the brass doorknob to reveal another door behind the first. This one was obviously metal but had been painted reddish brown to look like mahogany. There was a circular brass plate, a dial in the centre and a brass wheel below it.

We paused to observe it.

'How did Saunders make his money?' Swift asked Fossett.

'Somebody said he made loans, but they didn't know who he loaned to. I don't think it was to anyone local.' He gripped the wheel with both hands and tried to turn it. 'Won't budge, sir.'

Swift leaned in to read the plate: *"Milners' Patent - Thief Resisting."*

The words encircled a lion and unicorn supporting the English coat of arms, with a crown above it and a sash beneath which bore the imprints: "London" and "Liverpool".

I had a go at twisting the dial, which moved easily back and forth, but I didn't hear any clicks or anything. 'It must be the most elaborate silver vault I've ever seen.'

Swift glanced at me. 'You're familiar with them?'

'Yes, they're pretty common in big houses. It's where the silver's kept between fancy dinner parties. There's one at Melrose Court, but it's much older and the door is studded oak and iron.' I tapped the door to hear a metallic ring. 'This must have been built when the house was constructed.'

'Is the room arched all the way through?' Fossett gazed up at the domed ceiling.

'Yes, they're usually constructed between two stone walls, lined with bricks and vaulted,' I explained. 'Concrete is poured over the top of the arch to stop anyone breaking in from the floor above.' I knew this because my cousin Edgar and I had once pried up the floorboards in Melrose Court, thinking that we'd leap out and surprise the butler when he opened the vault door, only to be thwarted.

'What about below?' Swift asked.

'Also concrete,' I said.

'There must be a lot of silver in there,' Fossett remarked.

'I doubt it was only used for silver,' I replied. 'Not with this level of security.'

'No, it's as secure as a bank safe.' Swift frowned. 'We should go to the drawing room, and hear what they've got to say for themselves.'

That didn't particularly appeal to me, but I went along anyway. The drawing room was on the ground floor, unlike most large houses I was familiar with. Fossett explained the layout as we followed him down the stairs.

'This hall's in the middle.' He waved a hand toward the full height ceiling, then paused to stand on the bottom step. 'The billiard room's on the right at the front of the house, and the library is on the left.' He pointed toward each. 'I've looked in them but there's covers on everything, and you can see by the dust they've not been used in a long time,' Fossett explained earnestly. 'Behind the library is the dining room, which is under Mr Saunders' bedroom. The breakfast room is in the middle behind this hallway, and it has doors out onto the back terrace. So does the drawing room, which is in the west wing.' He led us in that direction. 'The kitchen, scullery, and stores are below stairs, and upstairs there's lots of bedrooms and there are three bathrooms – whoever heard of three bathrooms in a house! When I was growing up we had a pump in the yard and a thunderbox behind the pigsty.'

'We still have,' Swift said, then grinned.

'He lives in a castle,' I explained.

'You never do?' Fossett looked dubious.

'In Scotland,' I added. 'On a loch.'

The lad didn't seem convinced, but carried on. 'Yeah, well, there's more bathrooms and bedrooms in the attic, including Lady Clementine's. She said she'd rather be with the servants than the bunch of weasels infesting the house.'

I recalled the lady as fairly eccentric, although with a streak of good sense.

Swift was more interested in the particulars. 'If the dining room is on the ground floor, why is the silver vault upstairs?'

'Don't know, sir. Maybe it's safer up there?' Fossett guessed, probably correctly.

Ackroyd was lurking at the end of the passage. 'May I escort you to the drawing room, sirs?'

'Fine.' Swift nodded agreement. 'Did you find Lady Clementine?'

'Alas, no, sir,' he replied. 'She was not in her rooms.'

'You're remaining in post?' I asked the butler.

'You have commanded me to stay, sir, and so I shall

continue to perform my duties.' You'd think we'd signed his death warrant by the tone of his voice.

He opened the large double doors into a room bathed in sunshine, sumptuously decorated in rich burgundy and gold brocades with an overabundance of furniture and an enormous crystal chandelier.

'Ah, Major Lennox, there you are!' Margaret Saunders turned in her chair as we entered. There were four other people present. They were seated on three gilded sofas arranged to face a large unlit fireplace which sported a vase of gaudy orange and yellow gladioli.

'Ackroyd?' Cardhew was seated next to her. 'Are you back on duty?'

'As it would appear, sir.' The butler was frigidly polite.

'In that case we'd like some coffee.' The popinjay was still wearing his ridiculous red blazer.

Ackroyd didn't utter a word, merely flared his nostrils, turned on his heel and walked out.

'Where's Lady Clementine?' It was quite obvious she wasn't among them.

'I think she's gone for a walk,' a drably dressed woman said. I tried to recall her name, but couldn't.

'Everyone is supposed to be here for questioning,' Swift instantly objected.

A florid man, short, fleshy and with a head of white hair bounced in his seat. 'You can't order us about, don't you know who we are?'

'No,' I said. 'Who are you?'

'Really, Major Lennox,' Mrs Saunders replied in high

tone. 'I made introductions at the launch party, you must surely recall my husband's consortium?'

I had no desire to recall any of them and said nothing.

'We are the Royal Buckingham Financial Services,' the florid chap declared. 'One of the foremost investment companies in London.'

That made me stop and stare. I recognised the company, although I hadn't heard it mentioned at that damned dinner – not that I'd been listening.

'I want each of your names.' Swift pulled out his notebook.

They didn't look happy about that, either.

'I am Cedric Smedley the third,' the florid man replied, then pursed his pink lips as though he was guarding vital secrets.

Another man had been watching without a word. Black hair slicked back with scented oil I could smell across the room, he wore a dark suit, expensively tailored, with a silk waistcoat, a tie in pale grey, and pristine white shirt. 'Mrs Saunders informed us that you had retired from the force.' He addressed Swift, who stood next to me in front of the fireplace. 'What is your current status, please?' The man spoke formally with an accent I couldn't quite place, possibly because it was affected.

'We are consultants to Scotland Yard.' Swift spoke coldly. 'Your name?'

'Marcus Marriott, and this is my wife.' He didn't glance at her; she was the drab lady whose name I'd forgotten. 'Please present yourself, Gabriel.'

'I am Mrs Marcus Marriott.' The women next to him spoke quietly. 'You may call me Gabriel.' She looked up then quickly dropped her gaze again. She appeared the most natural among them; brown hair held back by a couple of pins, and large hazel eyes in a plain, unadorned face. Her dull green dress was in contrast to her city smart husband.

'Thank you, Mrs Marriott,' Swift replied in warmer tone, then addressed the rest of them. 'I understand there were two other people in the house when Mr Saunders was killed.'

'They're Mr and Mrs Palgrave, sir,' Fossett piped up. He'd remained beside the door and was now wearing his helmet.

'Where are they?' Swift demanded.

'I really don't know,' Mrs Saunders replied with a shrug. Swift's frown deepened.

'You're a dashed despot,' Cardhew suddenly accused him. 'Are you really going to make this house a prison and keep us confined here?'

'Yes,' Swift said, then stated formally, 'You are all suspects in a murder case. You may move around the house and grounds, but you must not leave the area.'

'Suspects?' Mrs Saunders' thin brows arched. 'Please don't be ridiculous, my husband was killed by someone from outside. We were all at breakfast.'

'Two days ago Devlin Saunders was murdered by someone *inside* this house,' Swift said in terse terms.

'That is a complete fabrication.' Marcus Marriott's

arrogant features hardened. 'If you've read all the statements you'll know the gardener passed the terrace before nine o'clock and didn't see any blood.'

'How do you know what's in the statements?' I snapped. Their arrogance was really irritating me.

'Because we read them while the constable and doctor were upstairs with the ambulance men,' Sebastian Cardhew answered for him. 'And why shouldn't we? It's our business, after all,' he added, looking smug.

'You shouldn't have done that, it's sneaking,' Fossett accused him.

'Well, you shouldn't have left them here unattended,' Cardhew countered.

'Not everybody had finished writing, so it was perfectly understandable the constable didn't take the statements away.' Gabriel Marriott spoke softly, but it was enough to shut them up.

'To return to my point,' Marcus Marriott said. 'Devlin was obviously killed after the gardener passed the terrace around nine o'clock, and we were all together at breakfast until his body was found.'

'There's no evidence to support the time of death,' Swift said bluntly, and without further explanation.

'I don't believe you, and none of us plotted to murder Devlin, the idea is farcical. We are reputable businessmen with very influential acquaintances,' Marriott retorted with an undertone of menace in his voice.

His wife shot him a glance.

'Why do you say "plotted"?' I eyed him narrowly.

Colour rose in his cheeks. 'Because it would be impossible for anyone to walk through the house with a bow and arrow without someone seeing what was happening,' he replied coldly. 'Which makes it a plot.'

He was quick to fabricate an excuse, even if it did sound hollow.

'All the more reason for you to remain here,' Swift rejoined.

'I will not be treated like a common criminal,' Marcus Marriott snapped. 'I have business in London. We will leave in the morning.'

'If you attempt to leave, you will be arrested.' Swift was in hawkish mood.

'Try and stop me,' Marriott challenged.

I sat down on a spare chair and leaned back on the plush cushions to enjoy the show.

'Fossett, handcuffs,' Swift ordered.

'Erm…sir?' He edged up to where Swift was standing. 'I left them in the station. I've never used them before,' he whispered sotto voce.

'Right, then you are under orders to arrest that man the moment he leaves the grounds,' Swift commanded.

'Yes, sir. I'll do that, sir.' Fossett snapped to attention and saluted, almost knocking his helmet awry.

'But I thought we had decided to stay, Marcus.' Gabriel Marriott appealed to her husband. 'We agreed to help Margaret through this dreadful ordeal.'

Margaret Saunders didn't look as though she was going through any sort of ordeal, but was quick to pick up on the cue. 'Thank you, dear Gabriel. I am so fortunate in my kind friends.' She dug the handkerchief out again and raised it to dab her eyes carefully around her make-up.

'I think you should know that I'm acquainted with a senior inspector at Scotland Yard.' Cedric Smedley the third decided to join in, his florid cheeks suffusing as Swift shot a glare at him.

'Which inspector?' Swift demanded.

'Jeremy Brent-Smythe.' Cedric Smedley shifted in his seat, the buttons of his yellow silk waistcoat straining against his girth. 'We are members of the same Lodge.'

Which meant they were Freemasons. I assumed he was fishing to find out if either of us were members too. He was out of luck.

'Brent-Smythe retired last year.' Swift was dismissive. 'What's your role here?'

Smedley turned petulant. 'I am the company accountant. I am considered a leading expert on the subject of finance.'

I judged Smedley to be the oldest of them all; over sixty, overweight, and over satisfied. He had white brows, puffy eyes, bulging cheeks and thick lips.

'Why are you all here?' I asked the question we should have started with.

'It's a meeting of the Royal Buckingham Financial Services,' Margaret Saunders replied. 'Devlin and I thought it would be a treat to bring everyone for a long weekend and have the meeting at the same time.'

'What was the meeting about?' Swift was poised with a sharpened pencil.

'If you must know,' Margaret sniffed, 'Devlin had decided to retire, and he was going to announce the new President.'

'Which will be me,' Marcus Marriott stated.

'Not necessarily,' Margaret replied, which caused Marriott to fix sharp eyes on her.

The door opened at that moment and two more people walked in.

'Ackroyd said the police are here!' the man blurted, then spotted Fossett and stopped in his tracks.

'Well, it appears he was right,' the woman with him said, then saw me. 'Ah, the handsome war hero.' Her voice slowed to a husky drawl. 'Hello again, Sir Heathcliff.'

'It's Lennox,' I replied, then remembered my manners and stood up. I hadn't forgotten her, she'd worn a very revealing dress at the dinner party and flirted with all the men. She'd tried her allures on me and I'd barely babbled my way out of it. Persi had thought it highly amusing and hadn't made any attempt to rescue me.

'Dolores Palgrave.' She held her hand out to Swift, who shook it briefly.

'Please sit down.' He remained the gruff detective.

She sat on a chair. A slender woman with long jet black hair held by a jewelled headband. She wore too much make-up, a drop waist dress in peach, and a long string of pearls. 'You've come to investigate us?'

'They've been sent by Scotland Yard,' Margaret Saunders said.

'He's not, he's from the Manor.' Alfred Palgrave pointed at me. The chap was the tall, gauche sort, his dark hair combed in waves, brown eyes uncertain and nervous – actually 'nervous' defined him, even his voice held a faint tremor of fear.

'She said "sent *by* Scotland Yard" not "*from* Scotland Yard", silly,' Dolores told him tartly, contempt curling her scarlet lips.

'Oh.' Palgrave broke into a timorous grin. 'Ha, sorry. I'm not one of those brain boxes, you know.'

Dolores rolled her eyes and reached for a cigarette case from her gold sequinned handbag. Alfred Palgrave perched on the arm of the sofa, trying to appear nonchalant.

'What is in the vault upstairs?' I asked before Swift began another interrogation.

That resulted in silence.

'It's the silver vault,' Margaret finally replied, patting a chestnut curl back from her face. 'My husband used it to store our valuables and some of his personal files.'

'We'd like to take a look, please.' Swift was coldly polite.

'So would we,' Marcus Marriott snapped. 'The code is missing; someone's hiding it.'

This led to an outbreak of bickering. Ackroyd arrived in the middle of it. 'Excuse me, sirs, but there is a dog in the garden. It is a gold-coloured spaniel. I believe it belongs to you, Major Lennox,' he addressed me.

'Mr Fogg.' I stood up.

'Oh, I say,' Alfred Palgrave blurted. 'Wasn't it a golden spaniel who peed on your aspidistra during that ghastly launch party, Margaret?' He turned to Mrs Saunders.

'Yes, it was.' She aimed a narrow stare at me, then realised what Palgrave had said. 'What do you mean "ghastly"?'

I made my way to the door as the volume of voices escalated.

'Well done, Ackroyd,' I said as I made an exit.

'For what, sir?'

'For providing an escape.'

'Lennox...' Swift called from behind me.

'Won't be long,' I replied, and strode quickly out of earshot.

I spotted Foggy meandering about the front garden, nose to the ground, possibly trying to trace me, or just bumbling about in his usual brainless manner. He must have escaped the Manor. I called him; he came racing over with tongue out and tail wagging and bounded around as if I'd been away for a month.

I ruffled his ears and then strolled off in the direction of the rear garden with him running ahead. I felt a pang of guilt, I should have stayed with Swift, but the inmates were irritating and I felt in need of some peaceful country air with my dog.

The gardens were smartly formal, easy to maintain and designed with no imagination whatsoever. I continued alongside the house with hands in pockets until arriving at the terrace.

I paused for an instant to gaze at the spots of blood below the balcony. Fogg took a sniff and promptly went to sit next to a stone urn on the lawn – he'd always hated anything dead, even the smell of blood upset him. I shifted my focus up to where dark rivulets could be clearly seen to have run down the stonework supporting the balcony.

Saunders hadn't been shot with an arrow, but if he had been, the killer would have had to be standing where I was, in full view of a large pair of glazed double doors. I walked between the pillars supporting the balcony and went to try the handle. It was locked, so I raised my hands to shield my view through the glass. The heavy satin curtains were open, revealing a dining room panelled in white painted wood with gold trim, currently devoid of life.

'Hello sweetie,' a woman's voice hailed me.

I spun around, then gave a grin. 'Greetings, Lady Clementine.'

# CHAPTER 5

She laughed gaily. 'Must I call you Lennox? Heathcliff suits you so much better.'

'I prefer Lennox.' I went over to where she was standing on the lawn in bright sunshine. Foggy came gambolling over to join us, his ears flapping behind him.

'Oh, and your doggy is just adorable.' She bent to stroke his head. He jumped up on his back legs, delighted at the attention.

'He's called Mr Fogg.'

'I remember him, he relieved himself on Margaret's aspidistra the evening of that dreadful dinner party.' Her blue eyes twinkled. 'I gave him a piece of beef as a reward. Clever little doggie,' she murmured, then straightened up to hold out a thin hand in my direction.

I pecked it in formal manner. 'We're questioning the household.'

'I know, young Fossett came to see me. He fetched my lion skin from the trunk. It was the one I shot.'

'Was it?'

'Yes, in Kenya. It ate my husband, which he thoroughly deserved. He was forever shooting things, no animal was safe from his rifle.'

'Apart from the lion,' I reminded her.

She trilled a musical laugh. 'And if the lion hadn't come after me, I would never have shot him, poor pussy cat.'

Lady Clementine had a habit of telling stories; it was an eccentricity, although it had caught me off guard when I'd first met her. She declared that she'd been made a pauper by her son-in-law, the recently deceased Devlin Saunders, and was reduced to begging for pennies in the street. She also said she'd met me in a previous life, which was rather disconcerting. Margaret Saunders, Lady Clementine's step-daughter, had told me quite clearly that I shouldn't believe a word her step-mother said. Hers hadn't been the only warning either.

'I thought your husband died of a heart attack.'

'Oh, we only say that because it's conventional. Margaret can't contemplate anything out of the ordinary.' Short and slim, with white hair tied in a bun high on her head, wispy strands falling about an elfin face, with sparkling eyes and a smile that still dazzled. Her beauty had matured into deep creases, hollowed cheeks and laughter lines, not that she seemed to care. She wore no cosmetics, although she made up for it with colourful clothes; a dress in turquoise silk, a bright yellow scarf tied about her waist, and a dazzling necklace of sapphires.

'The sort of convention that suggests her husband was murdered,' I replied.

'I think she's glad to be rid of him, I certainly am. I'm only surprised it has taken so long.'

'Do you know who did it?' I smiled down at her, she barely reached my shoulders.

'Oh, one of them, or all of them, it hardly matters.' She waved a dismissive hand, a gold bangle flashing in the sunlight. 'Now tell me, how is your lovely wife?'

'She's fine.' We began a slow stroll across the lawn. 'Where do you keep the bows and arrows?'

'Ah, you're sleuthing.' She glanced up at me. 'Are you going to be tedious about this?'

'Yes.'

'Can I help?'

'No.'

'Then I shall offer a reward.'

'Really?'

'To whoever killed Devlin.'

I laughed.

Swift emerged from the rear of the house. 'Lennox?'

We waited as he crossed the terrace onto the manicured lawn.

'Oh, my dear, it's been such a long time.' Lady Clementine gave him an appraising glance upon his arrival. 'How marvellous to see you again.'

Swift was about to give a perfunctory bow, but came to a confused halt. 'I'm sorry, have we met?'

'Of course we have. In one of our past lives.' She gazed up at him with gleaming eyes. 'We were lovers at the court of Louis quatorze.'

That flummoxed Swift. He stared and then straightened up. 'I'm afraid you are mistaken, madam. I was…I mean I am Detective Chief Inspector Swift of Scotland Yard. I'm a consultant…'

'Oh, I'm sure you are, but I recall you in your previous glory. What a lover you were, and still as handsome and virile in this life, I see.'

I grinned as the colour rose in Swift's lean cheeks. 'Madam, this is a murder enquiry.'

'I know, isn't it exciting!' Lady Clementine beamed.

Swift frowned then launched into an interrogation. 'Why did you have a fire in your room the day Devlin Saunders was killed?'

'Why shouldn't I? I was cold, so I lit the fire.' She wasn't in the least intimidated. 'You really are terribly fervent, aren't you?' She sighed in theatrical manner. 'But then you always were.'

'Lady Clementine has volunteered to show us the archery area,' I said before Swift blew a gasket. 'After you, my lady.' I held out my hand in encouragement.

'Of course, my dear.' She waltzed off ahead of us. 'Anything to help our handsome detectives!'

A high hedge of clipped yew formed a divide from the formal garden. We walked through an archway and discovered a paddock, fringed on one side by a copse of beech trees and the boundary wall on the other.

Three large round targets were propped on stands at the far end, and a pretty chalet-type shed stood in a corner surrounded by lilac bushes in full bloom.

Foggy headed straight for the copse, it being the sort of place where rabbits would hide. We strolled toward the shed.

'Who uses these targets?' Swift asked Lady Clementine.

'Oh, most everybody. Devlin was keen, so he made them come and practise with him,' she replied lightly. 'He wasn't terribly good, only Gabriel Marriott was truly proficient – she could give Robin Hood lessons.'

Swift opened the shed door to find hooks holding bows along one wall and another row opposite, supporting leather quivers. Each was filled with arrows, all had white feathers. Swift went to the nearest and plucked one out.

'It's the same,' he said.

'There's one missing,' Lady Clementine told him. 'Constable Fossett made the gardener count them. There should be ten in each bag, but there were only nine in that one.' She pointed to the middle quiver. 'Fossett fingerprinted them, but he didn't find anything.'

Swift began counting them in typical pedantic manner.

'What did Saunders actually do?' I asked Lady Clementine as we watched him.

'Anything that made money. He called himself a shark.'

'What sort of shark?' I wondered if this was another of her stories.

'A money lender to distressed gentlefolk,' she quipped. 'He preyed on the weak and vulnerable.' Her blue eyes met mine, a glint of anger in them.

'Usury,' Swift said. He'd finished counting arrows and held one up to examine minutely.

'Absolutely,' Lady Clementine agreed. 'He bled his victims dry with sky-high rates. I tried to warn those that I could, but they were utterly desperate and had nowhere to turn. They'll be so pleased to hear he's dead.'

Swift's brows drew closer together.

'If the money was loaned by Saunders' finance company, the loans won't die with him,' I said, being all too aware of the rules.

She pursed her lips. 'You may be right,' she said, then her eyes lit up. 'In which case there need to be a few more murders!'

'Lady Clementine—' Swift began in a very serious tone.

'Do you know the code for the silver vault?' I interrupted.

'Yes, you have to sing it,' she answered in all seriousness. 'But I can't recall the tune. Perhaps it will return to me later.'

'Would you have written it down?' I suggested.

'Oh, now that is a good thought! Perhaps I did.' She smiled vaguely. 'I will go to my room and search. Dear Ackroyd can help me,' she decided, and then raised a hand. 'Au revoir, mes chéries.'

'Absolutely barking,' Swift remarked once she was out of earshot.

'I'm not so sure. I think she plays games to amuse herself.'

'Well, we've got better things to do than provide amusement to eccentrics. Come on.' He marched off toward the nearest target, arrow in hand.

It was identical to any other archery target. Made of straw formed into a tight roundel and covered by a stretched canvas coloured with diminishing rings of white, black, blue, and red. There were a great many holes in it. Swift thrust the arrow through the canvas, then pulled it out again.

'That proves it.'

'Does it?' I said wryly.

'Yes, the force needed to push it into the straw is almost enough to break the shaft; it would never work as a murder weapon unless he'd already been stabbed.' He held the metal point up. 'It's not sharp enough…'

'Swift, I thought we'd already established that.'

'I know, but we had to be certain.' He shoved the arrow back into the target and turned to head to the house. 'No stone unturned, Lennox.'

I shook my head and followed.

'What did the suspects say?' I asked as Foggy came racing to catch up. His nose was grubby with soil, I assumed he'd been digging in a rabbit hole.

'Nothing of use. They just kept repeating they were all together when Saunders was found.'

'Didn't they wonder why Saunders hadn't joined them?'

'They said he didn't eat breakfast, he ate "brunch".'

'Hm.' I'd heard the term, it meant a mid-morning meal and was an anathema to me, breakfast being my favourite meal of the day. 'What are they doing now?'

'Complaining mostly, I let them return to whatever they were doing. Fossett's keeping an eye on things. We can fit at least one interview in before lunch.'

'Are you sure…' I pulled out my old fob watch, which had stopped. I shook it and shoved it back in my pocket. 'The girls are making a picnic, if we leave early—'

'It's only eleven thirty, Lennox,' he retorted as we walked across the short grass. 'I've arranged for Cedric Smedley to meet us in Saunders' bedroom. We'll use it as an incident room.'

We'd crossed the terrace then skirted a path alongside the house to enter a discreetly set servants door. It opened into a long passage leading to the central hall.

'I thought my library was the incident room,' I said.

'It is, but it wouldn't do any harm to have something here, too.'

I was about to object, but then thought it might be a good idea because the balcony was really rather pleasant, despite the blood stains, and it was quieter than my home at the moment. My life had changed considerably in the last couple of years since Swift had tried to pin a murder on me. Although I loved my wife, and enjoyed the company of my friends, I sometimes missed the peaceful simplicity of my old ways.

Nobody was in the bedroom when we arrived, but someone had been busy. Four chairs had been set up around the walnut writing table. The blotter, inkwell, a stack of blank papers and pot of pencils had been neatly arranged upon its gleaming surface. There was even a pencil sharpener with a winding handle and container for shavings.

Swift took a seat and began rearranging everything around him.

Foggy had followed us in and sniffed about the place, casting a wary eye towards the French windows and blood-stained balcony beyond. He crawled under the bed to snuffle about, then emerged to hop onto a small green sofa and settled down to watch what happened next.

Fossett came in. 'Hello, sirs.' He grinned. 'I've made it all ready for you, and Mr Smedley is coming up the stairs now. He's threatening to complain to Scotland Yard, but I said that he'd have to talk to you, like it or not.'

'Righto,' I said and sat in a chair next to Swift. 'Go and stand at the bottom of the stairs and don't let any of them up until we say so.'

'Oh, sir, can't I stay and listen?' He held his helmet under his arm.

'No,' Swift said.

'Righto, sir.' He sounded disappointed, then brightened. 'I'll just leave my helmet here for when I come back.' He put it on the sofa next to Foggy, then scooted off before either of us could reply.

Smedley arrived moments later, puffing with exertion. 'Well, you had better explain why you've dragged me up here,' he wheezed and dropped heavily onto the nearest chair. 'I've already told you everything, this is unnecessarily officious.'

'Sit down.' Swift didn't look up from the notebook he was leafing through.

'I'll have you know I'm a highly respected businessman,' Smedley blustered.

'You're a crook,' I said, which set proceedings off to a good start.

# CHAPTER 6

'I will not sit here and be called a crook,' Smedley fulminated.

'You can stand if you like,' I replied.

'Why is that dog in here?' Smedley pointed at Fogg, who cocked his ears. 'What sort of investigators bring a dog with them?'

'The sort who own a dog,' I said, thinking the man an idiot.

Swift finished sharpening his pencil and blew grains of graphite from its point. 'You're money lenders.'

Smedley shifted his outrage back to Swift. 'We are financiers. We provide funding for an exclusive clientele,' he said through gritted teeth. 'And there is nothing "crooked" about it.'

'Are you accredited?' Swift turned to a fresh page.

'The law does not require accreditation when private loans are made to private clients.' Smedley attempted superciliousness but sounded like a blustering windbag.

'How much interest do you charge?' I demanded.

'It depends on the risk associated with the client.' Smedley drew a handkerchief from his top pocket and wiped his forehead.

'You mean it's variable,' I said. 'Does it vary over the lifetime of the loan?' I had learned the meaning of these terms through bitter experience.

'Sometimes, yes,' Smedley admitted. 'Not that it's any business of yours—'

'Had Saunders received threats from any of your clients recently?' Swift interrupted with a policeman's question.

'No more than usual.' Smedley's colour began to rise. 'Threats are an unavoidable part of our business. People become desperate if they can't support their loans.' He must have realised he was digging himself deeper and attempted a different tack. 'Of course, it was probably one of them. Certainly an outsider. When I'm allowed to return to London, I will have a clerk search through correspondence to identify any dangerous malcontents.'

'Have you ever forced a foreclosure?' The threats I'd received recently were on my mind.

Smedley wiped his forehead again. 'Unfortunately that is sometimes necessary, it is part of the nature of our business.'

'You force families from their homes after you've bled them dry with sky-high rates of interest.' I raised my voice. 'You're nothing but damned bloodsuckers getting rich from unsuspecting chumps who don't understand what they're being led into.'

Smedley's eyes widened in shock at the fury in my voice.

'Lennox,' Swift warned. 'I'll handle the questioning.' He turned to Smedley. 'How much is The Royal Buckingham worth?'

'I'm not going to disclose…' Smedley began then grunted in irritation as he noted our expressions. 'Very well. The value stands at one hundred and six thousand, two hundred and ninety-three pounds, ten shillings and fourpence.'

I almost let out a gasp; even Swift was stunned.

'In cash?' I asked.

'No, the value is an accumulated figure.' Smedley said with more than a hint of contempt.

'Who owns the shares?' Swift recovered enough to write the enormous sum down on the page.

'Devlin was the president, his holdings were thirty-five percent, I have twenty, and the remaining forty-five percent are owned equally between the three directors.'

'That's Marriott, Sebastian Cardhew, and…' Swift turned back a page to find the remaining name. 'Alfred Palgrave.'

Smedley glanced at his immaculate fingernails. 'Correct.'

Swift made another note. 'Saunders was about to retire and you had come to this house to hear him announce the new president. Marriott said that it would be him.'

'There's no certainty who it will be,' Smedley replied, his fleshy lips pursing.

'Who inherits Saunders' shares?' I asked.

'I don't know. I assume it's Margaret. She certainly believes she will, anyway,' he huffed a reply.

'Where is Saunders' will?' Swift demanded.

'It's locked in the silver vault,' Smedley replied. A sheen of sweat had formed on his brow and he wiped it away again.

'You do realise Saunders' assets will be frozen until his will has gone through probate, don't you?' Swift watched the man closely as he dropped the bombshell.

'But... but you can't. The company has to function. We must decide the next president, it can't be held up...I...I mean we have informed our company lawyer, he didn't say a word about freezing assets.' Smedley began to bluster.

'Then you should have asked him, because he will confirm it's a legal requirement.' Swift spoke matter-of-factly.

'No, I will telephone him.' Smedley rose from his chair. 'This cannot be allowed to prevent the...' His breath started to come more rapidly, beads of sweat dripped from his brow. 'I...I think I may be unwell...' His face flushed bright red, he struggled to his feet gasping for breath, then suddenly staggered sideways, clutching at his chest. He heaved another gasp, reeled and let out a strangled cry before thudding to the floor like a felled tree.

'Oh hell.' Swift leapt from his chair. 'He's having a heart attack.'

I was inclined to say good, but decided against.

'I'll call an ambulance,' Swift shouted. 'There's a telephone on the landing. Stay with him,' he ordered and raced out.

I stood up and put my hands in my pockets to go and gaze at Smedley, flat out on the carpet. He was unconscious, but still breathing; he lay on his back like a beached whale, face turning mottled puce, white hair damp and clothes dishevelled. He didn't look at all well.

Foggy had pricked his ears and sat up to stare at Smedley with rounded eyes. He looked at me, then hopped down from the sofa and went to hide behind it.

'Operator, I need an ambulance.' I could hear Swift along the corridor, he spoke rapidly. 'I don't care if he's having his lunch it's an emergency…yes, we're at Ashton Hall…what? No, there is not a madman on the loose, it's a heart attack…yes, Dr Fletcher please, if you can find him.' He put the receiver down with a bang and stalked back into the room. 'Blasted operator.'

'Flossie Craddock?'

'Yes, and she still hasn't forgotten that skirmish I had with her last Christmas.' He came to kneel beside the comatose Smedley. 'Damn it, what can we do for him?'

'Aspirin under the tongue.'

'Do you have any?' He glanced up.

'No.'

'We might have to give him mouth to mouth.'

That was an appalling thought. 'Stay there, I'll look for some aspirin.' I went to the dressing table and started pulling drawers open.

'Sir, I heard you speaking into the telephone…' Ackroyd entered. 'Agh, what has happened to Mr Smedley?' He took a step backwards.

'Do you have any aspirin?' I demanded.

'He's having a heart attack,' Swift said.

Ackroyd wasn't listening. He raised his hands to his cheeks. 'Oh Good Lord, not another one. I simply cannot bear it.'

Fossett ran in. 'What is it, I heard Inspector Swift on the telephone...' He spotted Smedley. 'Gosh, there's another one gone.'

'He's not dead...' Swift began.

'The ambulance men should be here shortly,' I told him. 'Go and wait for them, then show them up.'

'Oh sir, you're always sending me away when it gets exciting,' Fossett complained.

'Go.' I pointed at the door. 'And don't let any of those damned people up here.'

He went off as the sound of loud questioning rose from downstairs.

'Ackroyd.' Swift spoke sharply. 'Do you have any aspirin?'

'Aspirin, sir?' He took a breath and pulled himself together. 'I believe there may be some in one of the bathrooms.'

'Go and get it,' Swift ordered.

Ackroyd dashed off.

'Well done, Swift.' I commended him. 'I'll wait on the balcony.' I headed for the French windows and warm sunshine.

'Lennox, you can't just leave...'

Ackroyd dashed back in again waving a box of tablets. 'I have found some, sir.'

They bent over him as I headed outside and went to lean on the railings, sidestepping the chalk outline and pool of

66

dried blood. It was peaceful out here; I watched a heron flap away from a distant brook, followed by a few crows, then became aware of people speaking in hissed tones. I couldn't see anyone, they must have been behind the yew hedge. Their voices were too low for me to make out the words, but the exchange was clearly angry; a staccato of short sentences which stopped abruptly. I waited, and saw Margaret Saunders emerge from behind the hedge and storm into the house via the breakfast room doors. A moment later Marcus Marriott stalked out and disappeared around the side of the house.

I decided I'd better return to duty, and wandered back through the French windows.

Smedley hadn't moved. Swift and Ackroyd were kneeling either side of him, watching the feeble movement of the man's chest.

'Ambulance has arrived, sir.' Fossett burst back into the room.

A minute later two large men in white coats arrived carrying a heavy stretcher between them. Cyril Fletcher followed on their heels.

'Another one gone?' He came to gaze at Smedley as Swift and Ackroyd rose to their feet.

'Not yet,' I remarked and turned to Fossett. 'Stop anyone else coming up here, will you.'

'Why do I...?' He sighed. 'Yes, sir,' he muttered and trudged out.

Fletcher put his medical bag down next to the patient. 'Best give him some aspirin.'

'We put a tablet under his tongue,' Swift told him.

'Ah, well done that man.' Cyril beamed. 'Better than mouth to mouth, eh!' He knelt to take Smedley's pulse then placed a stethoscope onto his chest. We all watched in silence.

'His lips are goin' a bit blue, sir,' one of the ambulance men remarked.

'Yes.' Fletcher rose stiffly to his feet. 'Best get him off to the hospital PDQ if he's to stand a chance.'

'We'll soon have 'im loaded,' the chap replied. 'Come on, Bob.'

'Right y'are, Jim,' his compatriot mumbled.

'He's a big 'un,' Jim said as they laid the stretcher alongside the bulging form of Smedley.

'I've seen bigger,' Bob replied as they heaved him none too gently, then tidied his arms and legs into place before fastening him down with leather straps. I assumed they were expecting a bumpy ride to the hospital.

'Actually, we'd better give him something for the road.' Fletcher held up a small bottle of tablets he'd retrieved from his bag. 'Nitroglycerine.' He squinted at the label, then unscrewed the lid and stuck one in Smedley's mouth.

'Isn't that an explosive?' I asked.

'Ha, yes, but it's only a minute quantity,' Fletcher explained. 'Not enough to blow his head off.'

Everyone stopped to see the effect, which was nothing very much. Smedley remained comatose, but the rise and fall of his chest improved perceptibly.

'He seems to be breathing more easily,' Swift observed.

'Yes, that's the reason I gave it to him,' Fletcher replied, his eyes fixed on the patient.

'Best put a blanket round 'im,' Jim told his mate.

'Aye. We'll do that, don't want him gettin' a chill.' Bob unrolled a blanket from the end of the stretcher and spread it over the patient.

'Right, I'll follow you. Let's be off,' Fletcher said, then gave me a grin. 'More drama to add to the mix, eh Heathcliff?'

'It seems to be the day for it,' I agreed.

They trooped out, the stretcher creaking as they went. Ackroyd followed for whatever reason.

Babbling voices rose as they made their way downstairs into the hall. I heard Sebastian Cardhew and Dolores Palgrave fire questions at Cyril Fletcher, with Fossett trying to call them to order as best he could.

'Lennox, we should search Smedley's room.' Swift turned to me.

'It's lunch time. The girls will have the picnic ready, Swift,' I reminded him. 'We can't be late.'

He didn't move. I knew the policeman in him wanted to stay, but his wife had prepared lunch, and would be waiting...

'Fossett can lock it, and guard the place,' I added.

Foggy emerged from behind the sofa. He wagged his tail and raised his ears in expectation.

I picked him up to carry under my arm. 'Swift?'

'Fine,' he replied, his shoulders slumped in defeat.

We locked the door behind us and made our way

downstairs. The throng advanced as we reached the bottom.

'I demand you tell us what is happening,' Marcus Marriott called out. He'd obviously made a return from the garden.

'Was it a serious heart attack?' Alfred Palgrave threw the question.

'Is he likely to survive?' Gabriel Marriott asked, her hands clasped together over the drab frock.

Fossett put his arms out wide as though trying to herd them. 'You've got to stop bothering the detectives. Wait until the doctor comes back and tells us what's going on.' He tried to marshal them back down the passage, toward the drawing room.

'Find the key to Cedric Smedley's bedroom door and lock it, Fossett,' Swift ordered. 'Then go down to the gate and stop anyone leaving.'

'Sir, they won't do as I tell them.' Fossett was still trying to hold back the irate crowd.

'You can blow your whistle if any of them step out of line,' I told him.

He gave a grin, felt in his jacket, then pulled out a large whistle on a chain. 'Right, you heard them, you've got to stop mithering or I'll have to arrest you,' he shouted and then blew the whistle loudly.

This created even more chaos, and we made an escape out of the front door while they all argued. It didn't take a moment to fire up the Bentley and motor off along the drive.

The gates were standing open, presumably left by the departing ambulance. About half a dozen villagers were gathered in the lane, peering toward the house. They stepped back as I slowed to putter through the gateway.

'Another 'un gone, Major?' Mr Trimbell called out. He was the local beekeeper.

'He's not dead,' I called back. 'Nothing to worry about. Just a heart attack.'

'Was he attacked? Or was it shock?' Shelley Bays, the baker's wife, asked. She held a basket full of delicious-smelling scones.

'No, just the usual sort of attack,' I replied, wondering if I should ask her for a half-dozen.

'I'll shut the gates behind you, shall I, Major Lennox?' Frank Wright stepped forward to offer. He was the local Beadle and Scout Master.

'Excellent, thank you,' I replied, then put my foot down and sped away before any more of them could chime in.

# CHAPTER 7

'Ah sir.' Greggs seemed to be the only inhabitant in the house. 'Both m'ladies are in the flower garden arranging the table.'

'Excellent,' I replied.

Foggy gave a yap of excitement and he dashed off towards the back door.

'I'm just going to the incident room, Lennox,' Swift said.

'You mean my library, Swift,' I reminded him. He ignored me. I stuck my hands in my pockets and went off to find my wife.

'Hello, my love.' She smiled when she spotted me. She and Florence were smoothing down a gingham cloth over the outdoor table. They made a perfect picture dressed in their pretty summer frocks under sunshine filtering through trees heavy with blossom and fresh green leaves.

The Jack Russell puppy, Nicky, ran directly for me, then swerved to make a turn about my ankles.

The little rascal was getting out of hand.

'Sit!' I raised my voice to parade-ground level.

The puppy stopped in its tracks, gazed up at me with bright eyes, then abruptly sat with his front paw raised.

'Stay,' I ordered. His ears drooped, then he ran to hide under the table.

'Oh, poor mite.' Florence ducked down to see where he was.

'Lennox, you frightened him,' Persi chided.

'Persi, he has to learn.'

'I know, and we've been trying to teach him.' She glanced to where Florence was kneeling below the spread of the tablecloth, the grass brushing against her white dress. 'We all have our own ways.'

Florence straightened up with the puppy in her arms. 'He's a wee darling,' she cooed, then brought him to me. 'But you are right, he needs to be taught to listen.'

I put my hand out to scratch the tyke's ear; he tried to lick my fingers. 'He's a good-natured little dog.'

'Apart from the nipping.' Florence passed him over to me. 'Here, you hold on to him, he'll be less trouble that way. I'll just go and fetch the lemonade – or would you rather something stronger?'

'Greggs will bring a bottle of Sancerre,' I replied. White wine had been the tradition in our family picnics, back in the days when my mother and father were still alive.

'You won't shout at him, will you?' Persi demanded, a frown on her brow.

'Cross my heart.'

'Well, you can make friends while we fetch the food,'

she ordered, then softened her voice. 'Don't frighten him, Lennox. You're more intimidating than you realise.'

'Nonsense.'

'If only they knew what an absolute softie you are...' She stood on tiptoe to kiss me on the lips, then followed Florence into the house.

I sat down on one of the wooden chairs and held the puppy in my hands to face me. He gazed back with his tongue hanging out and little tail wagging. 'Nicky, you need to learn to listen,' I lectured. 'When someone says "NO" it means stop whatever you're doing. And you must sit, and stay, and not bite people.'

His tail wagged more furiously. I put him on the table. 'Sit,' I ordered. He sat with one paw raised. 'Well done.' I patted his head. 'Right, now...next lesson.' I picked him up carefully and placed him down on the grass in front of me. 'Sit,' I ordered. He sat again, then lay down at my feet, seemingly content.

Lesson over, I leaned back in the chair, which creaked alarmingly, but held together.

I could see the gardeners had been busy, dark soil freshly dug between burgeoning flowers in hues of pink, purple, and blue. Delphiniums, carnations, early roses and peonies spread their fragrance to merge with the scent of nearby magnolia trees. Swallows soared about the house, arcing darts against the cloudless sky; blackbirds sang in loud melody, and sparrows, linnets, and mistle thrush chimed in trilling chorus. A small corner of heaven in our green and pleasant land; I loved my home and whatever was necessary to keep it, I swore I would do.

Swift arrived, striding along the gravel path. Nicky instantly made a dash for him and swung about to nip at his ankles.

'NO. Sit down!' he ordered. The pup suddenly sat as told. Swift looked surprised then grinned. 'There you are Lennox, all he needs is a firm voice.'

I glanced up. 'Apparently.'

'Good boy.' Swift leaned over to tickle the pup's ear. The pup gave him a quick lick, then spotted Fogg and Tubbs heading toward the orchard and raced off to join them.

'You don't happen to have a blackboard, do you, Lennox?' Swift looked hopeful.

'Why would I have a blackboard?'

'It would be useful...but never mind.' He took the chair across from me. 'I'm trying to frame the timeline. The murder was after eight fifteen, but before nine twenty-five, because there had to be time for the blood to pool and drip from the edge of the balcony.'

'I know, Swift.' I was wondering where Greggs was with the wine.

'I don't think either Ackroyd or the maid are likely suspects, they were together all that time, although we have to question her first.'

'Swift.'

'What?'

'Can we just enjoy lunch?'

He glanced at the vacant table. 'Yes, as soon as it arrives.

The motive is almost certainly money; we need to find someone who can open the vault. Scotland Yard should be able to help, unless you know anyone locally?'

'If you mean, do I know any safe crackers, the answer is no.'

'Hum, well, Oxford station probably have one or two on their books…'

Greggs emerged from the house and trod sedately across the lawn carrying a tray with a bottle in an ice bucket, and a number of glasses. The girls weren't far behind, Florence with two plates piled with sandwiches and pork pies, while Persi bore a platter of sliced apples, four different cheeses, tomatoes, celery, Cook's best pickle and some scotch eggs.

It didn't take a minute to spread the goodies, along with knives, forks, napkins and the usual whatnots. Greggs poured us each a glass of wine, although Swift would only take a small one as he was 'on duty'.

'Where's Angus?' Swift asked.

'Sound asleep in the parlour. He's been helping Brendan in the garden and worn himself out,' Florence answered in her soft Scottish accent.

'We're dying to hear what happened today.' Persi picked up a cheese sandwich. 'And which one of them did it!'

Swift studiously explained our suspicions about the spots of blood, and the arrow, and that Saunders' body had been moved from the wicker chair to the railings.

'It couldn't be Lady Clementine, then, she's very slim and wouldn't have the strength to lift him,' Persi remarked, glass of wine in hand.

'Indeed not,' Greggs said, then coughed discreetly and went off to fetch more goodies.

'I haven't met any of them.' Florence paused over the plate of sandwiches. 'Apart from Alfred Palgrave, he was walking along the track yesterday morning and introduced himself. He was quite sweet.' She smiled. 'I can't imagine he'd murder anyone.'

'His wife is a siren,' Persi said, having finished her sandwich. 'When we attended that awful dinner party last month she made eyes at every man in the room.'

'Dolores Palgrave,' Swift told Florence. 'According to her statement she didn't leave her bedroom until just before breakfast, but her husband wrote that he went and knocked on her door at twenty to nine, and there was no answer. He tried the door, and it was locked.'

'She lied!' Florence was shocked.

'Which was idiotic,' I said over a slice of pork pie. 'She should have checked with her husband first.'

'She may have simply been in the bathroom,' Persi suggested. 'Or he could have been lying.'

'Perhaps, but she didn't appear to have any respect for her husband,' Swift added. 'And they obviously don't share a room.'

'That's rather sad for him, poor man,' Florence said and reached over to squeeze Swift's hand.

'Margaret Saunders is a cold fish,' Persi remarked as she laid a slice of apple onto a sliver of Cheshire cheese.

'She's the top of my suspects list,' I said.

'And mine,' Persi agreed.

'Isn't she Lady Clementine's daughter?' Florence asked.

'Her step-daughter,' Swift corrected.

I told them Lady Clementine's story about the lion she supposedly shot, and why. They all laughed. I didn't mention her recollections of Swift and the court of Louis quatorze.

Nicky and Fogg returned from wherever they'd been and positioned themselves to watch us. We all passed titbits down to them. Nicky tried to snatch a crust from under Foggy's nose.

'No,' I told the pup.

He paused to look up at me.

'Sit,' Swift ordered. The pup instantly sat.

'Oh, how clever, well done, my love!' Florence beamed at her husband.

'You just have to be assertive,' he said, then patted the little tyke's head.

I didn't say a word.

'I felt sorry for Gabriel Marriott.' Persi swirled her glass of wine.

'Why?' Florence asked as she picked up a slice of scotch egg.

'Her husband, Marcus Marriott, is a bully,' Persi answered.

'And an arrogant blighter,' I added.

'He thinks he's going to step into Saunders' shoes,' Swift said.

'Not literally, I hope.' Persi smiled.

Swift grinned. 'Depends on the killer.'

'It must be rather disconcerting to think one is sharing a house with a murderer.' Florence wiped her hands on a napkin.

'They're convinced it was someone from outside,' I replied.

'But you must explain to them that the killer is among them,' Florence insisted.

'We did,' Swift said. 'We made it quite clear.'

'They refused to believe us, and anyway, there's unlikely to be any more deaths,' I added.

'Why were they all there?' Persi asked.

'Saunders had announced he was about to retire as president,' I answered. 'And now there's a bun fight over who's going to replace him.'

'Well that's a motive right there,' Persi observed.

'And the company is worth an extraordinary amount,' Swift added.

'Ah, that's why you said the motive is money,' Florence said.

'Exactly.' He smiled at her.

'Who inherits Saunders' estate?' Persi asked.

'Margaret Saunders, or so she thinks,' I told her. 'And his shareholding in the company.' I didn't add any more details, but it was playing on my mind.

Greggs arrived, bearing a tray holding four dishes filled with meringues, strawberries and clotted cream. 'Dr Fletcher telephoned, sir.'

Everyone pricked their ears up.

'What did he say?' I asked.

79

'One moment, sir.' He placed the tray at the end of the table, felt in his top pocket and pulled out a folded note. *'Cedric Smedley took a turn for the worse en route to the hospital.'* He squinted at the paper. *'Convulsions, sickness, followed by another heart attack. Died before we landed. Best check his medications, he may have taken too little, or too much.'*

There were a couple of shocked gasps and Swift decided to go and call Fletcher at the hospital.

'You just said there wouldn't be any more deaths.' Florence's eyes had widened. 'You don't think...'

'If it was murder, it's aimed at those in Ashton Hall. There's no danger to anyone here.' I tried to reassure her.

She didn't look entirely convinced and fidgeted for a few minutes before deciding to go and check on the sleeping Angus.

'I suppose we'd better return to the Hall.' I pulled my dessert dish towards me.

'I could come.' Persi sounded keen.

'I...' I knew how fearless she was, but I really didn't want to put her at risk. I decided on diversionary tactics. 'Actually it would be useful if you questioned the locals. Ask them if they know anything. A couple of local girls used to work as maids at the Hall, listen to what they have to say.'

'Lennox.' She gave a throaty laugh. 'I know you're just trying to protect me, but I'm perfectly capable of taking care of myself.'

I gave her a grin. 'I know, Kitsy, I remember the snakes and scorpions...'

'Damascus, yes.' She leaned both arms on the table and turned serious. 'Darling, I know you and Swift are trying to prove yourselves with Scotland Yard, but I don't want to be excluded from this part of your life.'

She was right, and it gave me pause for thought. 'I'll talk to Swift.'

'And if you don't, Florence will.' She smiled.

I sighed, why is it women always found ways to get just what they wanted. 'Fine,' I agreed and finished my dessert.

Swift returned. 'Fletcher had already left the hospital, but they're going to start the post mortem on Smedley later this afternoon. I told them it was urgent.' He didn't sit down, instead started pacing about the grass. 'I called Billings too, he thinks the answer's in the vault. He's having checks done on Saunders' finance company and his dealings. He said—'

'Swift.' I stood up. 'Come on.'

'Where?'

'Ashton Hall.'

'What about the events board, we need to—'

'Persi and Florence will do that,' I cut into his fretting. 'Won't you, Kitsy?'

'As you command, oh master,' she teased.

I leaned down to give her a peck on the cheek then went off with Swift at my side.

# CHAPTER 8

The Bentley's engine was still warm and a few minutes later we drove up to the gates of Ashton Hall. They'd been closed in our absence and almost a dozen denizens had gathered either side of the drive. A couple had brought deckchairs and were sitting in comfort on the grass verge.

I recognised most of the crowd. They shouted out light-hearted greetings. I assumed news of the latest death hadn't escaped yet.

'You go get 'em, Major,' Mr Briers called, raising his pipe.

'Will do, thank you,' I returned.

Mrs Tippet, the village busybody, waved; she held a panting Pekinese on a leash. Shelley Bays was handing out tea and biscuits. Fossett was nowhere to be seen.

Swift frowned.

'I'll open up, shall I, Major?' Frank Wright offered.

'If you would,' I called back.

A few of the others dashed forward to help and they pushed the gates wide.

'And you'd best shut them again, please.' I gave an

amiable wave and motored up the drive to park on the carefully raked gravel.

I let Swift rap on the knocker.

'Good afternoon, sirs.' Ackroyd opened the door. 'You will find the household in the breakfast room. They are partaking of lunch.'

He really was ridiculously punctilious.

'Not the dining room?' I remarked knowing it would pain him.

'This is not a house of consequence, sir,' he intoned with a sniff of disdain.

I hid a smile and followed Swift, who had marched off across the hall, his shoes echoing on the black and white marble floor.

'What happened to Cedric?' Margaret Saunders demanded as we walked into the breakfast room.

They had obviously just finished eating and were about to embark on tea. A maid flitted about with a silver teapot; her eyes darted in our direction as we arrived, but she carried on filling fancy porcelain cups. Dolores Palgrave was smoking a cigarette, a slim lighter and her gold sequinned bag on the table in front of her. The rest merely gazed at us in stony silence.

'Cedric Smedley died on the way to hospital,' Swift announced.

I'd expected the odd gasp of horror, but they seemed more annoyed by the news.

'Damn it, he was forever gorging himself, the bloody fool,' Marcus Marriott swore.

'There are ladies present, Marcus,' Dolores Palgrave reminded him, and turned to throw her cigarette into the unlit fireplace.

Marriott muttered something under his breath, but didn't apologise. The room was almost cosy with French wallpaper, two large oak dressers displaying decorative china, and a pair of glazed doors overlooking the terrace and gardens.

'Could you tell us the cause?' Alfred Palgrave asked politely.

'We don't know yet,' I said and sat in the nearest chair to better observe them. 'It may have been something he ate.'

They all stared at their empty plates.

'Do you believe that?' Gabriel Marriott turned to Swift.

He softened, ever the Galahad. 'No, we think it was merely a heart attack,' he reassured her, then threw a dark look at me.

'It was obviously the strain of poor Devlin's death,' Margaret Saunders declared. 'Whoever murdered my husband now has two deaths on their hands.'

'Will it delay us leaving?' Marriott demanded.

'Yes.' Swift sat down in the chair at the head of the table. 'Who was Smedley's doctor?' He pulled out his notebook and a newly sharpened pencil.

'Dr Rorke in Harley Street,' Alfred Palgrave answered. 'Cedric has been on heart medication for the last year.'

'How do you know that?' I asked.

'He told me,' he replied, blinking rapidly.

Swift made a note in his book. 'What medication was he taking?'

'Digitalis,' Palgrave fidgeted in his seat. 'My father has the same problem, that's the reason Cedric and I had discussed the subject.'

I suspected everyone knew the effects and dangers of digitalis; beneficial to the heart in low doses, deadly in excess. Rather like most things, I supposed.

'How long are we going to be held here, now?' the Honourable Sebastian Cardhew demanded.

'Until I say so,' Swift replied and turned a page.

'It's rather sad for Cedric,' Gabriel Marriott said quietly. Nobody echoed her sentiment.

'I suppose his death doesn't make any difference, all bets are off now anyway,' Dolores Palgrave said brusquely, and pushed a strand of black hair away from her fine-boned face.

'Dolores, be careful what you're saying,' Marcus Marriott snapped at her.

'Oh, for Heaven's sake, Marcus.' Dolores wasn't in the least cowed. 'It's irrelevant, she's got what she wanted.' She glared at Margaret Saunders.

'That's enough, you've no right to blurt our business in front of the police.' Sebastian Cardhew joined in.

Swift and I sat back in our chairs as the suppressed tension exploded into open hostility.

'You would say that, wouldn't you, Sebastian,' Dolores snapped back. 'You've been sucking up to Margaret since Devlin's death.'

'That's outrageous, and you've no room to talk. Don't think we don't see the games you've been playing, Dolores,' Cardhew retaliated.

'Games *I've been playing*?' she rasped. 'You think the company is yours for the asking, now, don't you?'

'Sebastian would run it very well.' Margaret put her teacup clattering down onto the saucer.

'He would be a disaster.' Marriott leaned forward to glare at Margaret across the table. 'Do you really want the company run into the ground by that ignorant fool, or by Palgrave?' He stabbed a finger toward them. 'Neither of them are competent. The business will fall apart and the income will go with it. You'll be penniless within months. I'm the only one fit to take Devlin's place.'

'You would think that.' Dolores challenged him, her grey eyes flashing. 'You're nothing but an arrogant misogynist.'

He turned on her. 'Are you telling me you think you could run the company?' he sneered.

She suddenly slapped him across the face. 'Don't equate me with your stupid wife,' she hissed. 'I'm just as capable as you are.'

Marriott glowered, his cheek reddening. I saw him clench his fists, so did Gabriel, she moved to put a restraining hand on his arm and whisper something quietly to him.

'Dolores, must you make such a spectacle of yourself?' Alfred Palgrave objected, which I thought brave of him.

'Don't dare talk to me like that, you simpleton,' she retaliated. 'Don't you understand what's happening? We're all sunk, and we know who's behind it.' She turned blazing eyes on Margaret Saunders. 'You did it, didn't you? You've got it all now. Everything you wanted.'

Margaret stared in astonishment. 'Are you accusing me of killing Devlin?'

'Of course it was you. You've got your claws on Devlin's shares, and you're so besotted with Sebastian, you're going to give them to him, aren't you?' Dolores stood up and raged at her.

'That's completely unwarranted,' Cardhew objected, jumping to his feet. 'And you should not shout at Margaret like that.'

'That's enough,' Swift shouted. 'Sit down.'

They both did so. Dolores crossed her arms, her brow creased in fury, scarlet lipstick puckering around her mouth.

'You need to explain what this is about,' Swift demanded, turning to Marcus Marriott.

He glowered. 'Devlin announced he was going to retire and he would sell his shares to one of us, that's why we came here.' He spoke through gritted teeth. 'The sale was to be by auction, we were expected to bid against each other.'

It took a moment to register the meaning of that. We'd been told Saunders was going to announce the next president, this was something new.

'But now that Saunders is dead, his shares will be distributed according to his will?' Swift surmised. 'Is that correct?' He addressed Margaret Saunders.

'Yes,' she replied with a shrug. 'He will have left them to me.'

'And you intend giving them to Cardhew?' I asked and glanced at him. His smooth face turned as red as his blazer.

'I haven't decided what I'm going to do.' There was no sign of the 'bereft widow' now.

'Actually, the bidding will have to go ahead because Devlin signed a covenant that required his shares to be sold within a certain time,' Arthur Palgrave spoke up.

'What?' Marriott demanded as all eyes fixed on Palgrave. 'How do you know that?'

'Cedric told me last evening,' Palgrave explained. 'He said it was legally binding and there's no getting out of it. The lawyer advised Devlin to do it.'

'I don't believe you,' Sebastian Cardhew broke in. 'Nobody told me about it, and besides, we aren't able to raise any funds without Cedric, so there can't be any bidding.'

'Smedley was arranging loans for you all?' I aimed a calculated guess.

Marriott glowered. 'Precisely.'

Now it was beginning to make sense. 'Who's eligible to bid for the shares?'

'Directors only,' Marriott replied, then turned to Alfred Palgrave. 'What was the time limit on the auction?'

'By the end of this week,' Palgrave responded.

'Nobody has explained any of this to me. What does it mean?' Margaret Saunders seemed confused.

Dolores Palgrave suddenly burst out laughing. 'It means all your plans have just gone up in smoke, Margaret.'

'Sebastian, will you explain what they're talking about?' Margaret sounded close to hysterics.

Cardhew didn't answer, he seemed just as confounded.

'Devlin's shares must be sold according to the covenant he signed, regardless of whoever inherited them,' Marcus Marriott was quicker to understand the implications. 'But without Cedric to arrange loans for us, nobody can borrow any more money, so we can only pay according to our means.' He fixed cold eyes on Margaret. 'If you have inherited Devlin's shares, and are forced to sell, you'll have to accept whatever we offer.' He straightened up. 'In which case, I propose a bid of one pound a share.'

'Then I'll go to two pounds,' Alfred Palgrave declared. His wife's head swivelled to stare at him.

'Three would be my maximum,' Sebastian Cardhew suddenly piped up, and then laughed.

Even I recognised that was a brutal betrayal, even if it were only meant as a joke.

Margaret Saunders' mouth open and closed as her eyes widened; the realisation of what was happening slowly sinking in. 'Sebastian, you...you fiend. All of you – you are treacherous. How dare you do this to me, how dare you!' She turned on them. 'Well, it won't do you any good because I'll overturn that stupid covenant. I will inherit the majority holding and I'll control the company.'

'Alfred said the covenant is legally binding,' Marriott reminded her. 'You can't rescind it, Margaret.'

That caused another outburst of argument and we let them shout at each other for a few minutes before Swift interrupted.

'Quiet,' he yelled, then had to repeat himself.

They shut up in red-faced anger, apart from Gabriel Marriott who was quietly watching her husband.

'One question,' I said before anyone else spoke. 'Who did Cedric Smedley leave his shares to?'

# CHAPTER 9

Nobody knew the answer to that question.

'We need Tremayne,' Marriott stated.

'Who's Tremayne?' Swift demanded.

'The company lawyer,' Sebastian Cardhew answered.

'Why didn't you ask him to come earlier?' I added, as it seemed ridiculous they hadn't.

'We did, but he said it was the weekend and he had to wait to gather some paperwork from his office first,' Cardhew continued in petulant tone. 'We'd have returned to London to see him there if your stupid constable hadn't stopped us.'

'He's not stupid,' I retorted. 'And I'll remind you that one of the people in this house is a murderer and no-one's going anywhere until we find them.'

'Poppycock,' Cardhew retorted.

'I'm going to telephone Tremayne this minute,' Margaret Saunders snapped then stalked out of the door and slammed it behind her.

A moment's silence hung in the room as they looked at each other.

'I've had enough,' Dolores announced. 'This is a stupid mess.'

'Dolores, I really don't think...' Alfred began an objection.

'You should have told me what Cedric said.' She aimed her fury at him.

'I didn't have a chance...' he tried to explain.

'Oh, just shut up, you unutterable idiot,' she yelled in his face before flouncing out.

'I have affairs to attend to.' Marriott stood up. 'Gabriel.' He held his hand out to his wife. She rose and slipped her hand into his, her face almost serene.

Swift didn't object to them leaving; they all took their cue and filed from the room.

'If you don't put a stop to this,' Sebastian Cardhew paused to accuse us. 'They'll be at each other's throats, and it will be all your fault.'

'Our fault...' I was astounded. 'How the hell can it be our fault?' I was wasting my breath because the damned popinjay just stalked off.

Swift watched him go. 'He's the self-absorbed sort, Lennox. Everything is someone else's fault.'

'They're all the damned same, every single one of them, self-centred, avaricious money-grubbers.'

'I doubt Gabriel Marriott is.' He slipped his notebook back into his pocket. 'Come on, we need to find Fossett, and I want to search Smedley's room.' He led the way out.

'Do you know where it is?'

'Upstairs probably,' he replied glibly. For some reason his

mood had improved. Perhaps he enjoyed being on the trail of a bunch of suspects who were almost uniformly awful.

'I heard the hubbub, sir. It is most unbecoming.' We found Ackroyd at the foot of the stairs. 'But I am resigned to expect nothing else in this house.' He was as inclined to martyrdom as Greggs was.

'Smedley's bedroom,' I said, not being in the mood for martyrs.

'I will escort you, sirs. You will find Constable Fossett already in place.'

'Is he, now,' Swift remarked, as we followed the stiff-backed butler upstairs.

Voices could be heard from inside.

'You're not supposed to be in here,' Fossett was telling Lady Clementine as we entered.

'It's my house, I can go wherever I choose,' she replied with utter insouciance.

'Fossett,' Swift said.

'Ah...' He spun around. 'Sir, I've been telling her ladyship that she's not allowed...'

'Oh, don't mind me, I'm just keeping him company,' she replied lightly.

'If you wouldn't mind, Lady Clementine...' Swift indicated the door, which Ackroyd was still holding open.

'Oh, you are so manly! Just as you always were.' She beamed up at Swift as she sauntered out past him.

Swift waited until Ackroyd closed the door behind him. 'Absolutely barking.' He shook his head, then fixed steely eyes on Fossett. 'You were supposed to be guarding the gate.'

'Half the village are down there, sir. They'd soon tell me if any of 'em tried to run off,' he explained. 'And my uncle works at the railway, so they can't escape by train, either,' he added in a hurt tone.

Swift wasn't quick to forgive. 'Have you fingerprinted the room?' He looked around, it was obvious the lad hadn't.

'Not yet, sir, but I did find something you'd want to see.' Fossett attempted to re-establish himself. 'It's by his bed, look.' He went over to the bedside cabinet. It held a glass and water carafe on a circular tray. Fossett had donned white cotton gloves and picked up the glass to show Swift. 'See, there's bits left in it.'

'Residue from powder, or crystals,' Swift observed. 'He took digitalis, have you found any medications?'

'I have, sir, it's in a fancy box in the top drawer. I covered it with a handkerchief.' He pulled open the drawer, lifted out an object wrapped in a square of white cotton and carefully unveiled it with a look of studious concentration of his face. 'There!' he said in triumph.

It was a silver cigarette box the size of a small book, the lid heavily ornamented, depicting a hunting scene with horses, riders, hounds, and even a fox.

'What's inside?' Swift drew his magnifying glass from his pocket.

'Papers with powder in 'em.' Fossett pressed a catch and the lid sprang open. It was like watching an amateur magic show.

The scent of tobacco wafted from the box, but it held

neatly folded sachets of powder. Tucked against the side was a small pile of used papers tightly screwed along their length.

'I counted them. There's eight twisted papers and there's twenty-three sachets not been opened yet,' Fossett told us.

'Thirty-one papers,' Swift was quick to calculate.

'It's May, one for each day of the month,' I said.

'Yep.' Fossett nodded. 'And it's only the seventh today, but there's eight used sachets.' He picked up one of the twisted papers. 'And one of them's been screwed the wrong way.' He held it up between the finger and thumb of his gloves. 'All the others are twisted over an' under, but this'uns been twisted under an' over. I reckon someone poured an extra dose into his glass, screwed up the paper and put it back in the box thinking it was done like the others.'

'Well done, Fossett.' Swift broke into a broad grin.

'Excellent, that man,' I congratulated him.

He beamed from ear to ear. 'I didn't say a word about it to Lady Clementine, nor anybody.'

'And you wore gloves,' I added to the laudations.

'Mr Ackroyd has lots of pairs of white gloves, he gave them to me. I needed some so's to be careful about fingerprints, but they're a bit tight.' He waggled them at us.

'Ackroyd probably never milked cows,' I remarked.

'Doubt he ever did sir.' Fossett grinned.

'What?' Swift looked at me.

'Anyone who's grown up milking cows has big hands,' I explained.

'Or chopped logs, or hauled coal.' Fossett warmed to the theme. 'Or done any proper work.'

Swift gave a brief shake of his head. 'Right, Fossett, we'll dust for fingerprints. Lennox, you can make a search, see what else we can turn up.'

'I've got another pair of gloves, if you need 'em, sir,' Fossett offered and delved into his satchel to tug them out.

The seams ripped as I pulled them on. I gave them back without a word.

'Too small, Major?' Fossett remarked. 'I'm not surprised, you being a proper countryman.'

They set to work in companionable silence, busy with brush and copious amounts of powder. Fossett spread it carefully across the surface of the silver cigarette box, Swift aimed his magnifying glass as he went. I shoved my hands in my pockets and gazed about, not being keen on rifling through Smedley's drawers.

'He must have had a briefcase,' I remarked.

'He did,' Fossett replied, his face fixed in concentration on the brush. 'It was locked up in the silver vault according to Mr Ackroyd. Probably still in there, I'd guess.'

'Damn.' I sighed, I supposed I'd have to go through Smedley's clothes. I threw open the wardrobe. A knock sounded at the door.

'Come in,' I called out.

Ackroyd entered. 'I would like to inform you, sirs, that Sir Edwin Tremayne will be arriving tomorrow morning on the 10 o'clock train,' he announced as though proclaiming the next King of England. 'I have been instructed that he will be staying in this room. I must therefore prepare it.'

'Not until we've finished,' Swift said. He'd brought along the sheet of inky fingerprints Fossett had taken from the house guests on the day of Saunders' murder, and was now studying it closely.

'You can search for clues, that will speed the process,' I said to the butler.

Ackroyd brightened at that. 'Clues, sir? Very well, how should I commence?'

'Go through drawers, cupboards, wardrobes and whatever else you can think, and show your findings to Inspector Swift,' I told him. 'I'll see you later.'

'Lennox?' Swift called as I strode out of the door and out of earshot.

I'd intended to go in search of Lady Clementine, but didn't get very far. Margaret Saunders was stalking along the corridor, and instantly pounced.

'Major Lennox, I simply must speak to you.'

'Must you,' I said dourly.

'Come with me,' she demanded and led off. 'I need a man.'

That gave me pause.

'Well, come along.' She turned to glare at me, then marched to a door and yanked it open. It was a bedroom, hers presumably judging by the full-length stand-up mirror, range of perfume bottles on the dressing table, and ruched bedspread in a ghastly shade of mauve.

'This is my room,' she announced, needlessly. The room

was the same size as her late husband's, which occupied the opposite wing of the house, as far from hers as possible.

She advanced on me. I backed away to the window. It was an ordinary one. 'You don't have a balcony,' I said, glancing at the sweep of back lawn.

'The builders ran out of money, apparently.' She dropped onto a small pink sofa. 'But I didn't ask you here to discuss architecture, Major Lennox. Please be seated.' She patted the sofa.

I went to sit on the chair opposite.

'I don't bite you know.'

'Why do you need "a man"?' I asked.

'To stand up for me. Sebastian obviously won't. You heard him, he's with them and they're determined to beggar me.' Gone was her archly deferential attitude, she was brittle and angry. 'It's unconscionable, it's…it's unscrupulous, how could they do this?' She clenched her hand into a fist and banged it on the arm of the sofa. 'They don't care what happens to me, they'll do anything for money, they're rapacious, grasping, and will stop at nothing.'

'Isn't that the basic qualification for money grubbers?' I remarked.

Her eyes flashed in irritation, but she ignored the provocation. 'If they think they're going to cheat me, they've got another think coming!' She carried on. 'I won't let them win, they'll see. I'm the majority shareholder now, I'll find a way to overturn their stupid rules.'

Normally I'd be sympathetic to a widow's plight, but it was quite clear she was as bad as the rest of the sharks in the house. 'Are you certain your husband left you his shares?'

'Of course he did, who else would he leave them to? And I'll prove it.' She became imperious. 'His will is in the vault, you must open it.'

'How?'

'I've no idea, surely you must be able to do it.' She had crossed her legs and her foot twitched in irritation, causing sunlight to glint on her black patent shoes. 'Or you know someone, or that inspector of yours does. I mean what are you here for, otherwise?' The high colour of her anger enhanced her allure. Manicured and maquillaged, primped and permed, the sort of woman who always looked her best, even when she wasn't on her best behaviour.

I decided not to answer her question on the principle that it was fatuous. 'I thought you'd just called your lawyer, surely he can answer your questions about your husband's will?'

'He might, but Devlin was quite secretive...very secretive actually, and anyway, Edwin Tremayne is a stickler. He'll follow the law, he won't take sides. I can't rely on him to bend any rules.'

'And neither will we,' I retorted.

She flashed another set of daggers at me then looked down at her shiny shoes. 'No, well, why would you...We're not good people, I know that.'

'Do you really?' I drawled in disbelief.

'Of course.' Her voice dropped. 'Nobody's taken in. Only the desperate would borrow money from Devlin.

He'd come out of a meeting and say, "There's another fool for the fleecing". Then he and Cedric would go and calculate how long it would take to bankrupt them so they could foreclose on their properties.'

I could feel my blood beginning to boil, given my own situation. 'Were loans always made against clients' homes?'

'Yes, it was their "business model".' She glanced at me. 'It wasn't greed, although everyone thinks it is, but it's actually the hunt. They're predators, or they were…It's so hard to believe they're both gone.' Her voice sounded almost normal, I'd only ever heard her speak in strident tones. 'They picked off the weak and the foolish. That's what everyone does in their circle. The people they knew were all the same. Hyenas, sharks, wolves, jackals.' She waved a hand. 'They'd all call themselves something like that. It was a joke between them, and we wives had to accept it…'

'Are you trying to say you didn't want all the trappings of wealth?' I didn't believe her for a moment.

'Oh, we enjoyed the lifestyle – who wouldn't? Dressing to the nines, glittering with gold and jewellery, playing the perfect hostess. It's every girl's dream, isn't it?' She smiled suddenly. I wasn't amused.

'Was your husband faithful to you?' My tone was cold as I asked a proper detective's question.

She let out a peel of harsh laughter. 'No, never. It wasn't expected, and it would have made no difference if it were.'

'Has he had…' I sought a delicate phrase. 'A relationship with any of the ladies here?'

'Dolores, of course, but then she's an alley cat, so what do you expect.' Her face flushed, the brazen mask slipping. 'She wants to run the company! Isn't that ludicrous. A woman, can you imagine! And she's not even clever, she's just venal.'

'Who else has Dolores had liaisons with?' I wondered if I should take my notebook out and write things down, then I remembered I'd left it at home.

'I don't know.' She shrugged. 'All of them probably.'

Her words didn't ring true. 'Including Marcus Marriott?'

'No, not Marcus, he's besotted with his little mousey wife.'

That raised my brows. 'Really? He doesn't seem the sort to be besotted.'

'No, it's a joke isn't it.' She didn't look amused. 'Marcus in love, and with such a bland creature. He cares for her, protects her, he's even faithful to her.' She closed her painted lips and dropped her gaze. The actions of her 'friends', the way they'd turned on her, seemed to have scored a deep hurt. 'What does it take to be loved?' she suddenly asked. 'I did everything Devlin wanted – played the role to perfection; I kept my mouth shut, looked the other way. I was exactly the wife he wanted, and he paid me well for it – that's how he put it – he said I was bought and paid for...But he never loved me.'

'I'm sorry,' I said, and almost meant it.

'Do you love your wife?' She looked me in the eyes.

'More than life.'

She suddenly burst into tears, and leaned to slump onto the sofa, deep painful sobs racking her body.

I stood up, not sure what to do, then realised there wasn't anything I could do, so I left quietly, closing the door behind me.

# CHAPTER 10

I returned to Smedley's bedroom, thinking Swift was probably steaming by now.

'Lennox, this room is a crime scene and might hold clues to the murderer. You should have stayed to help,' he hissed at me while Fossett and Ackroyd assiduously rifled through drawers, pretending they weren't listening.

'And has it?' I asked.

He frowned. 'No, but…'

'Fine, come to Devlin Saunders' bedroom,' I said and led the way out.

'It's the on-site incident room.' He corrected me as we walked along the corridor.

I swear he made these things up as he went along.

'Did you find anything?' he continued.

'Not particularly.'

I heard his sigh of exasperation. 'And you shouldn't have asked Ackroyd to help in the search, he hasn't been cleared.' He began a mild rant. 'I had to tell Fossett to keep an eye on him.'

'Righto,' I said. Fossett's "Police" sign had slipped to the floor. I picked it up and pinned it back in place then entered the 'on-site incident room'. It was, if anything, even brighter than before, the afternoon sun now shinning directly through the French windows.

We took up positions on either side of the walnut writing table.

'You're certain Smedley didn't just take a double dose by accident?'

'Yes, we're certain.' Swift picked up a sheet of paper. 'We tested it ourselves. You're right-handed, and likely to screw the paper by twisting it with your right hand away from you, and your left hand towards you...like this.' He demonstrated.

I took a sheet of writing paper from the desk, folded it along its length then screwed it laterally. I checked the paper in my hand – he was right.

'Smedley was left-handed, and seven of the used papers were wound with the left hand away and right toward. Only one of them was twisted right away and left toward,' Swift added helpfully.

'Hum...' I turned my piece around to see if the twist changed. It didn't. 'How do you know Smedley was left-handed?'

'Ackroyd noticed, and he's also left-handed, so we experimented on him.'

I glanced up at that but he was absorbed with twisting paper. 'So you're convinced a right-handed person somehow poured an extra powder into his glass of water when he wasn't looking?' I was dubious.

'It's more likely they added it to the remains of the water in the carafe. Ackroyd said the maid fills them every morning at around ten o'clock when she makes the beds, and Smedley's carafe was usually empty by the time she arrived.'

'Had she refilled his carafe this morning?' I recalled Fossett showing us the powder residue in the glass. 'Or cleaned up?'

'No, Fossett ordered the whole household to stay downstairs when he arrived. She hasn't cleaned any of the bedrooms today.'

'Smedley's room was quite neat,' I recalled.

'He was another tidy sort according to Ackroyd, it was the only good thing he had to say about him.'

I nodded. 'Did you find any residue in the carafe?'

'A tiny amount. We'll send that with the glass to the laboratory for testing. There weren't any fingerprints, the killer probably poured the powder in without touching the carafe.'

I thought about it. 'So it was added sometime after ten o'clock yesterday.'

'Or early this morning.' He'd taken his notebook and pencil out. 'The sachets were lined up in neat order in the cigarette box. Smedley probably picked one out every morning, emptied it into his glass of water then twisted the used paper in case he needed to double-check how many he'd taken.'

'He was an accountant, so it sounds reasonable,' I agreed.

105

Swift nodded and wrote a line in his notebook.

'Margaret Saunders cornered me,' I told him.

He glanced up. 'Serves you right for clearing off.'

I grinned, then told him the tale. 'It's a pretty shabby set-up,' I remarked at the end.

'The price of greed.' His lean features sharpened.

'They pretend it's "the hunt" but I don't believe it.' I leaned back in my chair. 'I have never understood why people can't be content with just having enough. Why must they grab everything, including whatever anyone else has?'

'I've always thought it comes from hatred.' Swift paused in contemplation. 'The few avaricious people I've dealt with have been totally obnoxious. They've been nasty from childhood and shunned as a consequence, and their response is to fight.'

'Schoolground bullies?'

'That's usually where it starts. They can't get attention any other way, their only interaction with the rest of the human race is through aggression. They rouse antipathy, and it engenders anger; the bully lashes out and in many cases makes the other party pay. Whatever they gain is considered restitution, and a sort of trophy…a symbol of their power.'

'And they feel entirely justified,' I added, recalling the type from school. I'd always been too big to bully, but I'd stood up for the poor saps who were undersized or too passive for their own good. 'From the descriptions of Saunders, I'd say he fitted the type, but did Smedley?'

Swift shook his head. 'He didn't seem the bullying sort, just greedy.'

The door opened. Alfred Palgrave sidled in.

'Could I stay in here for a while?' He shut the door quietly and came over. 'My wife's on the warpath, and I recall you said you wanted to interview us, so I thought I'd kill two birds with one stone, haha.'

His laughter was forced. He had the look of a maltreated hound facing another whipping.

'Sit down, man,' I told him.

Swift reverted to police mode and flicked through his notebook. 'You're Alfred Palgrave, a director and share-holder of Royal Buckingham Financial...' he began.

'Oh God, don't remind me.' Palgrave slumped in his seat, his forced smile sinking into misery. 'This a nightmare.'

Swift glanced up. 'In what way?'

'Everything...absolutely everything.' Palgrave raised a hand to run through his carefully combed hair, ruining the style. 'I don't know what to do, there doesn't seem any way out.' His accent was as refined and authentic as mine. Whichever path had led him to the Royal Buckingham, it had started in an upper-crust household.

'Who's your family?' I asked.

His eyes flicked to mine. 'We're a branch of the Somersets.'

'Somersets?' Swift asked.

'Duke of Somerset, he's the paterfamilias, they used to own the place.' He meant the county.

'How far removed are you?' I continued.

'Oh, younger son of many younger sons. We're about as minor as you can get.' Palgrave sounded desolate. 'Most of us are penniless with no discernible talent. Pa's a clergyman, Ma the daughter of another clergyman, none of us ever had a bean to rub together.'

'But more of a pedigree than any others in the Royal Buckingham?' I guessed.

He nodded.

'What about the Honourable Sebastian Cardhew?' Swift asked.

'He's not an "Hon.",' Palgrave replied. 'He's a charlatan.'

'But you've got actual connections?' I affirmed.

He gave a mirthless laugh. 'Exactly, old chap. I've benefitted from public schooling, and am occasionally privileged to rub shoulders with my illustrious cousins.'

'You're bait,' Swift stated.

'Bravo, exquisitely deduced.' Palgrave tried another grin, then folded his arms and let his chin sink to his chest. His shoulders shuddered but he managed to keep himself under control.

I pulled out my hip flask and unscrewed the top, which doubled as a cup. 'Drink?'

He looked up. 'Won't say no.' He reached for the cap as I filled it with amber liquid. 'I'm not a lush, you know.'

I grinned. 'Neither am I. It's Braeburn whisky from Swift's wife's estate.'

'You're a toff, too?' Palgrave asked Swift.

'No.' Swift extracted his own flask. We all drank in

quiet contemplation, giving the chap time to pull himself together.

'How did you come to own shares in the company?' I asked by way of an opening.

'Dolores.' He clutched the silver cap in his slim hand. 'I met her in a club in Soho. She was with a loud group, I was with a bunch of pals, it was just after the war and we were making a night of it. We got together and by the end of the year we were married.'

'Children?' Swift asked.

'No, nor will there be.' Palgrave finished his whisky. 'She wants a divorce, but not until I've nabbed a bigger share of the company.' His voice trembled, so did his hand.

'What does being "bait" entail?' Swift shifted the subject as Palgrave was obviously distressed.

'It varies. They wanted me to draw in the gilded side of my family. I kept telling them that they're too smart and too well advised to be caught out. After a while Devlin realised it was true but he knew I had other connections. Sometimes I'd hear through the grapevine that so-and-so was in financial trouble. Devlin would send me in to soften up the poor sap, assure them that we were proper people. Trustworthy, you know.' His lips twisted. 'Once I'd calmed their nerves, I'd pass them either to Sebastian or Marcus. They'd talk them into the deal, and eventually have them sign the contract.' He let out a breath. 'At first I didn't realise how it really worked, as I said, I'm not much of a brain box. But one day one of my close friends asked me to arrange a loan for him. I passed him to Sebastian, he gave him the usual slick patter, and then my friend marched back in to see me – he was absolutely blazing. He accused me of being a bloodsucker, and a traitor, and… and worse. He said I was deliberately manoeuvring him into penury. I think I'd known it, but hadn't wanted to admit it, not to myself. My friend told everyone what I was doing, and I became an outcast – none of my pals wanted to know me. I told Dolores I had to quit, and she exploded in fury. We'd just bought a flat, Devlin had lent the money, she raged at me, telling me I had to carry on with the company or we'd lose everything. And now I have anyway…'

We stopped talking and drank more whisky. It didn't take a genius to see how he'd been drawn in, or how the victims had been netted.

'Why did Smedley tell only you about the legal covenant requiring Saunders' shares to be sold?' I asked.

He shrugged. 'We were discussing money, my loan, actually, and he just came out with it.' His voice cracked again.

Swift stepped in with a neutral question. 'How was the bidding for Saunders' shares arranged?'

'Oh,' he sighed. 'It was to be a real bloodbath. Devlin thought it highly amusing, of course.' He blinked rapidly. 'It was a few weeks ago. He called us into his office in London and announced he was going to retire. We duly applauded, offered the usual accolades, and the others started calculating how to carve up the company without him. Then he said his shares were for sale and he'd accept the highest offer. That caused a massive row, Marcus thought he was going to take over, he still does actually. As soon as he realised he'd have to find the funds to outbid everyone else, he hit the roof.'

'Did Cedric Smedley join in the bidding?' Swift asked.

'At first, yes, and then he calculated he could make money by arranging loans for the rest of us. Cedric's even older than Devlin, he didn't actually want to run the company,' Palgrave explained. 'Anyway, the offer of loans fuelled the frenzy. Without loans, our bids were limited by how much cash we each had, but once everyone could borrow, the bids flew sky-high. Then Devlin said he would hold an auction because the arguments were disrupting the running of the company. It was typical of him, always changing the rules to suit himself. He informed us it would be held at his 'country residence' which meant here, and it was set to be today, actually.'

'You intended bidding?' I watched him, his eyes glinting with tears, and fear. He was completely out of his depth.

'Yes, I had to, Dolores insisted. I didn't know at the time that she wanted to divorce me…that came after I'd signed the agreement with Cedric.'

'What agreement?' Swift had been quietly making notes.

'To borrow twenty-one thousand pounds…' His voice broke on the words.

Swift shook his head in silence. I stared at Palgrave; the sum was three times the amount I was in hock for.

'This was the loan you were discussing when Smedley

told you about the covenant Saunders had signed.' I put two and two together. 'Were you trying to get out of it?'

He nodded as tears began to spill from his eyes. 'But by then, he'd already transferred the funds into my account and he said I couldn't wriggle out.'

'Your wife wants the shares as part of your divorce settlement?' Swift said softly.

'Yes.' Palgrave reached for his handkerchief and blew into it. It sounded the sort of situation that would drive a man to madness.

'What about your flat?' Swift had stopped writing.

'The one in London? Dolores wants that too, she's told me to move out…I'm at the end, I can't take much more…' He suddenly stood up, tears streaming down his cheeks. He put the cap down and stumbled toward the door, handkerchief balled in his fist. We didn't speak as the door closed behind him.

'If ever anyone has a motive to murder, it's him,' Swift observed, and wrote it in his notebook.

# CHAPTER 11

'That's two in a row,' I remarked.

'Dead?' Swift glanced up from his notebook.

'No, in tears.'

'You seem to have that effect on them.'

'Hm.' I frowned. 'Palgrave went to see Smedley last evening to ask him to dissolve the loan because he thought the bidding would be called off.'

'And Smedley told him about the covenant, and that the auction had to go ahead,' Swift added then put pencil to paper. 'Palgrave must be a desperate man indeed.'

'And forced into a corner by his awful wife,' I said. 'Margaret Saunders described her as an alley cat.'

Swift continued making notes. 'What else did she say?'

'I've already told you.'

'I need to write it down.'

I rolled my eyes. 'Fine. She said Dolores had affairs with all the men, apart from Marcus Marriott who loves his wife. She's convinced she'll inherit her husband's shares and overturn the covenant to take control of the company, and then she said Dolores is as shallow and venal as the rest of them.'

He looked up. 'She said that?'

'Well, not in those exact words.'

He added another note.

'She might be putting a target on her back,' I mused.

He paused, then shook his head. 'Alfred Palgrave's the prime suspect, why would he kill Margaret? His problem is with his wife.'

'I can't imagine Alfred Palgrave as a cold-blooded killer.'

'It's not a popularity contest, Lennox,' he said dryly.

'I know, but why didn't he simply murder Dolores?'

'Because he'd be suspect number one,' he countered, which didn't make any sense.

I let out a sigh, then switched to something that had been churning in the back of my mind. 'Cedric Smedley was organising loans for the directors to bid for Saunders' shares,' I began. 'He didn't include himself in the running because he intended retiring, or simply didn't want the extra work.'

Swift put his pencil down. 'And could make more from arranging the loans.'

'What if he were playing kingmaker,' I suggested.

'Hmm…' He leaned back in his chair. 'Which one would he make king, and why?'

'Marcus Marriott is probably the most intelligent of the lot,' I said.

'Then why not just give him the role?' Swift countered.

'Because that's not their style is it, they'd have wanted to maximise their profits.'

'In which case Saunders and Smedley were conniving together,' Swift concluded.

'Yes…that's likely isn't it,' I agreed. 'Smedley offered them loans, thus profiting Saunders by the increased bids, and Smedley would earn commission.'

'And interest,' Swift added, then mused, 'Assuming they did want Marriott to win, Smedley would have to know the savings each man had because they'd be able to add that to whatever he agreed to loan them.'

'Both Smedley and Saunders would know how much the men earned, they'd have been able to make a rough calculation,' I replied.

He nodded. 'If you're right, then Saunders and Smedley may have been found out and killed for it.' His eyes darkened as he mulled the implications.

'In which case, Marcus Marriott is the most likely killer,' I suggested.

'Not necessarily,' Swift replied. 'Any of them would be furious at the manipulation, and we've already established Alfred Palgrave was desperate. And Sebastian Cardhew thought Margaret would hand the shares over to him, so that's motivation in itself.'

'Which doesn't really get us any further forward, Swift,' I said. 'And all this talk of shares, loans, and financial machinations is beginning to make my head spin.'

'Fine. Let's deal with the facts we have, rather than supposition.' He reached for the papers Fossett had given him. 'These are the statements the household made after Saunders was murdered…' He placed them side by side across the table top and jabbed a finger on the first. 'Marcus Marriott was with his wife, Gabriel, in their room. He rose at six o'clock and worked on some figures until eight thirty, then he went to shave and bathe in the bathroom along the corridor. He said this took around twenty minutes.'

'Where is their bathroom?' I asked.

'There are three bathrooms on the first floor; the Marriotts use the one located between their bedroom and Margaret Saunders' suite, which she also uses.' He pointed to a line drawing of the first floor, it had the look of Fossett's handiwork.

'So their bedroom is in the opposite wing to here,' I remarked thinking that if it were one of them, they'd have to come all the way along the passage without being spotted. 'Is there a servants' stair anywhere?'

'No, this is a modern house,' Swift replied.

'Gabriel Marriott must have used the bathroom at some time, too, so both were without an alibi for at least twenty minutes,' I stated.

'Exactly, and Sebastian Cardhew slept alone, as did everyone else.'

'Dolores Palgrave's door was locked at twenty to nine, according to Alfred Palgrave.' I put a hand on the signed paper. 'But she wrote that she was in her room at the time.'

'These are of no help.' Swift gathered the statements back together and put them aside. 'None of them can be trusted to tell the truth.'

'What about Lady Clementine?'

'Her rooms are on the third floor, she said she was

reading,' he replied. 'And we know she lit her fire, but didn't include that in her statement.'

'Why would she?' I said in the lady's defence.

A knock sounded on the door. Fossett entered then stood aside to admit Dr Fletcher.

'Another one dead!' Cyril Fletcher said with a touch of drama. 'Snoring one moment, expired the next, according to the medics. Apparently the man just stopped breathing. Scarcely credit it, can you.' Fletcher plonked down onto a spare chair, as natty as ever, despite events. 'I was tootling along in my car behind the ambulance when it suddenly swerved off the road. I did the same and ran to help. We all tried pounding his chest – one of the chaps even had a go at mouth to mouth, quite heroic actually. Anyway, it didn't make the slightest bit of difference, he was already gone. I followed on to the hospital, but didn't want to stay and see him cut up – I've had enough of that. So I stopped at a delightful place on the way back and had a bite to eat,' he added and leaned back in his chair. 'Now young Fossett tells me the man was taking digitalis and there's a theory about a double dose.'

'Yes, sir, and—' Fossett tried to add something, but Swift held his hand up to quieten him.

'He'd been prescribed daily doses of digitalis.' Swift proceeded to explain in detail to Dr Fletcher about the sachets and twisted papers. He even demonstrated the theory to him.

'Well, that would do it.' Fletcher flicked the end of his moustache. 'The man brought it on himself. Unhealthy specimen. Overweight, arteries probably choked with fat, valves stiff as boards. I'd say the extra dose was added to his water yesterday afternoon. Takes a while for the drug to build up to toxic levels. When he took another sachet this morning, it would have been just enough to push him over the edge.' He reached into the capacious pockets of his plus fours. 'Got something for you. The bods thought you might need it, it's Devlin Saunders' wallet,' he said and tossed it onto the table. 'They found it in his dressing gown pocket.'

'You should have spotted this, Fossett.' Swift looked at him.

'I did, sir. It was stuffed full of money and that inspector from Oxford said it should stay with the body, 'cause it was part of the evidence,' Fossett explained, then bit his lip. 'I think I might have forgotten to tell you, sir. Sorry, sir.'

Swift's brows closed together.

'They must have been looking for it the day after he died, that's why they made Ackroyd unlock the door,' I said, trying to create a diversion. 'And the maid cleaned up after them.'

Swift flipped open the bulging leather wallet and pulled out the contents to make a pile on the table. Most of it consisted of five-pound notes. I heard Fossett draw a breath when he saw just how much money there was. 'His doctor's details.' Swift slid an engraved card from under the white notes, then another. 'A house of ill repute...' He tossed the black and red card aside. Fletcher picked it up to peruse more closely. 'And...' Swift had picked up a piece of tightly folded paper in his hands. He carefully undid it to reveal a creased page covered in numbers. He grinned. 'This could be part of the code to the safe.'

That instantly drew our attention. The numbers were written in black ink, two in each row and four rows in total.

I leaned forward for a closer look. 'It's been cut in half,' I said, although it was blindingly obvious.

'And I've found the other half!' Fossett finally gained our attention. He held out a similar piece of paper to the one from Devlin Saunders' wallet. 'I've been trying to tell you, sir. It was in Mr Smedley's bedroom.'

'Show me.' Swift put his hand out. Fossett duly delivered the slip to Swift who placed it on the desk next to the unfolded one.

'Where was it?' Swift asked.

'It was rolled up tightly and pushed into the folds in the silk lampshade beside his bed,' he answered.

We both looked at him in surprise.

'What made you search there?' I asked.

'I didn't. The sun shone through the window and lit it up and I spotted it,' Fossett explained. 'I could see it was cut in half, and I've been looking for the other half. I made Mr Ackroyd help me search for it. We turned over the mattress, and the rugs, and looked at gaps in the floorboards. We even poked about in a mouse hole but we couldn't find it.'

Swift pushed the two pieces of paper together to form a grid of sixteen numbers in a four by four block.

'56, 79, 8, 33,' I read out. '18, 10...I thought combinations were only three or four numbers?'

Swift's brows furrowed. 'They are, and it should state if the turn is right or left.'

'More of an aide-mémoire, perhaps?' Cyril Fletcher suggested. 'I use 'em all the time.'

Swift was rubbing his chin. 'No, the paper was split between them. It may have been an emergency system if something happened to one of them.'

'Which failed,' I said.

Swift reached for the jar of glue on the table and carefully stuck the two pieces onto a clean card, then blotted the whole. 'There, they won't be lost now.'

'Could we try the numbers out, sir?' Fossett was keen.

'Yes, why not, there's nothing to lose,' I added by way of encouragement.

'Let me make a copy first.' He duly noted the numbers in his notebook, then stood up. 'Right, come on.'

'Excellent stuff!' Cyril Fletcher beamed. 'Tally-ho.'

We went along the corridor to form a small crowd around the door to the vault. Swift designated himself as chief safe cracker and we stood at his shoulders to watch. He decided to turn it into a lesson, for some reason.

'The mechanism needs to be cleared of all previous attempts to open it,' he lectured. 'The dial should be turned all the way to the right, which is clockwise, then left...' He twirled the black dial in the centre of the door. 'This will reset the cogs...' He glanced at the card in his hand, then passed it to Fossett. 'We will assume the first number is turned counterclockwise, and alternate through each combination. If it doesn't work, we'll start at the beginning going clockwise.' He was as pedantic us usual. 'Fossett, read out the numbers.'

'Yes, sir. The first one's 56.'

Swift duly turned the dial counterclockwise. 'And the second number?'

'79.'

'Clockwise...79.' Swift twirled the dial once more. 'Next?'

'8, sir.'

'Counterclockwise to 8,' Swift continued.

'And 33.'

'Right.' Swift turned the dial to the fourth number, then grabbed the brass handle and tugged. Nothing happened. He tugged again.

'Best have a bash at the next set of numbers, old chap,' Fletcher advised him.

Swift took the numbers from Fossett and began the whole process again.

Ackroyd had spotted us and come up behind to peer over Fossett's shoulder.

'Ackroyd, go and find Lady Clementine and ask her to come here. Do not take no for an answer, and do not come back without her,' I instructed very firmly.

He dragged his eyes from the dial. 'Very well, sir, if I must.' He went off muttering to himself.

'D'you think the divine Lady Clementine has a talent for safe cracking, Heathcliff?' Fletcher chortled.

'Lady Clementine told me she knew the code, but couldn't remember it,' I replied. 'She said it was a song.'

'I heard her singing in the garden,' Fossett said. 'She can't sing for toffee, it was awful.'

'What was she singing?' I asked as Swift twirled the dial again.

'Row, row, row your boat,' Fossett replied, then started humming it.

'I have a stethoscope in my medical bag, if you want to listen for clicks,' Fletcher told Swift.

Swift didn't reply; his lips were set in grim determination. He tried the next set of numbers, with no luck.

'Hello sweetie, are you breaking in?' Lady Clementine arrived minutes later with Ackroyd two steps behind.

'Do you have the code?' I asked.

'I heard you singing a tune, m'lady,' Fossett said, then began singing, 'Row, row, row your boat, gently down the stream. Merrily, merrily, merrily, merrily, life is but a dream.'

'Ah, yes, that was it.' She beamed up at us. 'Such a pretty song.'

'Is it part of the code?' Swift demanded, having finally given up.

'It is, and it's terribly clever,' she replied, her blue eyes alight with amusement. 'Should I tell you?' She turned to me. 'Or will opening the safe merely lead to more murders?'

'We need the code, Lady Clementine.' Swift was adamant.

'Well, on your head be it,' she said. 'It's the first three letters of the third word in each line, so the first word is "row".'

'What?' I said.

'R-O-W,' and you have to add it together,' she replied.

'Do the numbers start with 'A'?' I asked.

'They do,' she laughed in delight.

'Fifty-six,' I said.

'Oh how clever of you, Heathcliff!' She clapped her hands.

'How did you do that, sir?' Fossett was astonished.

"A' is one, it's very simple,' Swift answered and turned to Fossett. 'Which line is 56 on?'

Fossett looked at the numbers. 'Top corner, sir,' he replied.

'Clockwise or counterclockwise?' I asked Lady Clementine.

'There's a comma before the word, so it is to the left,' she explained, her smile fading. 'And I do hope you know what you are doing.'

'Counterclockwise to 56.' Swift was already turning the dial. 'What next?'

I made a quick calculation. "T-H-E' which is... 33.'

'Fossett?'

The lad found the number. 'That's on the other corner, sir.'

'Which way?' Swift asked Lady Clementine.

'Without a comma, which means it's to the right,' she replied.

Swift twirled the dial rapidly.

'Next is 'M-E-R' from merrily…36,' I said.

'With a comma in front, sir.' Fossett had been following closely. 'And that's in the bottom corner.' He was staring at the paper.

'So, 36 counterclockwise.' Swift turned the dial accordingly.

'Oh, sir, if you look really carefully, you can see a little dot under each number in the corners. That's how they knew which ones they were!'

'Marvellous, well spotted young man,' Fletcher congratulated him.

'What's the last number?' Swift asked.

'"B-U-T" which is 43.' I added, 'And no comma, so it's clockwise.'

Swift stopped the dial at the number, and gripped the brass handle once more. It moved easily as though well oiled, and he tugged it to pull the heavy steel door slowly open.

# CHAPTER 12

'Good heavens. What a dreadful mess!' Lady Clementine exclaimed. 'I'm sure Devlin wouldn't have left it like this.'

Swift bent down to pick up a handful of fragments from the concrete floor. 'It's been torn into little pieces.'

He passed some of the fragments to me. Fossett leaned over my shoulder for a better look, then scooped some up for himself.

'It looks like a typed list of names.' Swift was picking up the pieces and turning them over in his fingers.

I lined a few up along my palm, trying to read the letters. '...nley Cou. Mr. Wi...' I read. '...Ond. £12,560. SW1. 00.5s 4d.' I looked at Swift. 'It could be a list of debtors.'

He nodded. 'I agree.' Then scanned the scattered fragments covering the floor. 'We need to re-assemble it.'

'Fossett.' I turned to him. 'Find a box or something and collect every single scrap of paper.'

'Righto, sir.' He nodded. 'Where d'you keep the boxes?'

He turned to ask Ackroyd, who had remained at the rear trying to pretend he wasn't there.

'They are stored in the store cupboard,' Ackroyd replied haughtily. 'I will fetch one, and bring a brush and dustpan.' He went off, rigid-backed as usual.

'At least he's stopped complaining,' Cyril Fletcher remarked.

'No, he hasn't.' Fossett knelt down to sweep the pieces of paper into a corner with his hand. 'Should have heard him when we were searching Mr Smedley's room. Moaning on about the folk in the house, how none of them was proper gentry. They didn't know how to treat staff, they ordered him around like he was just a nobody.' He was clearing the floor quickly; we all stepped back, out of his way. 'He takes being a butler seriously though, and I think he's proud of what he does, and them being rude to him is demeaning. Not everyone's born to do great things, but it doesn't mean it doesn't matter to them.' He made a neat pile of the torn papers, then stood up. 'There you go, sirs.'

'Well done, Constable,' Swift told him.

The lad grinned and sketched a salute. 'Proper policing this is.'

'I am going to my room to change,' Lady Clementine suddenly declared.

'What?' Fletcher's brows shot up. 'But it's just getting exciting, dear lady, you will miss it.'

'Dear Cyril, we have had two deaths in a matter of days with complete chaos between, and I have no doubt there is more to come.' She smiled sweetly as she spoke.

'You can tell me all about it at dinner, later,' she said and then left us.

'Well, where shall we begin?' Cyril Fletcher clapped his hands, gazing at the range of shelves lining the brick walls.

The top two racks on both sides were groaning under the weight of silverware, most of it heavily gilded. Below were delicate porcelain tureens, plates in all sizes, and teapots, coffee pots, saucers, jugs and cups. On the end wall was another set of shelves bearing neatly stacked box files held shut by red ribbons tied tightly together.

'We'll note each one and take them to the Manor,' Swift declared. There was a black briefcase on the lower shelf, it had Cedric Smedley's initials stamped into the leather. Swift picked it up and put it under his arm.

'You must let us root through them first,' Fletcher objected. 'And find out who's inherited Devlin Saunders' ill-gotten gains.'

'No.' Swift was adamant. 'Fossett. Write down the order in which these boxes are stacked, note every label you find and then we'll take them to your car, Lennox.'

I was actually in agreement with Cyril Fletcher, but realised it was not only past afternoon tea, it was fast approaching drinks time. 'Fine,' I said. 'I'll see you outside.'

Swift muttered something under his breath. Fletcher decided to come downstairs with me.

'I'd join you, old chap, but I have arranged to take Lady Clementine to the Wheatsheaf later and I really must change.'

That raised an eyebrow. 'You're taking her to the pub?'

'In Northleach, yes, they've started serving food.' He trotted along beside me. 'Found themselves a French chef, would you believe.'

'Really? Where on earth did they find a French chef around here?'

'Oxford. Apparently it's becoming quite cosmopolitan, they even have Italians outside the colleges selling gelato, don't you know.'

We crossed the hall and exited into the bright sunshine. Tommy was polishing the headlamps of my car, he had a grubby handkerchief in his hand and was rubbing it very slowly across the lenses whilst staring up at the windows of the house.

'Tommy, what are you doing here?' I demanded as we crunched across the gravel.

'Finished school and came to the gate to see where you were. Everyone said there's another'un dead!' he exclaimed with relish. 'They all reckon there's a mad murderer around, sir, and anybody might get done in at any minute. So I thought I'd best come and see that you was alright.' He looked up at me with bright eyes from beneath his crumpled school cap.

'If there's a mad murderer in the vicinity, you should be at home protecting the household,' I told him.

He stopped polishing the car and shoved the handkerchief in his pocket. 'But no-one's really goin' to come sneakin' about, are they, sir? An' if they did, you'd shoot them. Just like all them Germans in the war. I could learn to shoot. You could teach me, then I'll be on guard whenever you're gone away—'

'Tommy,' Fletcher interrupted the lad's enthusiastic chatter, 'I'll drop you off on my way past the Manor.' He placed his hand on the boy's shoulder. 'Come along, into the car with you.' He aimed Tommy at the smart red Riley almost hidden behind my Bentley. They climbed in, Tommy still chattering, as Fletcher drove off in a puff of exhaust smoke.

I cranked the engine and was about to hop into the driver's seat when Fossett emerged from the house, followed by Swift and then Ackroyd. They were carrying a stack of files each, plus a cardboard box. Swift was clutching the briefcase to his chest.

'They'll have to go on the back seat,' I called out, which was pretty obvious as the trunk wasn't strapped to the rear. It didn't take a moment to stack everything and cover them with the tartan rug.

'We'll see you later,' I told Fossett. 'Don't let any of them escape.' I nodded towards the house.

'Aye, sir.' He gazed longingly at the car, then turned to trudge back towards the front door.

'Wait. Stop,' Marcus Marriott shouted as he ran out from the house. 'I saw the vault door open. Where's Devlin's will, and the company papers?'

'Sequestered,' Swift said, as I swung the wheel about.

'No. I told you to stop.' Marriott raced to catch up. 'I demand you give me those files, you can't remove company property. I'll have the law on you.' He was running alongside the car, his oiled hair whipping into disarray, his feet scattering the gravel.

'We are the law,' Swift shouted back above the noise of the engine.

'Those documents are mine. Damn you,' Marriott gasped as I put my foot down and roared the car away to leave him panting for breath.

The gates were held open by Frank Wright and a couple of chaps from the village. They saluted as we went past. I gave them a wave and motored homewards through the winding lanes, fragrant with spring time blossom.

'I'll help unload, shall I, sir?' Tommy was waiting on the doorstep, Fletcher having just dropped him off. Foggy came down the steps bounding in excitement and raced about my feet in circles when I jumped out of the car.

'Take everything to my library,' I instructed.

'Careful with that cardboard box.' Swift pointed. 'Wait, I'll carry it,' he decided. He already had the briefcase under one arm.

Greggs stepped from the front door. 'Ah, sir. I do hope there have been no more tragedies.'

'Not since this morning.' I bent to ruffle my dog's ears. 'Where's Lady Persi?'

'She and Lady Florence are in the library, sir. We have constructed a chart.'

Swift stopped in his tracks. 'What sort of chart?'

'A coloured chart, sir, with suspects and a map of the house and grounds, and the times of death of the victims, and the names the household.' He simpered a smile. 'I have been assisting in the design.'

'Well done, old chap.' I grinned. 'I'm sure it will be just what we need.' I congratulated him.

Swift frowned, and marched indoors.

'I can help, Mr Greggs. I'll talk to m'lady. I'll make an ace detective.' Tommy had gathered a stack of box files to fetch in and could barely see over the top of them.

Greggs took the rest and I led the procession into the house.

'But you should really have waited for me, Florence,' Swift was saying to his wife. Persi was next to her and both were leaning over a long length of white wallpaper, which they'd unrolled along the reading table. It was covered in colourful markings.

'I know my love, but you described how you'd made an incident board like this during one of your cases, and when Persi and I began discussing it, we thought it a fine idea to make one for you,' Florence explained.

'And Greggs helped,' Persi added as though that clinched it.

'Where should we put the files, sir?' Tommy called out.

'On the desk,' I ordered.

Persi went to push aside the ink pots, pens, pile of old mail and whatnots strewn across my desk.

Tommy placed the box files down with a thud.

Greggs placed his more carefully, then went off, brushing dust from his waistcoat.

'What's in them?' Persi asked as she bent to read the labels.

'Secrets,' I said, then gave her a peck on the cheek. 'And possibly Devlin Saunders' will.'

That raised her brows. Florence looked equally intrigued.

'And there's a puzzle for you.' Swift had kept hold of the cardboard box, and placed it on top of the 'incident board' wallpaper. He removed the lid and carefully pulled out a handful of torn fragments 'This has to be reconstructed.'

Florence's eyes rounded. 'Jonathan, you can't seriously...' she began, and then realised he was entirely serious. 'But how?'

'Glue the fragments to a piece of paper, or card,' he replied as though it were the simplest thing in the world.

Greggs arrived with a tray. 'I have prepared a jug of Pimms, sir, with cheese and crackers.'

'Excellent.' I grinned. 'Just what the doctor ordered, and we aren't going to open a single file until we've had a drink.'

We took seats around the reading table and waited for Greggs to do the honours. He'd added sliced strawberries, chunks of ice cubes and fresh mint to the Pimms, and was careful not to let the fruit spill while he poured the liquid into four glasses.

'Can I have one, sir?' Tommy watched the proceedings.

'No,' I told him. 'And you'd best go and help Cook.'

'Angus is with her, they're making chocolate biscuits,' Florence called out.

'Oh, but...' Tommy began then realised what Florence had said. 'I'd best go and help then, Angus gets chocolate everywhere!' He dashed off.

'What happened to Cedric Smedley?' Florence asked.

'He died of an overdose,' Swift answered and then explained all over again about the sachets of digitalis and twists of paper as we sipped Pimms and nibbled cheese and crackers. The girls demanded a demonstration so Swift showed them how the lengths of paper were screwed up. They tried it for themselves, Florence was left-handed and her example clinched it.

'How clever of you.' Persi smiled.

'Actually, Fossett spotted it,' I said.

'He's really quite an asset,' Florence remarked. 'Don't you think so Jonathan?'

'Hmm,' Swift was non committal.

Persi made a note of the digitalis on their chart in green crayon, then drew a box around it, and Smedley's name, in black.

'And this mustn't go any further,' Swift warned them.

'What mustn't?' Florence asked him.

'About the sachets, and the means by which Smedley was murdered,' Swift told her. 'It's information only the killer would know.'

'Ah.' Florence regarded him. 'And the same applies to the way Devlin Saunders was killed?'

'Exactly,' Swift said. 'Only a handful of us know that Saunders was killed by a dagger and not by the arrow.'

'But you will warn them at the house,' Florence repeated a plea she'd made earlier. 'That they must be careful.'

'Yes, of course,' he reassured her.

'Right,' I declared now that we were onto our second glasses of Pimms. 'We can open the files.'

Swift would only allow one to be opened at a time, and insisted on making notes of everything we found – which was more tedious than I'd expected. Various company documents, incorporation deeds, and black bound ledgers filled most of them. One box file contained a stack of threatening letters, some with very colourful language.

The last file held Saunders' personal papers, including his birth certificate, his shares in the company, the marriage licence to Margaret, and his last will and testament.

I put my glass of Pimms down, picked up the will, then began flicking through the bound pages.

'Who inherits?' Persi asked, trying to peer over my shoulder.

'Just a moment.' I was scanning the words, but realised it was far more complex than simply reading a name out. 'He's made a number of conditions about who dies first, including the other directors, and how his assets are to be distributed…this must have been written before he decided to retire.' I skipped through the flowery legal phrases trying to find the nub of the matter.

'Lennox, will you let me read it?' Swift held his hand out.

'Just a moment,' I repeated and turned another stiff page of parchment over. They were crowded around me, even Greggs was craning on tiptoe to read the carefully crafted words in curling copperplate. 'Devlin Saunders' entire shareholding in the Royal Buckingham Financial Services have been left to…' I had to turn yet another page. 'Lady Clementine Elizabeth Annabelle Knox.'

# CHAPTER 13

'Lady Clementine!' they exclaimed almost as one.

'But why would Mr Saunders leave his shares to his mother-in-law?' Greggs said, which seemed a particularly pertinent remark, to my mind.

'She can't really be expected to take an interest in running the company.' Florence sounded astonished.

'There'll be a reason.' Swift took the will to read each word carefully.

Persi looked at me. 'Do you think she knew?'

I gave it some thought. 'Yes,' I said, then sighed. 'She had the code, but she only gave it to us when she saw we had already found it.'

'And she realised we'd eventually work out the combination,' Swift added, without taking his eyes from the will. 'The four numbers were in each corner of the block of sixteen.'

I had to explain what that meant, and the girls made him show them the spliced paper glued to the card.

'But surely you do not imagine Lady Clementine to

be the culprit, sir?' Greggs seemed confounded by the disclosure.

'No,' I answered immediately.

'She knows more than she's telling us,' Swift said, his voice coldly professional. 'And she had a fire in her room the day Saunders was killed.'

'Why is that significant?' Persi asked.

'There were pages missing from Saunders' newspaper, we think the killer splashed blood onto them,' I explained.

'Ah…' Persi picked up a red crayon. 'We didn't have that information.'

'Or the code to the vault.' Florence moved some of the files off the length of wallpaper. 'Here.' She pointed to a column headed *"Suspicious Activity"*. 'And we should cross reference that to Lady Clementine.'

'We may have to designate her "red"?' Persi was poised with the crayon.

'Is red for primary suspect?' I asked, being quite sure of the answer.

'Of course,' Persi replied and then underlined Lady Clementine's name in the colour. This was under the column marked "suspects". I was half expecting them to find little wooden figures like those used in the war to follow troop movements on maps of Europe.

'Her bedroom is on the third floor.' Florence pointed to the series of plans they'd drawn in the centre of their diagram. It showed each floor, and included labels of who slept where and had two black X's; one on Saunders' balcony, the other in Smedley's bedroom.

'Sir, I am certain Lady Clementine would have nothing to do with murder.' Greggs' enthusiasm was losing its fizz.

'We must keep an open mind,' Swift reminded him, then turned to Florence. 'How did you know the layout of the house?'

She beamed. 'We spoke to the maids from the village, the ones who worked for Margaret Saunders until she was rude to them. They explained the layout to us, and they said there was hanky-panky going on.'

'Between who?' Swift asked.

'Margaret Saunders,' she replied.

'And?' I prompted because she'd closed her mouth, her eyes alight.

'Sebastian Cardhew!' Persi answered.

'We knew that,' I said.

'Fine, but I'll bet you didn't have an eyewitness,' she replied, to which I conceded with a grin.

Swift made a note in his notebook. 'Did they tell you anything else?'

'Not of significance,' Persi said. 'But they didn't like the people in the house at all, the only ones who were pleasant were Lady Clementine and Alfred Palgrave. They said Palgrave seemed rather lost and sad. They felt sorry for him.'

'That's a shame,' I said. 'Because he's suspect number two.'

That wasn't well received and they both argued why it couldn't be either of them.

'We haven't looked in the briefcase, yet,' I reminded Swift, which managed to divert attention.

'Ah yes.' He retrieved it from under his chair. 'Too many distractions,' he muttered.

We waited as he proceeded at his usual pedantic pace. He pulled out a newspaper, which was the *Daily Mail*, then a half bottle of brandy, a couple of pens and a plain white envelope.

'Is that all?' I asked.

Swift was feeling the sides of the interior for anything hidden. 'It seems to be.'

'I'd expected the signed loan contracts at least,' I said as I reached for the envelope.

'So had I.' Swift stopped searching and put the briefcase back on the floor. 'Lennox, let me...' He reached for the white envelope but he was too late. I swiped it and slit it open with my penknife.

Persi and Florence both leaned forward to see what was in it.

I pulled it out. 'A train ticket.'

'Where to?' Persi asked.

'Monte Carlo.' I gazed at the red, white, and blue printed card. It was very prettily done, and written entirely in French. 'It's for Le Train Bleu.' I turned it over. 'The day after tomorrow,' I said then stopped. Persi and I had returned on the Blue Train when I'd gone all the way to Egypt to propose to her; the train had been a magical ride.

'What?' Swift reached over and all but snatched it out of my hands. 'It's not for Cedric Smedley, it's in the name of Devlin Saunders.'

'Smedley must have been hiding it for him,' Persi instantly guessed.

'Hmm, which is probably why it was locked in the vault,' Swift said. 'I wonder if he intended going alone.'

Tommy came in carrying a sleepy Angus, his face smeared with chocolate. Swift and Florence immediately jumped up to take him. They excused themselves to take the little boy for a bath and to bed. I took the chance to escape.

'Come on.' I grabbed Persi's hand.

'Where are we going?' She smiled.

'The lake,' I told her as I led her out of the back door.

The lake was my favourite spot and we wandered hand in hand, Foggy trotting ahead, along the deer path leading through the meadows and woods to emerge at the jetty overhanging the water's edge.

Mayflies danced across the still surface; a trout rose to snatch one, leaving ripples across the mirror-like water. Ducks and coots nestled amongst the reeds, and a kingfisher darted away in flash of viridian and blue.

I'd mended my row boat some weeks ago, and now steadied it for my lovely wife to step down. Foggy hopped in and I pushed off for a slow meander in the warmth of the fading day. Long rays of pink and amber spread from the horizon, suffusing the light with roseate hues. I let the oars rest and gathered Persi in my arms, her soft cheek next to mine. The scent of her hair, the warmth of her body; I doubt I could have ever imagined such simple joys as these moments. I kissed her, and murmured my love, then Foggy wriggled his way between us and insisted on his own cuddle.

Dusk had fallen towards darkness by the time we returned to the house to change for dinner.

'Will Lady Clementine be able to take control of the Royal Buckingham?' Florence asked as we started on the first course of quails' eggs and blue cheese salad.

'I doubt it,' I replied and began to explain about Saunders having signed a binding covenant forcing the sale of the shares. We explained about the bidding, until Greggs removed our salad dishes and replaced them with plates of lamb with new potatoes and greens smothered in butter.

'Will the shares actually be worth anything if the sale is forced?' Persi asked.

I knew they were trying to undermine our suspicions of Lady Clementine.

'Their lawyer is arriving tomorrow, he will clarify that.' Swift's reply was dry.

'Did you find out anything more about Devlin Saunders' character?' Florence asked as she speared French beans.

'A greedy bully obsessed with getting rich, and didn't care who he destroyed in the process,' Swift replied.

I related what Margaret Saunders had told me in her bedroom. 'Apparently the wives put up with their husbands' behaviour because they enjoy the wealthy life.'

'Does that mean they would ditch their husbands if they were suddenly made poor?' Persi was caustic.

'It sounds more like a commercial arrangement, to me.' Florence spoke quietly. 'And rather abhorrent.'

'Broken people,' Swift said between forkfuls.

'Do you think so?' Florence turned to him. 'In what way?'

He thought about it for a moment. 'Well, my greatest joy comes from being with you and Angus, not gathering riches. Love and contentment drive my life, but Saunders and the rest seem to be obsessed with possessions. And no amount of gold could ever replace you, my love.' He held his hand out to her.

'Do you think some of them could appreciate both?' Persi asked.

'Possibly,' he replied. 'But would you have time for love if you dedicated yourself to grabbing whatever you can?'

'Love didn't come into the matter, according to Margaret Saunders,' I remarked.

'I think these types are only one part of a spectrum,' Persi said. 'I've known men utterly dedicated to inventing things, or discovering something, and they do understand love, and probably cherish it, but can't find time for it. I don't think they even realise they are in the grip of obsession.'

'Well, work is obviously necessary, and there's nothing wrong with professionalism.' Swift sounded defensive.

'And we all have to keep a roof over our heads,' I said, thinking of my own in particular.

'Indeed, there has to be a balance,' Florence said diplomatically.

'But these sharks, or however they call themselves, don't have that balance.' Swift lined up his knife and fork precisely on his plate. 'They have no integrity, no basic moral foundation, and no comprehension of the joy to be found through loving relationships. As I said, they're broken.'

'And yet Margaret Saunders was upset,' Persi countered. 'That implies she realises there's something missing in her life.'

'Which she wants, just as she wants everything else,' Swift rejoined.

'So she feels guilt, and perhaps the others do, too,' Florence said. 'Everyone knows right from wrong, however hard they try to ignore it.'

'It seems to me that they've done pretty well at ignoring any conscience they might have,' I remarked.

'But that's the basis of their rage,' Florence said, which didn't entirely make sense to me.

'They take whatever they can from others because they're hated, and they hate in return,' Persi concluded. 'They know it's wrong, but they do it to inflict punishment.'

This was much the same point Swift had made earlier in the day.

'Well, whatever the cause, someone is punishing them now,' I said as Greggs cleared the table in readiness for dessert.

'Do you think that's the motive?' Florence's lovely eyes turned to me.

'If it is, then who would it be?' Persi answered. 'Surely if it were revenge, or punishment, it would come from outside.'

'It could be punishment based on betrayal,' Swift

mooted. 'We know Margaret Saunders is having an affair with Sebastian Cardhew.'

'*Was* having an affair. I think that's over now,' I said.

'She said Dolores Palgrave was an alley cat who's had affairs with all of the men.' Persi aimed that at me.

'Apart from Marcus Marriott,' Swift added.

'We can't be sure of that,' I said. 'There's no proof she's had an affair with anyone. It could have been said in mere spite.'

'Given that their mutual interest is money, greed is the more likely motive,' Swift stated.

'In that case it's Marcus Marriott,' I said. 'He wants the shares, and he killed Saunders and Smedley for trying to exploit him.'

'But Lady Clementine has Saunders' shares, now,' Swift rejoined. 'Which is further reason for her to be at the top of the suspects list.'

'No.' Both girls objected, so did Greggs, and then coughed to hide the indiscretion.

Discussion of motives kept us busy through the rest of the meal until the conversation turned to more domestic matters. I didn't want to bring up one obvious fact they all seemed to be ignoring. Lady Clementine had the code to the vault and had avoided giving it to us. And Alfred Palgrave said that Dolores had demanded his shares as part of a divorce settlement, which didn't make sense because she was in no position to demand anything. So what did she have on Alfred?

We broke up for an early night after what felt like a long and eventful day.

The morning brought bright sunshine filtering through

the curtains. I'd no sooner reached to entwine my wife in my arms when both dogs suddenly started barking frantically downstairs.

'What is the cause of that damn racket, Greggs?' I called as I ran down the treads.

Greggs was in the hall, gazing up at the grandfather clock. 'Mr Tubbs caught a squirrel, sir, and let it loose in the house. It has taken up residence within the mechanism, and Mr Fogg and Nicky are keen to apprehend it.'

The dogs were sitting on the stone-flagged floor, eyes fixed keenly on the clock face. Nicky held one paw up and was quivering with excitement.

'I suppose it's no worse than wasps in the kitchen.' I stood to gaze with them.

'It was not a wasp, sir. Cook had a case of tinnitus.'

'Ah. She'd better consult Dr Fletcher.'

A twitching red nose appeared from the side vent of the clock head, quickly followed by the rest of the squirrel. It climbed onto the decorated top and sat with long bushy tail wrapped about its feet to wash its whiskers. The dogs erupted into another frenzy of barking until I yelled an order for them to stop.

'Aaaaeuungggg…' Angus ran into the hall, arms out wide in aeroplane mode, circled twice around us, then sped out again. We watched him head for the kitchen where the sound of muted voices and clinking pots and plates could be heard.

'We used to be a haven of peace and quiet, Greggs,' I mused. 'When did life become so animated?'

'I believe life is supposed to be animated, sir,' he replied in amiable tone. 'And it is rather agreeable to see the house returning to its old bustle.'

'Hmm…' I knew he was right, and that I'd almost turned the place into a hermit cell after the war. 'Was there any post?'

'A letter from London, sir. I left it on the mantelpiece in the library.'

Tubbs came in, his stubby black tail sticking straight up in the air. He sauntered over to the dogs to join them and sat to stare up at the squirrel in wide-eyed innocence, as though he'd had nothing whatsoever to do with it being there.

I went in search of the mail. I could tell from the postmark, and typed address, that it was another letter from my financial adviser. It would be a repeat of the previous threat, no doubt. I picked it up, tore it in two, then tossed it in the fire grate with a lighted match to follow.

'Lennox?' Swift called out. 'Did you know there's a squirrel on top of the grandfather clock?'

'Yes.' I returned to the hall. 'I'm going for breakfast.'

We strolled to the morning room, bright rays of sunlight falling over an embroidered cloth on the circular table set in the window. A vase of spring flowers stood on its centre, signs my wife had already been busy.

'We'll start with Lady Clementine,' Swift began. 'The lawyer arrives today so we should be prepared for him, too.'

Greggs entered with plates of heaven-scented bacon, eggs, black pudding, fried bread, and mushrooms. 'M'lady has gone to collect eggs in the orchard with Tommy and Angus, sir.'

'Fine,' I said as I picked up my knife and fork. 'And the squirrel?'

'Still on top of the grandfather clock, sir.' He placed a steaming cup of tea at my elbow. 'I have spoken to the gardeners. Brendan will endeavour to remove it after breakfast.'

'He's not going to shoot it, is he?' Swift paused over a sausage.

'M'lady has expressly forbidden it, sir, and Brendan is fond of animals. He would not harm it.' He went off again.

'Swift,' I said. 'The torn shreds of paper...'

'Yes, the girls are going to stick them together.'

I put my fork down. 'You'll find my name on it.'

He stopped eating. 'How? I thought your loan was with the bank.'

'No, there was a letter waiting for me when we returned from Lancashire. It informed me that my debt had been sold to the Royal Buckingham. Apparently they're allowed to do this without even asking.' I spoke with barely suppressed anger. 'And the Royal Buckingham promptly doubled the interest rate. They even charged me an administration fee for switching lenders.'

'Lowlife bloodsuckers...' he swore under his breath.

I sliced off the end of a sausage then gave it to Foggy. The injustice of the bloody loan was almost enough to affect my appetite.

'How much is the total now, Lennox?'

146

'Seven thousand pounds,' I muttered through gritted teeth.

He closed his eyes for a moment. 'There must be something we can do.'

'Yes, catch the blighter and claim the reward, at least it will pay off some of the loan. Although none of them deserve a penny of my money.'

'Agreed.' Swift took a bite of bacon and chewed it while he deliberated. 'If Billings found out, he'd remove you from the case through conflict of interest.'

'He won't find out, Swift, and I'm quite capable of being objective,' I retorted, although we both knew this wasn't entirely true.

He glanced at me. 'Don't worry, we'll keep it to ourselves.'

# CHAPTER 14

'Lady Clementine, would you please be seated?' Swift was formally polite. We were gathered around the writing table in the late Devlin Saunders' bedroom.

'Of course…oh, you've brought your doggie!' she exclaimed as Fogg ran from under the table to greet her, tail wagging madly. 'How delightful.' She bent to give him a fuss.

I'd decided to bring Fogg with me, given the loose squirrel in the Manor.

Ackroyd had escorted her ladyship and remained by the door. He moved quickly to pull a chair out. 'M'lady,' he said and bowed.

'Thank you, dear boy.' She sat down to face us. 'Will there be tea?' She had dressed in gay colours, a yellow silk blouse with a flowing skirt in peacock blue, and red shoes, which was an interesting combination.

'Ackroyd?' Swift glanced at the butler.

'Certainly sir, may I ask for how many?'

'Three,' I replied. 'Earl Grey.'

'Very well, sir.' He went off, nostrils flaring.

Swift turned to Lady Clementine. 'You tore up the list of debtors in the vault, didn't you?'

'Oh, how clever of you to deduce that.' She laughed. 'I would have burned it, but I wanted the weasels to see it was destroyed when the vault door was finally opened.'

'There will be ledgers, and contracts at Saunders' offices in London,' I said.

She sighed. 'Yes, I realise that now, but I was so terribly angry. They didn't care about Devlin dying, and neither did I, but all they thought about were his shares and money and how they could profit by his death. So, in the quiet of night I went down, opened the vault, and tore their list of debtors into tiny pieces.'

'One of the names on the list may have been the murderer's,' Swift said.

'Exactly, and can you blame them!' She beamed, her blue eyes sparkling with mischief. She was enjoying the attention.

'The code would have allowed us to open the vault sooner. You have obstructed a murder enquiry, Lady Clementine,' Swift continued. 'You should have given it to us.'

'I wanted to be sure of you first,' she replied in pure provocation.

'And yet you said you'd known me in another life,' Swift countered, which was incongruous, although he had a habit of throwing in the unexpected.

She broke into peals of laughter. 'Touché, my dear Inspector. You haven't lost your sense of humour.'

He had the grace to smile.

'We think Smedley and Saunders were working together to manipulate the bidding,' I said.

'Were they?' Her eyes widened in surprise. 'I don't understand the implication I'm afraid, I've always tried to avoid their financial shenanigans.'

'And yet Devlin Saunders left his shares to you.' Swift slipped in the accusation with an assassin's touch.

She didn't bat an eyelid. 'Yes, because he wanted this house, and I told him I'd leave it to him in exchange for his shares.'

I'd half expected this. I leaned back in my chair as Swift frowned.

'So you do own this house?' Swift sounded surprised. 'I had the impression your step-daughter owned it.'

'Just because Margaret thinks she is entitled to everything that is mine, does not make it true,' she said with a touch of asperity in her voice.

Swift made a note with a freshly sharpened pencil. 'You must have been aware Devlin Saunders was about to sell his shares. Would you have been entitled to the full value of them if he had done so?'

'I would think so,' she agreed. 'But he thought I was certain to die before him, and even if I didn't, he assumed I would leave everything to Margaret.'

'And will you?' I asked.

She laughed. 'Not at all, I'm going to leave it the local cats' home. I have every intention of coming back as a cat. One of those lovely exotic breeds — slinky and sleek with a long tail and dazzling blue eyes. And then I will live off my inheritance in sybaritic luxury.'

'Lady Clementine, this is a serious interview,' Swift reminded her sharply.

'Oh, you were always so passionate, Jonathan, especially when you're angry,' she said, then sighed loudly. 'I'm so pleased this new life hasn't changed you.'

I was determined not to laugh. Swift looked as though he were about to erupt. Ackroyd knocked on the door and came in bearing a tray, providing a welcome distraction.

'Tea, and a sampling of Cook's chocolate dips,' he announced and placed the tray on the nearby dressing table. He busied himself pouring dainty cups of tea, then served them with finicky finesse. 'The biscuits are of a simple butter-crumble base stirred with marinated cherries and dipped in chocolate. I trust they will be to your satisfaction, m'lady.' He bowed as he presented the plate of goodies to her.

'Oh, I'm sure they will be utterly delicious,' she replied with a beaming smile.

He simpered and put them down at her elbow, then cleared off without offering any to us.

'Lady Clementine,' Swift began as she nibbled a biscuit. 'You must realise this puts you in a very difficult situation. Devlin Saunders was found murdered and you will directly benefit from his death.'

She gazed at us appraisingly. She was no fool. 'Margaret told me what happened when the weasels heard Cedric Smedley died. They offered her a few pounds a share, and if that's their game, I will not benefit from either death, will I?'

'The offer of a few pounds a share was a nasty joke, and you wouldn't have known that would be the outcome either,' Swift replied dryly. 'Most people would expect the shares to retain their value, especially if they don't involve themselves in "financial shenanigans".'

She gazed at him, then carried on nibbling her biscuit.

'Did you tell Margaret that you had made a deal to inherit Saunders' shares?' I asked.

'Good heavens, no,' she replied. 'She would have never given me a moment's peace.'

'What happened to her, and her father?' I thought to turn the subject to more neutral ground.

'Her mother died before I arrived in Kenya.' She brushed crumbs from her skirt. 'She was a lonely child. Her father was a big game hunter...' She seemed to drift into a daydream.

'Who was eaten by a lion,' I said, which brought the smile back to her lips.

'Perhaps he wasn't, but he should have been.' She became serious. 'He'd made a fortune in industry and decided he had no need to work again. He moved to Kenya to take up hunting – it was quite fashionable at the time and he teamed up with various pals and visitors on safari.' She glanced up. 'You know the type, idling about in tents, drinking all day, eating off fine china surrounded by scurrying servants. Reginald wasn't a big brave hunter, he simply had his guide show him an animal, harmlessly grazing or snoozing, and he would aim his rifle and shoot it.' She paused as her brows drew together. 'I didn't realise any of this at the time. I'd been recently widowed; my husband was Sir Anthony Latham and we had lived and loved with all the passion of youth. He ran one of the family companies, exporting spices from Zanzibar. It was such fun... And then he died of a fever.' Age suddenly crept into her face, lines and creases filling the hollows with melancholy. 'I moved back to Kenya where my parents lived. They were awfully old, at least as old as I am now and they died soon after. It was really rather awful, then along came Reginald with his hunter's mystique and marvellous stories, and like a fool I fell for his nonsense and we wed. Margaret had just finished school and came to join us for a while, but she and her father had a difficult relationship, and she yearned for the glittering life. She moved to London to live with an aunt until the woman died of something or other.' She pushed a tendril of white hair from her forehead. 'Anyway, I had inherited a great deal of money, and Reginald promptly set about enjoying it. I discovered that his career as an industrialist was somewhat exaggerated. He'd have reduced me to penury if he hadn't had the heart attack. I was so relieved when it happened.'

'So he did die of a heart attack,' I said.

'Yes.' She sounded sincere. 'Just before the lion pounced.'

I laughed, then saw Swift's face. 'Right...were there any witnesses to his death?'

'Only me and the lion.'

'Lady Clementine.' Swift sounded pained. 'Would you

please relate your movements the morning Devlin Saunders died?' He leafed through the pile of statements and found hers.

I drank my tea.

'Would you like a biscuit?' Lady Clementine held the plate out. I took one. Swift shook his head, and waited with pencil poised over his notebook.

'Well, I felt rather cold,' she began. 'So I lit the fire. Dolly helped. And then she went and fetched my breakfast, I don't eat very much—'

'Dolly?' Swift broke in.

'The maid – haven't you spoken to her?'

'I…no, not yet,' Swift muttered.

'Well, you should.'

'Yes, thank you, we will. Please continue.' Swift jotted a note.

The biscuit was delicious, particularly the chocolate and marinated cherries.

'Well, I had a boiled egg at the table in my room – I have two rooms upstairs, a bedroom and a small drawing room so that I don't have to endure that pack of weasels Margaret has foisted upon me.'

'What time did you eat breakfast?' Swift continued without looking up.

'Eight o'clock, which is my usual time. Dolly came back soon afterwards to take my tray away,' she said and suddenly stood up. 'Well, do you think he's finished?'

'What?' Swift frowned.

'Young Fossett. You sent him to search my rooms while you questioned me, didn't you?'

This was true, but we thought she wouldn't realise.

'We need to search everyone's rooms, Lady Clementine,' Swift said by way of apology.

'I have nothing to hide.' She smiled. 'And you are always welcome to come up and see me, Jonathan.'

Two red spots appeared in Swift's lean cheeks. He cleared his throat noisily.

'You're quite observant,' I remarked to her.

'When I take an interest in things,' she agreed.

'Your rooms overlook the rear of the house.' I knew this from the drawings Persi and Florence had made on the wallpaper. 'Can you see the balcony?' I nodded towards the French windows.

'I can.' She smiled.

Swift's frown deepened. 'Did you see Saunders' body, or whoever killed him?'

'I did not, but if I had I would have cheered them on.' She was unrepentant. 'He was alive and just as disagreeable when I saw him at half past eight with Marcus—'

'What?' Swift broke in. 'Where did you see them?'

'They were on the balcony,' she replied. 'I saw them from my window not long before I went for a walk. So I missed witnessing anything.'

Swift had her statement in his hand. 'You didn't write any of this down.' He sounded outraged. 'You stated you were in the breakfast room with the other "inmates".'

'And did any of them say I wasn't?' she asked, her head tilted slightly to one side.

Swift bit his lip, then muttered, 'No.'

'Well, you can't really believe what anyone says, then, can you.' She made to leave.

'Wait. Where did you go for a walk?' I asked.

'Into the village. I spoke to the lady who operates the switchboard. She is really quite delightful, we chatted about this and that for simply ages.'

'What time was this?' Swift recommenced writing.

'Oh, I have no idea. I left the house at about five to nine...' she mused. 'I didn't return until half past, by which time they'd found Devlin and had started running around like headless chickens. Ackroyd will be able to give you the exact details. He let me in and out of the front door. Toodle-oo, mes chéries.' She blew a kiss and went out, leaving the door open behind her.

Swift went to shut it with a bang, then stalked back to sit down.

'She must have been talking to Flossie Craddock at the time Saunders was killed,' I said.

'We don't know for certain what time he was killed. And Ackroyd said he was with the maid serving break-fast, but according to Lady Clementine he opened the front door to let her in and out.' He was turning tetchy. 'Damn it, there's no certainty where any of them were at any particular moment.'

'So everyone, including the staff, could be the killer.'

'That's what I just said, Lennox.'

He fulminated for a moment more, then began furiously writing notes. I ate the remaining biscuit.

A knock sounded on the door. Fossett entered. Foggy

greeted him with a yip of excitement, then went to lie on the sofa in a shaft of sunshine. The young constable put his helmet on the dressing table and came to make a report. 'Didn't find nothing, sirs, but she's got loads of jewellery, and a gun.'

'A gun?' Swift asked.

'Pocket pistol, sir. No ammo in it, so I left it where it was.' He came and sat down. 'What did she say about inheriting all them shares?'

We'd told him, on pain of death not to repeat it.

'She'd made a deal with Saunders.' Swift put his pencil down and leaned back in his chair with a sigh. 'And she said she saw Marriott with Saunders on the balcony at half past eight the morning of the murder.' He banged a hand on the table. 'They've just lied, the whole damn lot of them. We can't pin anything down.'

'Oh, it'll work out, sir,' Fossett said in supportive tones. 'Everyone says Major Lennox is brilliant at detecting murder, so you don't need to worry yourself.'

That didn't seem to bring him much joy. 'Has the lawyer arrived yet?' he snapped.

'Not yet, sir, but Mr Marriott has walked to the station to meet him. My cousin is following him, and I already told you my uncle is the Station Master. He wouldn't let the train leave the station if any of the suspects were on it.'

'He could catch a bus,' Swift said tersely.

'Mr Wright's nephew drives it, and he's been warned as well,' Fossett assured him.

I laughed. 'There you are Swift, no-one's going to escape the Cotswolds while the local militia are on guard.'

He didn't look reassured, actually his brows were almost meeting in the middle. 'We need to talk to the maid.'

'Righto, sir. She's called Dolly. She was just finishing making up Mr Smedley's bedroom ready for Sir whatsit Tremayne. I spoke to the cook, too, 'cause I went in the kitchen before coming here. She said Mrs Saunders is a right pain in the neck. Full of herself, always bossing folk about and playing the high lady, even though she wasn't and never has been. And there's something going on between her and Sebastian Cardhew.'

'Cook or Mrs Saunders?' I asked.

He grinned. 'Mrs Saunders. I thought Cook was a bit indiscreet, but she said it was common knowledge that Mrs Saunders has been chasing Mr Cardhew. Anyway, Mr Cardhew's not really that keen and they had a big row last night after we'd all gone home. Dolly and Cook heard it, and I bet the rest of the house did too.'

We both sat up at that.

'What was it about?' I asked.

'She says he betrayed her.' His face lit up as he regaled us. 'Not with a woman, but by only offering a few quid apiece for the shares. She thought he loved her, but he said he never had and it was all a figment of her imagination. Then he said she should stop making a scene because her husband had only just died, which made her cry, and she started throwing things, so he went out and slammed the door. Everyone stayed in their rooms after that and Dolly and Mr Ackroyd had to serve them all dinner on trays, except Lady Clementine because she was out for dinner with Dr Fletcher.'

'Did anyone go into the vault?' Swift demanded, showing no interest in the possible romance.

'Mr Marriott did, but there was nothing left worth looking at, except the silver, and that belongs to Lady Clementine anyway.'

Swift wrote all this down.

'You were supposed to come for a debriefing at the Manor last evening, Fossett,' I reminded him.

'Aye, sorry, sir. Mrs Rozier's cat got stuck up the tree again. I don't know why she keeps calling me.' He shook his head. 'I told her over and again – nobody has ever seen the skeleton of a cat up a tree; it'll come down when it's hungry. But she don't take the blindest bit of notice.'

I grinned. 'We've got a squirrel in our grandfather clock.'

'And it ain't for me to get it out,' he lectured. 'Wasting police time, that is. You'll have to ask your gardener to do it, if you pardon my sayin' so, sir.'

Swift was smiling too, but he bent more closely over his notebook to hide it.

'I'm sure Brendan will manage,' I replied gravely.

'Well, I've got a net on a long pole if he can't,' Fossett offered.

The door opened. Ackroyd entered without a word and admitted an elderly man, then shut the door quickly on himself. The chap stalked toward us; he was tall, thin, wore an old-fashioned suit and carried an ebony walking stick.

'Tremayne.' He spoke in stentorian tone. 'I am the lawyer. You are the detectives. We have matters to discuss.'

# CHAPTER 15

Fossett leapt to his feet and saluted stiffly to attention. Foggy sat up and gave a muffled *woof*; Tremayne paused at the sofa to rub the fur on his head and then advanced on us.

He held his hand out and we all shook in formal manner, then sat down again, apart from Fossett, who dithered. Swift told him to take notes, so he perched on a chair at the corner of the table as far from the intimidating lawyer as he could.

'Two dead.' Tremayne rested hands on his ebony stick. He must have been over seventy; Victorian in style and manner, white hair swept back in leonine fashion, hooked nose, cold, intelligent eyes and a face which could have been sculpted from stone. 'Have you apprehended the culprit?'

'Not yet,' I answered.

He gazed from under thick white brows. 'What facts have you ascertained?' His speech was as Victorian as his appearance.

Swift told him in as few words as possible, omitting the

more frivolous aspects, such as man-eating lions. He didn't
mention our theory about the arrow either, or Saunders
and Smedley working in cahoots.

'Marriott stands to benefit more,' Tremayne surmised,
then closed his lips in a tight line.

'What's Marriott's background?' I eyed the man,
his haughty manner and cold demeanour spoke of an
unflinching character with a misanthropic bent.

'Manchester. One of Barnardo's lost boys. They did their
best, but he's cold, calculating, and dangerous.'

'How is he dangerous?' I continued.

'War hero. Army captain. Fearless,' Tremayne explained.
'Led his men into battle, too many killed but he won more
fights than he lost. Not a congenial character, but effective.
His ambition is to control the Royal Buckingham.'

Fossett wrote diligently with his arm wrapped around
the notebook.

'Lady Clementine inherits Devlin Saunders' shares,'
Swift said. 'I assume you are already aware of that.'

'I am the lawyer, I facilitate the company's legal
requirements.'

I assumed that meant yes. 'Does it allow her to control
the company?'

'Hypothetically, but Devlin Saunders had entered into
a legally binding covenant wherein he committed to sell
his shares to the highest bidder. No party has the power
to overturn that order.'

'But until they're sold, Lady Clementine is the majority
shareholder?' Swift asked.

'Probate has not been granted and the will may yet be challenged. She cannot control the company for a number of reasons, not least the one I have just stated,' Tremayne intoned.

It was like drawing blood from a stone. 'She probably wouldn't realise that,' I said. 'Has she given you any orders in the meantime?'

'She has, although I have informed her that she lacks the power, and therefore her demands are null and void,' Tremayne replied.

'What did she order you to do?' Swift asked. 'And I remind you that this is a murder enquiry and Lady Clementine is a suspect.'

A tic showed in Tremayne's cheek. 'She requested the annulment of all private loans held by the company. I informed her that I was unable to comply.'

That made my heart lurch. It would have settled all my debts in one stroke. Swift glanced at me; he would have realised it too.

'Cedric Smedley had arranged loans for the other directors,' Swift stated. 'Did you draw up the contracts?'

Tremayne looked him in the eye. 'Was his death murder?'

'Almost certainly,' Swift replied.

'Almost?' Tremayne demanded.

Swift explained the twisted papers and number of unused sachets in the silver cigarette box. He made Fossett give a demonstration by screwing up papers. The lad was nervous but made a commendable job of it. Tremayne watched and listened attentively, asking only a couple of questions.

'Very well.' He nodded. 'You are correct Smedley was engaged in facilitating loans, but I was not commissioned to arrange any such contract, nor have I had sight of any.'

'Was Smedley in cahoots with Saunders?' I asked.

'Possibly,' Tremayne replied in noncommittal terms.

'Did any of the directors discuss this with you?' I continued.

'They did not, and I doubt Smedley would have been sufficiently careless to expose such a scheme,' he replied.

This set us to thinking about the intended outcome of Saunders and Smedley manipulations. The room fell quiet, apart from Fossett's scratching pencil, and the sound of birdsong beyond the balcony.

'Why did Saunders sign the covenant binding him into selling his shares?' I asked because it had puzzled me.

'He requested the document. I suspect it was part of whatever plan he and Smedley had devised.'

'You didn't ask?' Swift demanded.

'Nor did I advise,' Tremayne replied obliquely.

'What do you believe is the consequence of both men's deaths?' I switched back to the subject.

Tremayne leaned back in his chair, interlacing long fingers together. His gaze turned to the window. 'I imagine they had a particular man in mind to become president. Marriott is by far the most competent, and so my belief is that this was their intended outcome. However, now that both men are dead, loans cannot be raised and each bidder will be constrained by their personal financial circumstances. In consequence, Lady Clementine will receive a lesser sum than otherwise.' He leaned forward and raised a long finger. 'And that dilutes any motive you think she may have.'

'She'd have received nothing at all if Saunders hadn't died,' Swift stated coolly.

Tremayne lowered white brows.

'Where did Smedley source the money for the loans he made?' I asked, because I'd wondered.

Tremayne leaned back again. I swear I heard him creak. 'I assume a private bank, or personal funds.'

'Who will inherit Smedley's shares?' Swift asked the question.

'Lady Clementine,' he replied gravely.

'What?' We all said at once.

'Sorry, sirs.' Fossett's face glowed red and he hunched back over his note taking.

'She now owns...' I made the simple calculation: thirty-five plus twenty. 'Fifty-five percent!'

'How did she persuade Smedley to agree to that?' Swift asked, although the answer was predictable.

'That is a question you must address to Lady Clementine,' he replied.

'She made a deal with Saunders to leave him this house if he left her his shares,' I stated.

'Really?' Tremayne raised a brow as though this were news to him. I didn't swallow that for a minute.

'And I'll lay money that she did the same with Smedley,' I added.

Tremayne constrained a smile.

'If she had died first, how could both men inherit the house?' Swift demanded.

'An interesting question,' Tremayne replied.

We waited for an explanation. It didn't come.

'What's the answer?' Swift prompted.

'I imagine that would be for the courts to decide,' Tremayne intoned, which was hardly illuminating.

'There's a clause at the beginning of every will revoking all others,' I said, being reasonably well versed in matters of inheritance, as were most landowning gentry. 'So only her very last will would count.'

'Unless both wills were dated the same day,' Tremayne countered. 'In which case her lawyer would have to swear as to the hour.'

'But you're her lawyer,' I returned.

'I am the company lawyer. There is no reason I would involve myself in drawing up her ladyship's personal will,' he replied coolly. 'Notwithstanding, the answer is now moot given that both gentlemen are dead.'

Swift's frown indicated it wasn't moot at all, but he was still intent on gathering information. Tremayne, however, had other ideas. He rose to his feet, the ebony cane in his hand.

'Gentlemen, I wish you well in your endeavours. I am to remain here for two nights. The auction of Saunders' shares must proceed. I have decided it should take place tomorrow evening at five o'clock. I will leave the morning after the bidding has closed. Good day.' He made to go, pausing for a moment to ruffle Fogg's head. Fossett scrambled to open the door, then closed it after him.

'He's scary isn't he?' Fossett sat down again, then pushed Swift's notebook toward him.

'No, he's merely precise.' Swift peered at Fossett's notes.

'And he's playing games,' I said, then explained as they both turned to me. 'He could only know who Saunders and Smedley left their shares to if he drew up their wills.'

'Are you saying he knew what Lady Clementine had done?' Fossett looked astounded. 'But isn't that illegal, or something?'

'It would be fraud,' Swift stated. 'And I think he helped her do it.'

'Only if she used him to draw up her own will, and he said he hadn't. Anyway, it is now irrelevant unless anyone wants to go to court over it.' I was dismissive.

'Her step-daughter probably will,' Swift countered.

'Does it affect our list of suspects?' I changed tack.

Swift sighed. 'Not unless Lady Clementine is the next victim, no.'

'Right,' I continued. 'The bidding for Saunders' shares will take place at five o'clock tomorrow evening…'

Fossett put his elbow on the table and rested his chin. 'I don't understand all these shares and auctions and whatsits.'

Swift began a lengthy explanation. I glanced at my little dog.

'Need to take Fogg for a walk, Swift, I won't be long.' I made a rapid exit before he could protest, and was out and into the grounds behind the house in a matter of minutes.

Foggy bounded across the lawn, barking at whatever took his fancy. I strolled behind him, taking in the scent of May blossom drifting on the breeze.

My mind was buzzing with all that we'd learned and yet there was no actual evidence pointing to anyone. If Lady Clementine saw Saunders alive at eight thirty, then it narrowed the window down, and proved Marriott a liar. There was little we could pin down about Smedley's death though; the digitalis could have been added to his carafe at anytime the previous day.

Were they even all together at breakfast? Lady Clementine wasn't there, and nobody had mentioned it. I suppose it wasn't a lie, but rather an omission of truth. Perhaps they were all in it together? Actually, unless there were some very good actors among them, that seemed unlikely.

At least the motive was obvious. Money is the glue that binds them together, and whoever wins the auction, and becomes President of the company, will save a fortune now they're not forced to borrow from Cedric Smedley.

'Oy, your dog's digging up my flowers.' A shout broke into my musing.

I turned around. A bent old man was pointing a gnarled finger toward the miscreant busy excavating a hole in a flower bed.

'Fogg,' I called him. He was too occupied to hear me, his nose almost buried in the ground, his paws scrabbling at black earth.

'Got enough trouble with rabbits without addin' in a dog.' The old man hobbled over, leaning heavily on a hoe.

'You are Bent, I assume.'

'That I be, sir.' He was from the West Country, and pronounced it 'zur' – typical of the Somerset dialect. 'And he'll 'ave me lent-lilies up iffen 'e carries on.'

Lent-lilies were daffodils.

'Fogg.' I called him again and told him firmly to sit. Which he did, with his tongue hanging out and his eyes fixed firmly on the hole between two camellias.

'Best find me shovel and fill 'er in again.' Bent made to leave.

'Wait a moment,' I said. 'You found the blood?'

'Ah, ye're one of them policemen then?'

'Yes,' I replied. 'Well, actually I'm Major Lennox from the Manor.'

'Are ye now. I'm a furriner, y'know, I wed a girl from over Bloxford way. Then she died and I stayed on here… she were a lovely girl.' He shook his head, sadness in his voice. 'Anyways, me last job was too much work, but I saw a notice on the board, and asked the postboy. He said the folk weren't hardly ever here and it were quiet and peaceful like. He were wrong about that. Never seen such a to-do in all me life.' He shook his head. Poor chap, he was bent-backed and trying to gaze up at me by twisting his neck. His face was as gnarled as his hands, grey hair under a battered straw hat, a beard – rather unkempt – thick woven shirt, a woollen jerkin, dark corduroy breaches and hobnailed boots.

'What did you see the morning Mr Saunders' died?'

He leaned on the hoe to stare at the grass, probably

weary of trying to look up. 'I saw fresh blood on the flags, then the drip running down the stone, then his hand by the railin', and then the rest of 'im. He 'ad an arrow stuck out of 'im.' He paused to catch his breath. 'I went an' banged at the door, but no-one didn't 'ear me so I kept a bangin' and then Cook come. Mardy woman, she be, never so 'appy but she's miserable. I told 'er what I saw and she ran off bawlin'. Weren't more an' that I could do, so I went an' got on with me work.'

'Was there anything different about that morning? Apart from the murder.'

'Nope, an' there weren't none been in the garden, neither, 'cause there weren't no steps in the dew. Part from rabbits that is.'

That was interesting. 'Excellent, and thank you, Bent.'

'Ah, well, I don't be mindin' if you're bein' respectful, but the quality up there...' he nodded toward the house as best he could, '...they ain't proper gentry, them's city folk makin' out they's summat more.'

'Where are you from in Somerset?' I asked.

'Bishops Lydeard, near Taunton, an' I'm only stayed 'cause Lady Clementine be nice to me. She's a proper Lady, she is,' he said then tilted his head in Fogg's direction. 'Yer dog be diggin' agin.'

'Foggy.' I shouted at him. He'd crept away while we were talking and returned to the hole. He stopped digging when he realised he'd been caught out and sat down to gaze up at me, his ears down and black soil covering his paws.

'There's summat glintin'.' Bent hobbled over, using the hoe as a walking stick. He leaned down to reach in the ground. 'Well look'ee here then.'

# CHAPTER 16

'Don't touch it,' I warned him. I pulled out my handkerchief and used it to wrap around the handle of a knife stuck deep in the soil.

'What's it doin' in there?' Bent sounded astonished. 'Why'd some'un bury a dagger in the garden?' He watched as I carefully pulled the long slim knife out of the ground.

'It's evidence,' I said, which was hardly enlightening, but was as much as I was prepared to tell him. 'Keep it under your hat, would you.'

He took the tattered item off his head and scratched the grizzled hair below. 'Well, I don't s'pose there's any'un I'd tell.'

We both looked at Foggy, whose ears had pricked up, keen to see if I approved of his discovery.

'Good dog,' I said. He gave a *woof* of joy and ran over for a fuss, then trotted beside me back to the house, head held high and tail wagging proudly.

'A dagger!' Fossett was thrilled. 'So you were right about it bein' used to kill Mr Saunders, and the arrow was just a superfuge.'

'Look.' I pointed to a blackened stain riming to the underside of the hilt. 'That could be blood.'

'Gosh, so it is.' Fossett leaned in to peer at it. 'Real evidence! This is proper policing this is.'

Swift was equally excited although in more restrained manner. 'Fingerprint powder, Fossett,' he ordered.

'Yes, sir,' Fossett instantly replied and opened his satchel to rummage around. 'Here we are, and a couple of brushes.'

Fogg extended his front paws onto the edge of the table to watch with tongue hanging out. I leaned back in my chair and waited.

They laid the knife on the desk, the handkerchief spread beneath it, and painstakingly brushed the dirt away. Next stage was to sprinkle the soft grey powder, and then brush that away to show any prints. It took ages. Foggy gave up his vigil and lay down at my feet. I crossed my arms, then my legs. Eventually they were ready with a magnifying glass and the sheet of inky fingerprints taken from the suspects.

'Look, there's a clear set there, and another.' Fossett pointed at the handle of the dagger. It had a grip of polished steel, unembellished except for a foreign insignia I recognised as German. The blade was long and slim – a true assassin's weapon. Why the devil would anyone have buried it where it could be so easily found?

'The prints are...' Swift frowned over the sheet of fingerprints, names carefully written in Fossett's handwriting under each. 'It's Marcus Marriott's. Both of the prints are Marriott's,' he declared in triumph.

'Oh, sir, we got him!' Fossett's face lit up. 'Shall I go and fetch the handcuffs?'

'I brought some with me,' Swift stated, grim satisfaction in his tone. I didn't bother asking him why he was carrying handcuffs.

'I've never arrested anyone before.' Fossett's eyes were shining with enthusiasm. 'Oh, wait a minute. If we're going to lock him up in the station, I'll have to clean out the cell first – I've been usin' it for brooms and stuff.'

'Wait until we've heard what Marriott has to say before we do anything,' I cautioned.

'Aye, but we'll have to lock him up, won't we, sir?' He looked at Swift. 'At least until they come from Oxford to take him away?'

'Lennox is right, we need to talk to him first,' Swift agreed and passed him the handcuffs. But you can do the honours.'

'Thank you, sir.' Fossett's face was almost glowing. 'My first arrest.'

I stood up. 'I'll ring for Ackroyd, he can find him.' I tugged the bell pull before they had time to object.

'We should go and...' Swift began.

Ackroyd came in, he obviously hadn't been far away. 'I was just coming here, sir. Lady Persi sent a note, your boot boy brought it to the door. M'lady requests that you purchase eggs en route home. There was mention of a squirrel.'

'Fine,' I sighed. 'Would you ask Mr Marriott to come here, please.'

'I will indeed, sir.' Ackroyd flared his nostrils in

readiness. 'He is currently ensconced with Sir Edwin Tremayne.'

'I could go with him, just in case,' Fossett offered.

'No,' Swift replied. 'There's no need to raise an alarm.'

Ackroyd's thin brows arched at that, but he went off without a word, stiff-backed and nose in the air.

'We got him, sir. We got him!' Fossett was cock-a-hoop.

We remained silent; experience had taught us that things were rarely so easy.

'What the hell do you want now?' Marriott stalked in a few minutes later.

Foggy let out a low growl, the golden fur on his neck raised. I ruffled his top knot in reassurance.

'Sit down, please,' Swift told him.

He sat. Fossett manoeuvred around to the rear, hiding the handcuffs behind his back.

'Marcus Marriott, you are hereby cautioned that you need not say anything unless you desire to do so, but whatever you say will be taken down in writing and may be used in evidence against you. You are now under arrest on suspicion of the murder of Devlin Saunders,' Swift stated formally. 'If you do not cooperate or if you try to leave this room without permission, you will be handcuffed.'

'What?' Marriott made to rise.

'Stay where you are,' I snapped. He glared at me, grey eyes darkening, then did as he was told.

Fossett hesitated, the handcuffs ready in his hands.

'Remain by the door, Constable,' Swift told him.

'Aye, sir.' Fossett complied, a look of relief in his young face.

'You'd better explain yourself, Inspector,' Marriott rasped through gritted teeth.

Swift unwrapped the handkerchief to reveal the steel blade glinting in the sunshine. 'Is this yours?'

Marriott closed his eyes for an instant, then steadied his nerve. 'Somebody stole it.'

'Did you report it?' Swift spoke evenly, his tone remote and professional.

'I did not.'

'Why?' I asked. I was watching Marriott, or rather his profile; he was facing Swift across the writing table, his brows lowered against the light. His black hair immaculately styled and slicked back, his dark grey suit tailored to fit a tough physique. I could see the soldier in him, and I was angry because he'd been a hero and now he was a bloodsucking predator, leeching off hapless victims.

'I hadn't realised it was missing until yesterday. I didn't want to excite any more attention.' Marriott didn't look at me, he was looking at Swift, or rather through him. 'And Devlin was shot with an arrow, so it's not even relevant.'

'He was killed with that knife,' Swift said with conviction, even though we didn't actually have proof of that.

Marriott continued his distant gaze. 'You have evidence?'

'The post mortem confirmed he was killed with a blade,' I stated.

'What about Cedric?' he asked.

'He was murdered too,' Swift replied.

'It wasn't me,' Marriott stated.

'But it's your knife, your fingerprints, and you have every reason to kill them both,' I said. 'It all points to you.'

He dropped his gaze. 'I've been set up.'

And you deserved it, I thought but didn't say.

'Who would have set you up?' Swift wrote Marriott's name, along with the date, place, and time, across a fresh page.

'Cardhew, probably. I can't see Palgrave doing it, he hasn't the intelligence, or the backbone.'

'We know you lied in your written statement. Please explain what your actual movements were on the morning Devlin Saunders died?' Swift moved into full police mode.

Marriott lowered his gaze. 'We woke around half past six. I had some work to do, figures…' He paused and seemed to be struggling, perhaps reality was hitting him. 'Gabriel slept a little longer. I dressed, and then I went to see Devlin.'

'What time was this?' Swift instantly pounced.

'At half past eight.' He dropped his eyes to focus on Swift's note taking. His voice had lost the harshness, as though conceding defeat, or perhaps simply biding his time.

'You were seen,' I said.

'What?' He turned to look at me in surprise. 'How?'

'On the balcony,' I replied.

'The gardener,' he muttered under his breath. Actually, it was Lady Clementine, but none of us corrected him.

'What state was Saunders' bedroom in?' Swift asked the question.

'Tidy.' He shrugged. 'The usual.'

That tallied with Ackroyd's account, he said he'd made the bed at eight fifteen. 'Where was Saunders?'

'Sitting in the wicker chair reading the paper. He was in no mood to talk.'

'Why did you go to see him?' Swift asked. The questioning and answers had taken on a rhythm.

'I wanted his shares. The auction was a ridiculous idea. I told him to put a stop to it. If the company ended up with the wrong man everyone would lose out. It was stupid...I didn't use those words, but he understood.'

'Understood what?' Swift was busy writing.

'That if Sebastian took control, he'd lose the company. He's reckless. He'd put pressure on the clients, drive them too hard, and too fast. Too much pressure ruins the process, the clients begin to disappear, usually abroad, or end up shooting themselves. It happens. We have to tread a fine line...'

'Bleed them slowly you mean – get the most out of them until you've extracted all they have?' I said, my voice a low growl.

He glanced at me. 'They walked into it.'

'So have you,' I replied. 'And I'm going to see you hang.'

He looked away. 'I didn't do it.'

'You've done enough,' I snapped.

'Lennox,' Swift warned.

I closed my mouth and clenched my jaw.

'What did Saunders say when you told him you wanted control of the company?' Swift continued.

'He said it's every man for himself.'

'And your reply?' Swift prompted him.

'I said I'd pull out of the bidding,' Marriott said. 'He thought I was bluffing.'

'Were you?' Swift looked up from his note taking.

Marriott looked at his fingernails. 'Perhaps.'

'What time did you leave Saunders' bedroom?' Swift continued.

'Eight forty-five, or just after.' He folded his arms. 'And I want to talk to my wife now, she'll worry if she doesn't know where I am.'

'She'll be informed when we're ready,' Swift replied. 'Did anyone see you leave?'

Marriott looked mulish, but answered the question. 'Ackroyd may have done, he was crossing the hall downstairs when I walked by the top landing.'

I picked up a pencil from the desk and threw it at him. 'Catch.'

He instinctively grabbed it from the air. 'What the hell was that for?' He slammed it down on the table.

He was left-handed, which didn't fit with the paper twist theory. Swift noticed it too.

'What were you and Margaret Saunders arguing about in the garden yesterday?' I said as Swift made more notes.

His face tautened. 'She still wanted Sebastian Cardhew to take control of the company. She thought Devlin's shares were hers and she could do as she pleased with them. I informed her she couldn't.'

'They had a noisy argument last evening,' I stated.

His focus didn't shift. 'Cardhew showed his true colours when we heard Cedric Smedley died and he realised we didn't need loans. Margaret genuinely thought Cardhew cared for her...astonishingly naive.' He glanced up. 'Did she inherit Devlin's shares?'

'No,' I said.

He blinked at that. 'Who did?'

'Lady Clementine.'

He suddenly laughed deep in his throat. 'Bravo.'

'What will happen with the bidding now?' I continued.

He thought about it. 'The show we put on yesterday, after Cedric died, that was merely bravado. We still want Devlin's shares, or rather Sebastian and I do. Alfred's at the mercy of Dolores, she's pulling his strings.' He appeared to be telling the truth. 'The bidding will recommence, but at far lower levels. Whatever we offer now will have to be financed out of our own pockets and that will limit us.'

'Arthur Palgrave signed his loan with Cedric before he died and has the funds in his bank,' Swift said, watching Marriott intently.

Marriott's cold eyes slid toward him. 'Does he now... well that rather stirs up the hornets' nest, doesn't it. How much has he got?'

'That's confidential,' Swift replied.

'Why do you think Saunders was killed?' I asked.

He blinked, the question didn't appear to have occurred to him. 'Money I suppose, it's at the crux of everything.'

'We were told Dolores Palgrave had affairs with all the men,' I said trying to rattle him.

He shrugged. 'Not with me.'

'What about the others?' I continued.

'She plays games with the men, blows hot and cold around them, but I'm not sure it means anything. I can't imagine she'd have had an affair with Cedric, he's old enough to be her father, and Sebastian is an idiot.'

'Someone said she was close to Devlin Saunders before she met Alfred,' Swift said.

'Perhaps.' Marriott shrugged.

'Did it continue after her marriage?' Swift added.

'I've no idea.' He spoke coldly. 'Ask Margaret, she'll have kept tally on that score.'

I found his casual indifference to everyone else's feelings absolutely insufferable.

Swift remained professional. 'Was Margaret Saunders actually in a relationship with Sebastian Cardhew?'

'Only in her own mind. She's been chasing him for months, God knows why.' He glanced away, as though bored.

We didn't extract anything more of relevance from him and a short while later we frogmarched him to my car. Nobody from the house realised what was happening so it was done without drama, which was a relief.

He sat in the back, Fossett beside him, poker-faced and refusing to look right or left when we passed through the gate, despite the shouts of shock and surprise. Swift sat in the passenger seat, Foggy on his knee, tongue hanging out and thoroughly enjoying himself. It did rather detract from the seriousness of the occasion, but this was just a small village buried in the Cotswolds, after all.

We stood ready as Fossett locked the prisoner up – he had to remove brushes and buckets from the only cell in the station first. Marriott behaved impeccably through-out, which made us all suspicious. Once he was safely ensconced behind bars there didn't seem much to hang about for, so we went back to the Manor for lunch.

'It was Marcus Marriott!' Persi sounded astounded when we told the girls the morning's events.

'Oh, thank heavens.' Florence's pretty face showed shock. 'We were convinced you had decided it was Alfred Palgrave.' They were in my library, working on the colour-ful chart they'd devised.

'Why Palgrave, Kitsy?' I asked as I went to kiss my lovely wife.

'Because we thought he wanted to destroy the company.' Persi smiled up at me.

'That's like trying to cut the head off the hydra.' Swift gave Florence a peck on the cheek.

'Yes, but he's not terribly bright, so he wouldn't have understood that, would he?' Persi continued.

'Hum,' I replied. 'What's for lunch?'

'Egg and cress sandwiches,' Florence replied.

'Ah…about the eggs,' I began.

'Oh, did you forget?' Persi looked at me. 'I'm not sure you'll enjoy cress sandwiches.'

I grinned. 'You could add some ham and tomatoes.'

'What happened to the eggs?' Swift asked.

'The squirrel tried to escape and ended up in the kitchen,' Florence explained. 'Tommy and Brendan raced after it and in the chaos the basket of eggs was knocked off the table. Nicky ate the yolks off the floor, he's in his basket now feeling very sorry for himself.'

'But the squirrel jumped out of the window, so it wasn't a complete disaster.' Persi laughed. 'Come on, we can eat in the garden, the weather is lovely.'

And with that, we all trooped outside for a scrumptious lunch in the warm sunshine.

# CHAPTER 17

Swift declared we would interview Marriott formally at the station. I was ready to rebel.

'Lennox, you'll just have to get used to the fact that sometimes detecting can be tedious, and you should think of the reward Margaret Saunders offered,' he lectured.

'Fine,' I muttered and went to start the car. Lunch had engendered a feeling of contentment and I was more in the mood to take my fishing rod to the lake than to interview Marriott.

A small crowd had clustered outside the police station, and Fossett was on the doorstep with a broom.

'Sir, they won't go away,' he complained when we climbed out of the Bentley. 'And Mrs Marriott is sitting next to the cell talking to Mr Marriott, and she won't go away neither.'

'I'll talk to her,' I instantly decided.

'Lennox, we really should—' Swift began an objection.

'Nonsense, you and Fossett are perfectly capable of grilling Marriott, you don't need me.'

'Hello, Major Lennox,' Mr Trimble called out. 'You've got him then? We knew you would.'

This was followed by a few choruses of 'well done' and 'I thought it was him'.

We left Fossett to argue with the craning crowd and entered the cool confines of the police station.

'Mrs Marriott.' I spotted her first.

She rose to her feet. She'd been sitting on a stool, conversing with her husband through the bars of the cell.

'My husband did not kill anyone,' she began in a quiet voice.

'He was in the war,' I replied, thinking that he most certainly had.

'I meant anyone here.' Her cheeks flushed pink and she looked away.

'Lennox, I expect you to watch your step around my wife,' Marriott growled.

I ignored him. 'Would you like to come for a walk?' I asked her and held my hand out in invitation.

She glanced at Marriott, who was frowning, but he nodded his agreement.

'Move away from the door.' Swift had found the keys to the cell and ordered Marriott back. He did as told, and Swift let himself in with a loud jangle of metal as he unlocked the door and slid back the bolt. Fossett came in, broom at the ready.

The crowd fell quiet as I emerged with Gabriel, and stood respectfully aside.

I aimed her toward the road leading into the village. 'May I call you Gabriel?'

She hesitated. 'I'd rather not be stared at, could we walk by the stream?'

'Of course.' I turned toward the path through the woods that led to the brook and water meadows beyond.

'And you may call me Gabriel,' she said in her serious voice.

'Thank you,' I replied.

'Why are you holding my husband?'

I thought that was pretty obvious. 'We found evidence connecting him to Devlin Saunders' murder.'

'His dagger,' she murmured, then spoke a little louder. 'We realised it was missing. Marcus was annoyed, but we didn't connect it with Devlin's death.'

'Where did you meet Marcus?' I asked in a conversational tone.

'At the palace, just after the war.'

That raised my brows. 'Buckingham Palace?'

'Yes, it was an awards ceremony. The King was presenting medals. I was there with my father.'

I took another look at her. Her dress was dark blue, and as drab and shapeless as the one she wore yesterday. 'Your father?'

'Admiral Sir Rupert Paisley.'

'Hm.' I nodded, rather dumbfounded. I'd heard of Admiral Paisley, everyone had, he was one of the defence chiefs during the war. 'I read his obituary in *The Times*.'

'Two years ago,' she replied, her brown hair falling limply either side of her face.

Sunlight fell through the trees, the leaves catching the

light to throw dappled shadows across our path; a simple beaten track winding through pretty woodland scented with wild garlic, borage, and loosestrife.

I recalled Admiral Paisley's extensive obituary; his son had inherited his estate in Hampshire, there had been no mention of a daughter. 'I'm sorry, you must miss him.'

She didn't reply, merely pursed her lips. She wasn't actually unattractive, but somehow made herself so. Soft cheeks, a little too thin, but with clear skin and thick lashes framing hazel eyes, which were dull and lacking any sparkle. I didn't believe she was the meek woman she appeared to be, her tightly clenched jaw indicated a determined character.

We walked in silence for some yards, birdsong trilling through the canopy, a woodpecker's *rat-a-tat-tat* echoing from a hollow trunk.

'I assume you met your husband at the palace because he was also receiving a medal?'

'Yes, he was, for valour. He's very brave.' A smile hovered on her lips and warmth glowed in her eyes, which she was quick to switch off.

'He was a Barnado's boy?'

'From Manchester.' She nodded. 'His mother abandoned him. He never knew who his father was.'

'Did he ever find her?'

'His mother? No, she killed herself. We didn't discover this until after the war. Barnado's held back the information until Marcus attained his majority.' She cast me a fleeting glance. 'They believe such actions can influence impressionable youngsters – and it was self-murder, after all.'

It was a long time since I'd heard suicide described as self-murder. It sounded almost accusatory. 'How long have you been married?'

'Two years. Papa wouldn't allow it. We married after he died.' She spoke matter-of-factly, which surprised me given the sensitive subject matter.

'Doesn't it bother you that your husband is destroying people's lives?' I quelled the anger in my tone.

Her eyes flicked to mine. 'These "people" have run up debts, many of them through gambling, or stupidity. I was born into the upper classes, Major Lennox, just as you were. I have seen many instances where people have squandered their fortunes away, mostly through vice. This modern world is falling under the control of those who are commercially minded and clever. People with intellect and ability are taking over – those who were merely born in the right bed must learn to adapt, or perish.' She said this in a complete monotone, as though it had been learned by rote.

We reached the brook and stepped onto the wooden bridge spanning the crystal clear water. I stopped to lean on the rail.

'Do you believe that?' A fat trout hung in the water below me, half hidden between reeds swaying gently in the flow.

'Believe what?' She stood on the end of the bridge, nervously picking at her nails.

'What you just said.'

I swore I heard stifled laughter in her throat but her voice held no hint of it. 'I am merely my husband's wife, Major Lennox, I believe what I am told.' She took a step backwards. 'I would like to return to the Hall now.'

I sighed. I hadn't so much as scratched the surface. She was a complete enigma and I had no idea what she was hiding – but I was certain that whatever it was was buried deep. 'Fine, but please do not leave the area,' I cautioned her.

'I have no intention of doing so until my husband's name is cleared,' she said then made her way through the woodland path leading to Ashton Hall.

I retraced my steps back to the police station. Swift and Fossett were sitting in the tiny office beyond the reception area.

'Waste of time,' Fossett said. 'He just clammed up and demanded the lawyer. I called and asked Sir Tremayne if he'd come, and he said no, so that was that.'

'Gabriel Marriott wouldn't open up either.' I sat down at the rickety table which served as a desk. 'She's Admiral Rupert Paisley's daughter.'

Swift looked up from his writing. 'I thought he was dead?'

'He is, and Gabriel and Marcus didn't marry until after he died. He didn't approve, apparently.'

'Hardly a surprise,' Swift remarked dryly.

'I'd have thought Mr Marriott was too clever to do something as stupid as burying his knife in the soil where the gardener could find it,' Fossett said.

We both glanced at him. It was exactly what I'd been thinking.

'Have you arranged for Oxford to come and take him into custody?' I asked Swift.

He shook his head. 'No, I'm not...' He broke off on a sigh. 'It doesn't really add up, Lennox.'

'Perhaps it's a double bluff?' I suggested.

'Then it would be a stupid one, because it would confirm we knew Saunders was killed with a knife and not an arrow,' he replied tartly.

Which was a jolly good point, and I should have realised it. 'You're just going to leave him to stew?'

'Yes, for a while, anyway.' Swift ran fingers through his hair, he was never comfortable with ambiguity. 'Come on, we need to interview Sebastian Cardhew.'

'Righto, sir.' Fossett was instantly on his feet.

'You have to remain here and guard the prisoner,' Swift told him.

'And don't let his wife back in,' I ordered.

He sat down again, his face falling glum. 'Yes, sir.'

The bang of the front door being pushed open, followed by stomping in the reception area, made us all look around.

'Major Lennox!' The bulky figure of Flossie Craddock filled the doorframe. 'And Inspector Swift, as was.'

'Mrs Craddock...' we all began, but she was having none of it.

'Now, you'd best listen to what I have to say, because I don't want you going off on the wrong track. Lady

Clementine was with me Saturday morning when that man, Devlin Saunders, was killed, and I know exactly what time it was because I heard the church bell strike.' She was in full flow, billowing chest filling her floral blouse. 'It was nine o'clock, so don't you go accusing her ladyship of nothing, because if you do, you'll have me to deal with.' A flush had risen in her round cheeks, her small eyes alight with righteousness.

'Mrs Craddock, we have just taken Mr Marriott—'

'I know. I've heard what's gone on, and it's all nonsense because it was just a knife found, and we all know that man was shot with an arrow. So you're either playing silly beggars or you've got it all wrong, and if you don't know what you're doing, you'd best let some proper police take your place.'

'Yes, thank you, Mrs Craddock.' I stood up. 'PC Fossett will take your statement if you'd like to sit down.' I pulled the chair out for her. 'Swift, come on,' I said and walked out before she could draw another breath.

# CHAPTER 18

We returned to Ashton Hall to find an even larger crowd at the gate, which surprised me.

'Hello, Major Lennox,' Mrs Tippet called out.

'Goin' to lock up any of them others?' Mr Briers shouted.

'Major, we were led to believe the murder weapon was an arrow,' Frank Wright said as I paused to wait for him to push the gates open for us.

'There's muttering in the village, Major,' Mr Trimble said.

'Things are always more complicated than they seem,' was all I was prepared to say, and then motored off up the drive.

Ackroyd must have been waiting because he was on the doorstep as we stalked towards the portal.

'Sir Edwin would like a word, sirs,' he intoned as we entered.

'He can wait.' Swift was in no mood for diversions. 'Find Sebastian Cardhew, would you, and send him to the incident room.'

'You mean Mr Saunders' bedroom, sir.' Ackroyd was even more pedantic than Swift.

Swift glared at him.

'*Ahem*...very well, sir.' Ackroyd cleared his throat and went off.

I went straight onto the balcony to enjoy the warmth of the day and keep an eye out for my little dog, just in case. We'd left him at home because prison cells weren't likely to appeal to him, unless there was food included, of course. He didn't appear to be in the garden so I sat on the late Devlin Saunders' wicker chair and put my feet up. Someone had cleaned the tiles and there was now no trace of blood, chalk, or anything else akin to violent death, which was much more to my liking. It was rather a shame the newspaper wasn't still here, although I can't imagine I'd make much sense of the *Financial Times*.

'Lennox?' Swift called from inside the room. 'Why are you out there?'

I didn't answer.

Ackroyd returned, I could hear his voice.

'I have searched every room, sir, he is not in the house.'

'Are his clothes still in his room?'

'They are not, sir, nor is his suitcase.'

'Damn,' Swift replied, and banged something on the desk. 'Lennox?' He shouted.

I closed my eyes against the sunshine.

'Have you asked the people at the gate?' Swift continued interrogating the butler.

'Not yet, sir, but I will do so now,' Ackroyd replied.

The closing of a door sounded, then Swift walked out to throw a shadow over me.

'Lennox, we'll have to go and search for Cardhew, he's obviously taken the chance to escape.'

'He won't get far.' I crossed my legs and leaned back in the chair.

The shrill sound of a police whistle was heard somewhere in the distance, then shouting. Swift turned on his heel and marched out, allowing peace to descend. Fifteen minutes of quiet solitude later, the hullabaloo arrived. With a muttered curse under my breath, I stood up and went to confront the long arm of the law in the guise of Fossett and Swift, with the apprehended runaway, Sebastian Cardhew.

He was still wearing the red blazer, so he hadn't actually attempted to go incognito. His face was almost as red as his coat; he was fuming in petulant manner.

'You've arrested Marcus, so that's the end of it. There's no reason why I should stay here.' He threw himself into the chair opposite.

'He was trying to escape on the London train, sir.' Fossett had marched him in and was standing in accusatory manner. 'My uncle saw him, so did everyone, and they stopped the train until he got off. Uncle called me at the station and I went to fetch him, but he'd got in a taxi by then, and that was driven by Mr Feathers, and he wouldn't take him nowhere. Then when he saw me, he tried to run off.' Fossett glared at Cardhew. 'And that makes you a fugitive, that does.'

Swift hid a smile as he sat down in his customary chair.

'I am not a fugitive!' Cardhew raged. 'I have an appointment in London.'

'Aye, and you packed your bags too, so it weren't just an appointment, it were running away,' Fossett retorted. He was also red in the face, with arms akimbo and his helmet askew.

'I am perfectly entitled to leave if I want to.' Cardhew folded his arms tightly across his chest, creasing his silk cravat. 'You have no authority to stop me, you're just the local bobby. And you two...' He directed his focus at me and Swift. 'You're not even policemen. I'll have my lawyer after you, you mark my words.'

'Would that lawyer be Sir Edwin Tremayne?' I asked.

He dropped his arms. 'Yes, and, he'll....I mean, he will do as I say. I pay for his services, just like everyone in the company.' His bluster fizzled out and he dropped his eyes to stare at the tips of his dust spattered shoes.

'Fossett, you should return to the station,' Swift told the young constable.

'I'll do that, sir.' He straightened his helmet on his head and turned to Cardhew. 'And that cell's got room for two, ye know,' he said and then marched out, shutting the door with a bang behind him.

Nobody spoke for a moment.

'Marcus did it, so why shouldn't I leave,' Cardhew said sulkily.

'We're merely holding him for questioning.' Swift sharpened his pencil in the wind-up sharpener, then blew on the point. 'You are having an affair with Margaret Saunders.'

Cardhew's cheeks went from red to puce. 'I am not. She's been throwing herself at me and I have refused her attentions.'

'Marriott said she wanted you to take the majority holding,' Swift continued. 'Why would she do that?'

'I...I...you'll have to ask her,' Cardhew stammered.

'Did you conspire together to kill her husband?' Swift maintained the pressure.

'Oh, don't be ridiculous. You're not going to pin this on me, just because she wanted to be rid of him doesn't mean I would do it.'

That made us both stare.

'Do what?' I said.

He bit his lips.

'Wouldn't do what?' Swift demanded.

'Rid herself of him.' Having spilled the beans, Cardhew couldn't wait to bury Margaret Saunders in them. 'She talked about it more than once, said there must be someone who would take good money for it. And she could pay out of the proceeds of the inheritance.' He was almost gabbling. 'Or if I did it, she'd make sure I got the shares. I told her it was ridiculous, and she shouldn't talk like that. If Devlin got to hear of it, he'd probably have her done away with, which he would. He was ruthless.'

Swift watched him for a moment then wrote furiously.

I'd been surprised too.

'Did she actually search for someone to kill Saunders?' I demanded.

'You'll have to ask her,' he repeated. 'I wouldn't know

where to start. I mean where would one find an assassin? Put an ad in *The Times*? The whole thing was nonsense.'

'But she was serious about having him murdered?' I insisted.

'Possibly.' He reverted to sulkiness. 'Can I leave, now?' Having dropped Margaret in the mire he couldn't wait to slink off.

Swift wasn't finished. 'You were the last person to see Saunders alive.' I knew this to be an outright lie, but I didn't bat an eyelid.

'I wasn't, Lady Clementine was,' Cardhew said. 'She left his room at five to nine. I was about to go down for breakfast when I saw her. I shut my door again because she just makes fun of me when she sees me, but I kept it open a crack. She came from his room, walked past mine and went down the stairs.' He looked from one to the other of us, our faces obviously forgetting to freeze because he was suddenly cock-a-hoop. 'Ha, you didn't know that, did you!' He stood up, straightened his stupid blazer and walked out, preening himself as he went.

'God damn it!' Swift threw the pencil onto the desk. 'They're all bloody lying. Every one of them and they change their story by the minute.' He was fuming. 'Lady Clementine is in this up to her neck, and don't tell me she's charming, Lennox, because she's bonkers, and she's driving me the same way.' He went and hauled on the bell pull, then stomped back to the desk, ranting to himself.

The sound of music suddenly rose from below. I got up and went to look over the balcony rail.

My butler was dancing on the lawn with Lady Clementine. A gramophone complete with brass horn set on a table, a phonograph record rotating beneath the needle. Ackroyd stood to attention on the terrace, silver tray in hand bearing an ice bucket complete with ice and bottle of bubbly, along with champagne flutes. Foggy watched the performance, his head cocked to one side, no doubt as baffled as I.

'Greggs, what are you doing?' I called down.

Lady Clementine turned to look up. 'Oh Heathcliff, isn't dear Greggs divine. He is teaching me the tango.'

'Greggs, would you stop doing that, we need to talk to Lady Clementine.'

Greggs didn't stop, he carried on, they both did. It was rather amusing actually, and the music was very lively. Swift came out and stared down.

'Lady Clementine, this is a serious investigation,' he shouted, unnecessarily loudly.

'Oh phooey.' She was dismissive. 'I will come when we have finished. Adelante, dear Greggs,' she ordered, and they swung about to strut another Canyengue across the lawn.

We had to wait for two more performances before they stopped, and even then they'd have continued if Swift hadn't gone down to the terrace and swiped the needle off the record.

Greggs went off with a silly grin on his phiz and we took up vacant chairs on the terrace. Ackroyd served bubbly, which Swift declined because he was 'on duty'.

'Why didn't you tell us that you'd been to see Saunders before you'd gone into the village?' Swift demanded.

'Because I didn't see him.' Lady Clementine held her glass steady as Ackroyd topped up her champagne.

'Cardhew said he saw you leaving Saunders' room at five to nine.' Swift was sitting the other side of Lady Clementine trying his best to intimidate her. It wasn't working.

'Then he was mistaken. I knocked on Devlin's door but there was no answer, so I went away.' She took a sip of bubbly.

'You didn't go in?' I asked. The champagne was absolutely first class, Swift really was missing a treat.

'I couldn't, and I'd particularly wanted to talk to him. He was about to auction his shares and that would affect our arrangement over my will,' she explained perfectly rationally. 'Anyway, the door was locked, so that was that.'

'Locked?' Swift was instantly alert. 'From the inside?'

'I've no idea,' she replied, her blue eyes watching him over her champagne glass.

'You could have mentioned this before,' I admonished lightly.

'I thought it would only add to the confusion.' She smiled sweetly.

Swift's tetchy retort was interrupted by the arrival of Margaret Saunders stalking in our direction. Her hands were clamped into tight fists at her side, her face contorted in rage.

'Clementine,' she shrieked. 'How could you! How could you make that agreement with Devlin behind my back?'

Her eyes flashed, she towered over us like a valkyrie ready to swoop.

'If your husband chose not to confide in you, Margaret...' Lady Clementine was unperturbed.

'You know he never did,' she blazed. 'But you could have told me. You haven't said a word about it since he died. I had to hear it from Edwin.' Her voice rose a couple more octaves. 'You've made me destitute, you've taken everything that was mine.' She was leaning closer, scarlet lips drawn back from white teeth.

'Margaret, this is nonsense and you know it.' Lady Clementine fixed her with a stern stare. 'The house in London is yours, and so is whatever money Devlin had squirrelled away. He left me his shares because he thought he'd inherit this house from me.'

'So you own the company now and you think you're going to control us all.' Margaret was more interested in getting things off her chest. 'This is typical of you, you act like a featherbrain, but you're nothing of the sort. You always know exactly what you're doing.'

'When did you arrange to have your husband assassinated, Mrs Saunders?' I cut in with the sort of question Swift may have aimed.

That shut her up, which was fortuitous in itself. She stopped in confusion, then raised her hands to her cheeks. 'I didn't...I never would have,' she stammered, then got a grip. 'Sebastian told you that, didn't he? The rat. Why did I ever think he would...' She stopped again, realising she was digging herself deeper. 'I am going to have this out with him,' she hissed. 'He is nothing but a lying, cheating weasel.' She stormed off, high heels clicking across the terrace.

'Well done, Heathcliff.' Lady Clementine beamed. 'She really can be quite a termagant when there's loot involved.'

'What do you know of this planned assassination?' Swift looked at her shrewdly, it was obvious the news hadn't come as a surprise to her.

'It was just wild words. Dolores had been flirting with Devlin again, and Sebastian was playing hot and cold, and it all became too much for her.' Lady Clementine's gaze fell, and her smile with it. 'Margaret doesn't understand that you can not simply command love and affection. I've told her so many times, it has to be real, not negotiated.'

'Has she threatened to kill her husband before?' Swift asked, his tone hardening.

'Or anyone else?' I added.

'No, no, of course not.' She smiled reassuringly, although the smile didn't reach her eyes.

'You said her relationship with her father was difficult,' I reminded her.

'As are many such relationships. Please don't read anything into this, gentlemen.' She finished her drink. 'Now if you'll excuse me. I have business to attend with Sir Edwin.'

We stood up in gentlemanly fashion, and waited for her to leave. She waggled her fingers as she went, the smile returned to her lips.

Foggy came bounding over from whatever he'd been doing and started cavorting about my feet. I knew what that meant, it was approaching his supper time.

'Come on, Swift.' I drained my glass and stood up.

'Lennox, I want to talk to Dolores Palgrave.'

I didn't want to talk to anyone else from this damned house. 'Tomorrow, unless you want to walk home.'

He shoved his hands in his pockets and followed in dour mood.

'She should have told us. It's important. If Saunders' door was locked at five to nine, the killer may have been in there.'

'Yes,' I agreed in the hope of pacifying him. 'Or they'd already killed him and locked the door intending to return later.'

'It changes everything,' he continued as we crunched across the gravel drive.

'Do you think so?'

'I've no damned idea, Lennox,' he swore, then went on muttering under his breath until I started the car and we headed home.

# CHAPTER 19

We reached the Manor within a few minutes and it wasn't long before we were seated in the garden waiting for Greggs to arrive with the drinks tray. Angus ran circles around us, Tommy chased after him, and I gazed at Persi with a smile on my face. I would have been talking to her but the noisy youngsters had drowned us out.

'Go and play in the orchard!' Swift ordered when he returned from whatever he'd been doing indoors.

'Oh, sir…' Tommy began.

'Now.' He pointed a finger towards the walled garden.

'Dada.' Angus was undeterred by Swift's bad temper and came to kiss his daddy. Swift melted on the instant. He picked the boy up in his arms and carried him off with Tommy skipping alongside him. Tubbs, who'd been sunning himself on the kitchen windowsill, bounded after them in short-legged hops.

Peace descended in an instant and I told Persi everything we'd learned that afternoon, including Margaret Saunders' tantrum.

'Chilled white wine, sir.' Greggs arrived at exactly the right moment.

'Thank you, old man.' I gave him a grin.

So did Persi, which set him simpering.

'Is Jonathan going to let Marriott go?' she asked as Greggs served our drinks.

'Possibly. It was his knife and his fingerprints, but that doesn't actually prove he stabbed Saunders. And he's left-handed, which doesn't tie in with the twisted sachets either.'

'Could Gabriel have done it?' Persi reached for a crispy cheese roundel from the platter Greggs had placed between us.

'She doesn't seem the sort.' I mused over it. 'She's something of a closed book, but her feelings for her husband appear genuine.'

'Could they be in it together?'

I took a sip of my drink. 'Yes, but why bury the knife where it would inevitably be found, and with his fingerprints on the handle?' I returned to the obvious anomaly.

We both ate another snack while musing. Actually I was watching the sunlight playing on her shimmering blonde hair. Her brows were slightly creased above her blue eyes. She smiled when she noticed my gaze and extended her hand to mine across the tablecloth.

'Margaret is the most logical culprit, especially if her husband was having an affair with Dolores,' she reasoned.

'Cardhew may have been lying,' I reminded her. 'Or he could have fed the story of an affair to Margaret.'

She let go my hand and took another sip of wine. 'It's rather distasteful, isn't it? Money and affairs.'

'I suppose it depends on your outlook,' I said, although I agreed with her. 'They seem the type to want it all, and we're just happy with what we've got.'

That brought another smile to her lips. 'Well, it's caught up with them now.'

Tommy returned from the orchard holding a half dozen eggs in his school cap.

'Nicky's still not well, he's been in his basket all day since he lapped the broken eggs up. We've had to give him some kaolin to settle his tummy.' Tommy wanted to tell us his news. 'The squirrel raced around the kitchen and Auntie chased it with a broom, which just made it worse, and…' he lowered his voice in dramatic fashion, '…it wasn't the squirrel what broke the eggs, it was Auntie! She knocked the basket off the table when she took a swing at it.' He nodded.

Swift came up, pausing to slip Angus from his shoulders. The boy ran to take Tommy's hand and they went towards the kitchen, no doubt with food in mind.

'Lennox, we could modify the evidence chart,' Swift said hopefully.

'No, we couldn't, the girls are in charge of that.'

'We could show you what we've added to it today,' Persi offered.

'It's drinks time,' I said firmly.

Swift gave up and sat down. Greggs had been hovering, but came to pour a glass of wine for him, and then another for Florence as she arrived to take the chair next to me.

'Greggs said most of the villagers think it's Dolores Palgrave.' Florence glanced at him. He turned pink and decided to go off for another plate of snacks.

'Really? Why do they think it's her?' I asked.

'She went into the general store a couple of days ago and they didn't have the brand of cigarettes she wanted. She made a dreadful scene and was very rude,' Florence explained.

Swift had been watching his wife over the brim of his wine glass. 'Well, that solves it for me,' he joked.

She smiled at him.

'Greggs was teaching Lady Clementine the tango.' I told the tale to the girls.

Florence laughed in delight. 'Oh, I've always wanted to learn.'

'I tried it once, but I was quite hopeless,' Persi said.

'We can ask Greggs to show us the steps.' Florence looked hopeful.

'No, I'll teach you,' Swift said.

We all stared at him.

'Where did you learn the tango?' I asked in surprise.

'Argentina,' he replied offhandedly

'What were you doing in Argentina?' Florence's brows rose. 'You never mentioned you'd been there?'

'It was hush-hush,' he replied, straight-faced. 'After the war, and before I met you.'

That started an entirely different conversation which lasted through dinner. After dessert and a couple of bottles of wine, we badgered Greggs to bring the gramophone from his rooms, along with a phonograph record, and we made Swift show us the moves. Greggs offered helpful hints. It was utterly ridiculous and tremendous fun. We danced on the lawn until late with pulsating music thrumming in our ears and a great deal of laughter.

Next morning started without a squirrel but with a rather insistent schoolboy. I was bleary-eyed, mildly hungover and had been looking forward to a solitary breakfast in peace.

'Sir, can I go to the police station this morning and talk to that bloke incriminated there, sir? Can I?' Tommy was up early and clutching a paper and pencil.

'No.'

'But, sir, I'm on the school paper and I'm going to write a report on what it's like to be in prison.'

I'd barely sat down and hadn't even had time to take a sip of tea. 'No, and it's incarcerated, not incriminated.'

'But Mrs Summerour said I could write what I like. She's just started teaching at school and the newspaper was my idea and she thinks it's terrific.' Tommy wasn't giving up.

'I doubt she had interviewing criminals in mind.' I tried another sip of tea and wondered how long breakfast would be.

'Well, actually, she thought we would speak to the old folk about local history an' all that, but I thought I'd do something more interestin'.' He was fidgeting as he spoke, his tie askew as usual, school blazer too big for him, shorts a tad too long; he was still quite small for his age.

'You can speak to PC Fossett and ask him what it's like

to be a policeman, and,' I eyed him sternly, 'you are not to speak to anyone from Ashton Hall.'

His face fell. 'Oh, sir, I never spoke to a murderer before, and it'll be like his last talk before he gets hanged.'

'All the more reason to leave him alone,' I said. 'Now go and find out where Mr Greggs is, and my breakfast.'

He trailed out as Persi came in. She looked particularly beautiful in a peach-coloured dress and her hair caught in a loose bun. I told her about Tommy's latest ploy to garner information to spread about the neighbourhood.

She laughed delightedly. 'I was talking to Nell Summerour yesterday, she's from Oxford. She has some very clever ideas about education. I think a school paper's a marvellous idea.'

'Hmm...' My mind was elsewhere, actually it was mostly on breakfast.

Swift arrived, smartly turned out and itching to start the day. 'We need to question him again,' he said after he'd greeted us.

'Marriott?' I asked as Greggs arrived with a plate of bacon, eggs, mushrooms and fried bread to place before me. He fussed around with napkins and then headed back to the kitchen for more plates of deliciousness for the latest arrivals.

'Of course Marriott, who else?' Swift replied tersely.

'Do you think the killer might drop their guard while Marriott is in prison?' Persi poured tea for Swift and herself from the china teapot.

'It's possible,' Swift replied and picked up his cup. 'Although none of it adds up.'

'The best place for the scoundrel is behind bars anyway,' I said between bites of egg and fried bread. 'And you said you wanted to talk to Dolores Palgrave,' I reminded him.

'Yes, there's more to her demands for a divorce than Alfred Palgrave has told us.' Swift glanced at me. 'We'll let Marriott stew while we rattle a few cages.'

I grinned but decided I might have a round of toast and marmalade first.

Ackroyd opened the door to Ashton Hall a half hour later. He was in peevish mood. 'I cannot be delayed, sirs. Cook has announced that she is "on strike" for the foreseeable future.'

'We want to talk to Mrs Palgrave,' Swift announced.

'In that case, I will send the maid to accompany you—'

'No need, I know where she is, she has the bedroom overlooking the front door,' Swift cut in, then aimed for the stairs without waiting for Ackroyd to finish. I was about to ask Swift how he knew where Dolores Palgrave's room was, then recalled the floor plan Persi and Florence had drawn on their 'evidence board'.

We knocked, then knocked again more loudly. We were trying the doorknob by the time Dolly, the maid, arrived.

'It's locked.' Swift stated the obvious.

'Perhaps she took a sleeping draught, sir,' Dolly suggested. 'She has them in her room. I noticed a box when I was tidying up.'

Swift bent to peer through the keyhole. 'She hasn't left the key in the lock, is there a spare key?'

'Mr Ackroyd would have one, sirs.' Dolly looked up,

her plain face serious under a white cap. She wore a black and white uniform and was rather a nondescript lady of middling years, albeit with a kindly expression. 'Or Mr Palgrave might, but they're not really on speaking terms.'

I raised a brow in query.

'More on shouting terms, if you know what I mean,' Dolly said, 'or she was, he just had to listen. I felt sorry for him, poor man.' She spoke with a London accent.

Swift rattled the doorknob once more, then went to the nearest bell pull and gave it a few sharp tugs.

'Swift, I think she would have heard us,' I said.

'I know,' he agreed and tried the door once more, then gave it a shove with his shoulder to test its strength. 'We'd need a sledgehammer to open this.'

'Mr Ackroyd should come in a moment,' Dolly said, a frown of worry creasing her forehead.

'What's going on?' Alfred Palgrave wandered along the corridor, hands in his tartan dressing gown pockets, slippers on bare feet.

'Do you have a key?' Swift demanded.

'Don't be ridiculous, old boy, she's hardly going to give one to me,' he replied glumly. 'Why are you so keen to see her, anyway? She'll only give you a lambasting at this time of the morning.'

I ignored him. 'Where the hell is Ackroyd,' I muttered. I had my favourite detecting kit in my pocket, but was wary of showing them off in public.

'Lockpicks, Lennox.' Swift took a step back.

'Swift…' I began an objection.

'There's a smell,' he said sotto voce, and frowned at me meaningfully.

'Right.' I extracted the lockpicks from my jacket.

Alfred Palgrave and the maid watched as I probed with the hooked shafts through the keyhole.

'Don't you think this is a bit dramatic,' Palgrave said. 'She'll have taken a powder...'

'Shh,' I hushed him. It took a moment more before I heard the soft clicks of brass latches disengaging. 'There.' I twisted the knob and pushed the door ajar.

'Garlic!' Swift shouted and yanked the door closed again.

'What the devil...?' I demanded.

'Open that window,' he ordered the maid, pointing to the sash window at the end of the passage.

She looked confused.

'Quickly!' Swift shouted and she ran over and pulled the bottom section of the sash up.

'What is it? Has something happened to her?' Alfred Palgrave suddenly panicked. 'Dolores.' He threw himself at the door.

'No,' Swift warned, holding his arm out, trying to hold him back. 'It's deadly...'

Too late, Palgrave had shoved past him and was already inside. Swift raced straight across the room to the window to throw it open, then pulled out his handkerchief and held it over his nose. 'Out, come on.' He grabbed Palgrave by the shoulder. I went in and helped manhandle him through the door.

'Dolores, Dolores,' Palgrave cried, reaching toward the figure lying prone in front of the fireplace. 'Oh dear God… Dolores.'

# CHAPTER 20

We shoved Palgrave into a chair next to the open window, where he collapsed into a state of shock and misery.

The damned popinjay, Sebastian Cardhew, stalked up just as Dolly ran downstairs in search of Ackroyd.

'What's all this blasted noise?' He was wearing a hairnet and had pulled a velvet dressing gown over silk pyjamas. 'Why are you here? I'm sick of you interfering, you're causing nothing but trouble—' He stopped abruptly as he caught sight of Palgrave.

'Why…what?' Cardhew stuttered.

'Dolores is dead,' I told him. 'Go and telephone Dr Fletcher, and ask for the ambulance as well.'

Cardhew stood with his mouth gaping open. 'But she can't be…'

'Move,' I shouted at parade-ground level, which put the wind up him.

He turned and scuttled off, his dressing gown flapping open as he went.

'Stay where you are,' Swift ordered Arthur Palgrave, who

hadn't moved an inch. 'I'll check the body…your wife, I mean,' he corrected himself then marched back into the room, hankie over his nose.

I followed, handkerchief at the ready.

'Arsenic,' he said, his voice muffled. 'The garlic smell is arsine gas.'

He went to kneel beside the body and felt for a pulse on her wrist. It seemed rather pointless; it was quite obvious she was dead.

'She must have lain there all night,' I remarked. Her lilac satin evening dress was badly creased, her stockinged legs tucked up as though she'd toppled sideways, her jet-black hair fallen over her face.

He nodded agreement and let go her wrist. 'It must have been in the paper.'

That didn't make sense. 'What?'

Swift indicated the fireplace. 'The paper must have contained arsenic.'

I stepped across the body to take a look. There was a ball of carbonised newspaper in the grate. I could just make out a pink edge where the flames had failed to catch. A slim gold cigarette lighter was lying on the marble-tiled hearth.

'Don't get too close,' Swift warned. 'We should let the air clear in here. We'll move her to the incident room.'

This seemed rather ambitious given that we were both effectively one-handed. I took a breath then put my hands under her shoulders. 'Get her legs.'

'Right.' He took her ankles. 'Come on.'

We lifted her. I could feel her skin clammily cold through the fabric of her dress; her limbs were stiff making her awkward to manoeuvre.

'Oh, good Lord, not another one!' Ackroyd arrived, key in hand and came to a horrified halt as we exited the bedroom.

'Aghhhh,' Palgrave let out an anguished wail when he spotted us with the body.

'Oh, I cannot endure this, I simply cannot,' Ackroyd wailed.

'Pull yourself together and shut the damn door,' Swift snapped. 'Lock it, and then take Mr Palgrave to his room and make sure he stays there.'

That galvanised Ackroyd and he tugged the door closed before staggering back. He closed his eyes for an instant, straightened his shoulders, then went to where Palgrave had collapsed back onto the chair.

'Go,' I hissed to Swift and we hauled Dolores in undig-nified fashion along to the late Devlin Saunders' room and put her unceremoniously on the bed.

Sebastian Cardhew dashed in, still wearing the ridicu-lous hairnet. 'I've telephoned the doctor, and the ambu-lance.' He sounded breathless. 'They're on their way.' He came to where we were standing over the body. 'She is dead, then?'

'Yes,' Swift said.

He shook his head. 'She was always so alive. I can't believe she's gone…just snuffed out like that.' He sighed. 'She was a monumental pain in the neck, but so vibrant and domineering. I'm astonished anyone had the nerve to tackle her. How did they do it?'

'That's what we need to determine.' Swift was giving nothing away. 'You must leave, go to your room and stay there until you're called.'

I expected him to argue, but the stuffing seemed to have been knocked out of him and he just nodded mutely and tramped off.

We waited as he shut the door behind him before Swift began a cursory examination. He pushed strands of black hair away from Dolores' face. All the allure she'd held in life was gone, her lips drawn back as though in a horrified gasp, lipstick smeared in a red line from the corner of her mouth almost to her ear. Her eyes were staring with pupils dilated, and her skin had turned an awful yellow colour as though she'd been doused in nicotine.

'Was it quick?' I asked, hoping she hadn't suffered.

'Almost instant.' Swift's voice was low, an element of sadness in it.

'I can still smell garlic.' It was quite strong and quite distinct.

'It's the effect of arsine gas, I think someone had sprinkled powder containing arsenic onto the paper, when she set it alight the powder would have converted to gas.'

'The paper was pink, it may be the missing pages from the *Financial Times*.'

'It's plausible.' He picked her hand up, his movements gentle and unhurried. 'Her cigarette lighter was lying on the hearth, she would have been very close to the fire when she lit it.'

I knew Swift's police training had familiarised him with poisons of all types. 'Does arsenic burn easily?'

'It does, and it's explosive. Setting it alight would have resulted in a small blast.' He turned Dolores' hand over and pulled back the stiff fingers curled over her palm. Smudges of black ink and grey dust were smeared over the flesh.

'If she hadn't burned the paper, would the residue have poisoned her?' I asked turning the possibilities over in my mind.

'You mean if she'd simply torn the paper up? Probably not, assuming she washed her hands immediately afterwards.' He straightened up. 'Damn it, Lennox, this is the third murder in less than a week and we're no closer to the killer.'

There wasn't much I could say to that.

'Sir, I just heard...' Fossett came running in, his face pink with exertion. 'Oh, so it's Mrs Palgrave. Flossie didn't know who it was.'

'You mean the operator told you?' Swift frowned.

'Yes, Flossie Craddock. She heard there was another death. She was worried it might be Lady Clementine, so I said I'd come and find out.' He came to stare at Dolores, then took off his helmet as though in respect. 'I'm glad it's not, but it's a rotten shame for the poor lady anyway. What happened to her?'

Swift began a lengthy explanation, pointing out the effects of the poison on the body.

I decided I was in need of some fresh air and some quiet deliberation, so I left them to it and went to sit on the balcony in Saunders' wicker chair in the warm sunshine.

Who had done it? It must have happened when Dolores returned from dinner – she was in an evening gown and hadn't removed her make-up. Perhaps the paper had been slipped under her door after she'd gone down to the dining room? It couldn't have been Marcus Marriott – could it be Gabriel? And where had the killer got the arsenic from? Actually, that was easy, every garden shed had a box of rat poison on a shelf.

Who was left alive? I counted them off: Lady Clementine, Sebastian Cardhew, Gabriel Marriott, Margaret Saunders, Alfred Palgrave. They were all directly connected to the Royal Buckingham Financial Services. So was Sir Edwin Tremayne, and he was a dark horse…not that he was in the house when Devlin Saunders was killed, or Cedric Smedley, but he could be in cahoots with one of them. And then there was the staff, we didn't actually know much about any of them.

At least Dolores' death proved that the killer was someone inside the house – assuming the papers were actually pushed under her door…

'What-ho, the great detectives!' Cyril Fletcher's voice rang from the bedroom. 'Another one bitten the dust, eh? Ah, shame to kill a lady, what in heaven's name is the world coming to.'

I thought I'd better go and join in.

'Arsenic,' I told Fletcher, by way of greeting. 'Had any experience of it, Cyril?'

'No, but I took myself off to London in my early days to watch a post mortem performed on a victim. It was all the rage in Victorian times you know, bumping off extraneous relatives with rat poison. Didn't slow down until some clever blighter found a way of detecting it in the body. Jolly good thing they did or none of us would be safe.'

'We think she inhaled arsine gas.' Swift was in full police mode. 'Created from arsenic powder.' He went on to explain his theory about Dolores burning the paper.

Dr Cyril Fletcher's mood grew grim as he listened to the details. He bent over the body, pulling back her lips to expose the pale gums and tongue. Then he and Swift scraped powder residue from her fingers into a small brown envelope.

'I'll take it to Oxford for testing, but the smell of garlic, and yellowed skin, gives the game away.' Cyril sighed.

Fossett had been standing at the end of the bed, taking it all in. 'There's rat poison in the shed, sir, and I saw an old bottle of Fowler's solution in the larder and we all know that has arsenic in it.'

'Yes, but not in large enough quantities,' I said, because even I'd read about the stuff.

'Would you fetch the box of rat poison from the shed?' Swift asked him. 'We can dust it for prints.'

'Aye, sir, and I'll be sure to wear my gloves.' Fossett rushed off, full of enthusiasm.

Ackroyd came in almost on Fossett's heels. 'The ambulance has arrived, sir, they are on their way upstairs.' He sounded shaken but in full control. 'Mr Palgrave is resting with a brandy, and Lady Clementine has offered to remain with him. Dolly is making tea, and I have informed the rest of the household of the tragic event, sir.' He paused to draw breath and raised his hand to his forehead. 'I fear that none will leave this cursed house alive, but regardless of the consequences, I will do my duty perforce,' he added in a dramatic tone worthy of my own butler.

Fletcher gave him a beaming grin. 'That's the spirit, old chap! See it through to the bitter end, eh. But I'm sure you're quite safe, it's only the money grubbers being bumped off.'

Ackroyd sniffed. 'If you say so, sir.'

A knock sounded on the door. Ackroyd went to open it to reveal the same two ambulance men who'd carted off Smedley.

'Got another 'un then?' Jim said on arrival. 'That's the third now.'

'Never been so busy,' his companion remarked as he proceeded to lay the rolled-up stretcher on the floor in preparation.

'A lady this time, is it? Don't seem right.' Jim shook his head as he gazed down at the mortal remains of Dolores Palgrave on the bed.

'Actually, you chaps can help me give her a more thorough examination while she's still relatively fresh,' Cyril Fletcher decided. He glanced at me. 'You'd probably rather not stay, Lennox.'

'Right,' I readily agreed.

'Do you need me?' Swift asked.

'Don't believe so.' Fletcher pulled off his jacket. 'Unless you'd like to officiate?'

'I need to track down the perpetrator,' he replied.

'May I be excused, sirs?' Ackroyd had blanched at the obvious preparations.

'Yes, yes, off you go.' Fletcher waved him away.

'Wait, give me the key to Mrs Palgrave's room.' I held my hand out to Ackroyd. He gave the bed a wide detour, dropped the key in my hand then scarpered.

'Right, come on, Lennox,' Swift said and strode towards the door.

The passageway was empty, actually the whole house was silent, as though holding its breath. Either that or the inhabitants had barricaded themselves behind their doors for fear it might be them next.

The window in the late Dolores Palgrave's bedroom was still wide open. Swift took a sniff.

'The smell has gone, it's safe,' he decided and went directly to the fireplace and picked up the cigarette lighter with his handkerchief. 'It's the same one she had yesterday.'

'Obviously,' I said because it was hardly likely to be anyone else's.

He slipped it into his pocket, then turned to observe the carbonised ball of paper in the grate.

'There's a note attached, look.' I pointed to a paler grey square that was just visible under the blackened mass.

Swift probed it with the end of a pencil, trying to shift the wad, but it merely crumbled into small flakes. 'I'll try and break off the unburned edge.' He spoke slowly as he carefully prised away the corner of pink paper that had survived the fire. 'There's a date!' He sounded excited.

I pulled out my magnifying glass. 'Lay it on the lens.'

'Good idea.' We were almost whispering, which was ridiculous. He slid the unburned fragment onto the magnifying glass as I held it flat.

'Well done,' I said as I carefully manoeuvred it away from the fire and stood up. 'Saturday May 5th,' I read. 'It's the date Saunders was killed.'

'Excellent!' Swift was thrilled. 'Real evidence at last.'

He pulled a white envelope from his inside pocket. I slid the fragment into the envelope and he closed it to tuck back into his inside jacket pocket.

I returned to the carbonised mass in the fireplace. 'I'm going to turn it over, Swift,' I said and then flipped the blackened ball over before he could stop me. Whole sections broke off into tiny fragments, but the pale card remained intact. I leaned in, magnifying glass to the fore and read the words still visible in black ink against the card they'd been written on. *'Your greed has found you out, and here's the proof.'* I read aloud. *'Sleep well, Jezebel, for tomorrow brings the noose.'* I sat back on my haunches. 'It doesn't scan terribly well.'

'It was obviously enough to enrage her though.' Swift was trying to extract his notebook. 'Don't disturb it, I need to write this down.'

'Ready?' I was poised with the magnifying glass.

He nodded, so I reread it to him.

'Perhaps if it was "Sleep well, you Jezebel", it would work better.'

'Lennox, it doesn't matter.' He was unnecessarily tetchy. 'What is the style of writing?'

'I've no idea, the only poetry I know is Shakespeare and that's because they made me read it at school.'

'I meant the shape of the letters. Are they angular, slanting, looped?'

'Here, have a look yourself.' I gave him the magnifying glass and stood up to move away.

While he wrote yet more notes, I had a wander about the room. It was rather small; a standard bed, wash stand, dresser, wardrobe and whatnots, with wallpaper in shades of pink. I wasn't inclined to delve into the drawers so went to gaze out of the window.

Her room overlooked the front of the house. I could see quite an assemblage had built up at the gate, word must have got out that another murder had occurred. Somehow, I suspected this didn't reflect well on Swift and me. The ambulance was parked almost below the window and I watched as the two medics came shuffling out of the house toward it. They'd covered Dolores with a blanket and carried her on the stretcher held between them. There was something solemn and awful about it, with a touch of macabre fascination.

Cyril Fletcher emerged to join them, calling out instructions and making a show of directing things – no doubt to impress the gate crowd. He finally banged the back of the ambulance, setting it off to beetle up the drive, then went and hopped in his car to follow. He waved at the onlookers as he exited the grounds but didn't stop long enough to answer questions.

'Have you looked through any of her clothes?' Swift rose from the hearth, brushing dust from his trousers.

'No, but they've finished with the body.'

'We need to carry out a thorough search.' He was in full detecting mode.

'I'll send Fossett along,' I volunteered and headed for the door.

'Lennox...wait...' he called. He was too late, I was already striding down the corridor.

# CHAPTER 21

'Fossett, Swift wants you at the scene of the crime,' I told him. He was still in the 'incident room' which was now free of dead bodies and medical men.

A grin spread across his face. 'Oh, sir, that's three now! And I never thought I'd ever see a single one.'

'Right.' I didn't share his enthusiasm. 'Did Marriott's wife stay long with him at the station last evening?'

'She did, sir. Until nearly ten o'clock. She'd brought him a dish of cottage pie from the kitchen, and they shared it. Then I told her I had to lock up and she ought to go home. She took a bit of persuading and even though I'm a proper constable, I can't go around arresting folk just because they won't do as they're told. Anyway, she went, and then she came back early this morning and she was still there when I left.'

'She's not likely to help him escape, is she?'

He shook his head. 'Not while I've got the key in my satchel, sir!' He tapped his battered leather bag. 'Oh, and Dr Fletcher told me to say he had a good look at Mrs

Palgrave, but he didn't find anything new. I stayed by the door, it didn't seem decent to watch.' He sketched a salute. 'Best be getting off, sir, Inspector Swift will be waiting for me. I left the box of rat poison on the writing table. There wasn't any prints on it.' He picked up his helmet from the dressing table, fixed it on his head and went out.

I had it in mind to fire a few questions at the grieving widower. The more murders that occurred in this benighted house, the more perfectly Alfred Palgrave fit the bill.

'I suppose you've come to interrogate me.' He looked up with red-rimmed eyes as I entered his bedroom. I hadn't bothered to knock.

'Something like that.' I drew up a chair to face him. He was sitting by the unlit fire. His room was smaller than the others I'd been in; decorated in dove grey, it held a narrow brass bed, a few bits of plain furniture and very little else. I felt in my jacket for my hip flask and offered it to him.

He downed the contents in a few gulps. 'Thank you.' He passed the flask back; I slipped it into my pocket.

'Was Dolores having an affair with Devlin Saunders?' I thought I might as well get the worst over with.

He dropped his gaze. 'Possibly.'

'Was he planning to leave Margaret?' The train ticket in his name indicated that.

'Hah,' he said in derision. 'He was never really *with* Margaret, she was a convenient hostess, that's all. Dolores was a real woman; *'flesh, blood and red-hot passion'* I used to say. God, I can't believe she's dead, or Devlin – they've dominated my life for years…And Cedric gone too.' He raked fingers through his thick hair. 'Do you think they're all in Hell sharing a cauldron? Being prodded by devils with pitchforks…Serves them right if they are,' he muttered half to himself.

'Dolores wanted you to bid for Saunders' shares and give them to her as part of the divorce settlement,' I said. 'How could she make that demand? You're not obliged to divorce her, and she certainly can't force you.'

Divorce law was complex and tortuous, as everyone was quite aware.

He looked away, towards the blue sky where swallows soared in sun swept freedom. 'She was blackmailing me over Gabriel, we were sweethearts before the war. Her father was Admiral Paisley, they had a place not far from us…' His voice softened. 'She was always rather intense; it takes a lot to coax a giggle from her, but once you break through the ice she's really quite adorable. We kept it secret, I was only nineteen you see, and she was younger. Anyway, it was no more than a dalliance, not serious or anything. Then a couple of years ago, Marcus announced he was to marry and brought his bride-to-be into the office to introduce her. I was astounded. I think she was too, but she played it straight-faced, and I did as best I could. I told Dolores about it when I got home and she thought it terribly amusing. Then she threatened to tell Marcus if I didn't do as she said.' He threw an anxious glance at me. 'He'd kill me, truly he would. You have to understand him, he grew up in an orphanage and it scarred him for life. Dolores explained it to me, she said deep down he's terrified; terrified of being lost and alone, of falling back into the black void. She's quite astute, actually. Was, I mean,' he said and looked away again. 'She said Gabriel provides his stability, his rock in a maelstrom of insecurity, and he'd do anything to keep her.' His knuckles showed white where he'd gripped his hands together. 'I don't want to cross him. He's a cold-blooded killer.'

'Have you ever seen him harm anyone?' I asked.

'He hit someone once. They'd made some stupid remark about Gabriel's dress behind her back and he felled the man with a single blow.' He fell silent for a moment. 'I suppose you know his war record?'

'I've heard he was decorated,' I replied.

He nodded. 'More iron on his chest than a battlefield forge,' he quoted. 'Utterly unflinching and brutally effective. I think he was on a suicide mission. He didn't care if he lived or died, but now he has Gabriel to love, and a life, and the security of wealth. He's not going to allow anyone to jeopardise that.'

I thought he was exaggerating his fears. Dolores may have fuelled them, but I couldn't see why he'd been so cowed by her threats. 'Surely Gabriel would explain to Marcus that your romance was just a youthful dalliance and she no longer cares for you.'

'You don't understand – he thought he was the first, and he wasn't. As soon as Gabriel and I were able to talk privately, she pleaded with me not to mention a word to Marcus. She said it would devastate him and might destroy their marriage. Naturally I agreed, but I'd already told Dolores by then.' His face fell into misery again, tears rimming his brown eyes.

I waited a moment, letting him pull himself together. I wondered if he were hiding something, but he seemed genuine. I switched tack. 'When did you last see Dolores alive?'

He dashed a hand over his cheek. 'Last night at dinner. We ate together. Marcus wasn't there of course, he was tucked up in clink. Gabriel had taken some food to him. Dolores was frosty and nobody spoke, apart from Sir Edwin and Lady Clementine. They were laughing and chatting as though nothing was amiss.' His voice caught, but he sniffed and carried on. 'Sebastian and Margaret sat at either end of the table and just glowered at each other. I think her dreams have gone up in smoke too...' His voice trailed off.

'She hoped Sebastian would...' I wasn't sure how to phrase this. 'Form a liaison?'

'You mean she thought Sebastian would step into Devlin's shoes?' He gave a harsh laugh. 'Not a chance. He just led her along, he was only ever interested in the money. He's not much of a ladies' man, actually.'

'Smedley forwarded you the loan.' I returned to the crux. 'Was it secured?'

Blood leached from his face. 'Yes,' he admitted hoarsely. 'Against the family estate. I mentioned my father was taking digitalis. His heart's giving out, he hasn't got long, and then it will come to me.'

I nodded, it was adding up. This was the Royal Buckingham's standard practise. 'Dolores knew, she told Devlin and they hatched a plan to force you to take out a loan you couldn't afford so that they could ultimately foreclose on your property.'

He screwed his eyes closed. 'I should have confronted them. Refused to do it and taken the consequences. I just couldn't. I told you, I'm not brave, I can't help it.'

'Is the estate worth more than the loan?' I asked, remembering that he said his side of the family were virtually penniless.

'If it were broken up and sold, yes,' Palgrave admitted. 'Pa made me swear I wouldn't do it, it's been handed down for aeons. There's over three hundred acres of farmland, and our local village. The rents are at peppercorn level, Pa doesn't agree with impoverishing the tenants.'

Three hundred acres of rich Somerset soil was a princely prize. No wonder Saunders was keen to grab it.

'You've benefited from every death,' I stated, watching him quietly. 'And you have every reason to kill each of them.'

'I would never kill Dolores, however awful she was to me.' He was vehement in reply, then asked, 'How did she die?'

'That's a matter for the post mortem,' I prevaricated. 'But her death was painless.' I'd no idea if that were true, but I could hardly tell him otherwise.

His lips trembled. 'She loved life, she wanted to experience it all, have it all. She was exciting, vibrant, desirable... God, what a waste.'

'Do you think she could have killed Saunders and Smedley?' I took pity and tried to find a way out for him, plus there was that poem she'd burned.

'No, why on earth would she? She had nothing to gain by their deaths. It wouldn't make sense.' He rose to his wife's defence, despite all the anguish she'd caused. 'You can't truly believe she did, why would you even think it?'

I sighed and switched tack. 'Does she have any family?'

'Yes, in London, a sister and mother. Dreadful people, fighting all the time, always with their hands out for money. She rarely visited...I suppose I had better call them.' That seemed to make him even more miserable

'By the way, do you take the *Financial Times*?'

'Good Lord, no. I'm a complete duffer at numbers, always have been.'

That was pretty obvious. 'Stay here, would you, there's a good chap.' I rose to my feet, gave him a nod of commiseration and strode out.

I felt for the man; he was weak, and not very bright, but he hadn't done anything to deserve the misery his wife had inflicted on him. He hadn't told me the entire truth either, I was certain there was more behind the blackmail than he was admitting to. I sighed. As things were, everything pointed to him and he'd be heading for the gallows when it all came out. I decided I'd do a little more enquiring before finding Swift and laying Palgrave's story bare.

'Sir!' Dolly jumped to her feet as I walked into the kitchen, suffused with the smell of baking bread, biscuits and other deliciousness of the like.

'Greetings,' I said and went to the pine table and sat down.

'Oy, folk ain't supposed to walk in without so much as a by your leave. We've got rights we 'ave.' A large lady dressed in traditional cook's uniform accosted me from a chair by the stove. She was as rotund as most of her ilk, complete with rosy cheeks and an air of irritation. I was never sure why cooks seemed to be ever thus, but it was a trait I'd frequently observed.

'Actually I rather hoped for a cup of tea.' I gave her my best grin.

It didn't work. 'Don't you think a handsome face will get past me!' She crossed her arms over a generous bosom. 'I'm on strike and I ain't making tea nor doin' nothin'. We've been locked up in this house and treated like criminals, and there's someone runnin' about killin' folk.' She wagged a plump finger at me. 'Not that they don't deserve it, but ye don't know who's goin' to be next.' She raised her voice. 'And no-one's never said nothin' to us about it, nor how long we're going to be stuck 'ere.'

'Well, we've been trying to track the blighter down,' I began in mollifying tone. 'But nobody's telling the truth. It would really help if we had some reliable information to go on.'

She huffed, but uncrossed her arms. 'Just 'cos we're below stairs don't mean we don't know nothin'.'

'I imagine you see and hear more than most.' I laid it on more thickly. 'And you alerted the house to Mr Saunders' demise.'

'That I did.' She nodded sharply. 'Mr Bent came and knocked on the door. I knew it were important the minute I heard what he said. I told Mr Ackroyd he'd best go and take a look. Mr Ackroyd might have some strange ways about him, and he don't know his way around a kitchen neither, but he does things right, and there's nothing wrong with that.'

'And what happened after Mr Saunders' body was discovered?' I encouraged her.

'Well...' She looked at Dolly, who had gone to stand near the door for some reason. 'I think we might have a cup o' tea after all, and there's biscuits in the jar for them as wants them.'

'I'll put the kettle on, shall I Mrs Wiggins?' Dolly volunteered.

'Aye, you do that, dearie.' Mrs Wiggins nodded, then turned to me, her beady blue eyes gleaming. 'It was a shock, y'know. Blood drippin' down off that balcony, and him lyin' there with an arrow stickin' out of his heart. Never seen anythin' like it in me life. That started the palaver, and it's not stopped since. The other bloke went next.'

'You mean Cedric Smedley?' I asked for accuracy's sake.

'Aye, the old bloke. Always fussin' about what he could eat and what he couldn't. Had to have everythin' just so, not over cooked, not too much meat, and then he'd be askin' for seconds, 'specially pudding.' She paused for breath as the kettle began whistling. 'Dolly, never mind the biscuits, there's them doughnuts in the back of the larder that I made yesterday. Fetch them, will you.'

That made me sit up, doughnuts were a particular treat. 'We think Mr Smedley may have inadvertently taken too much of his medication,' I volunteered.

'Hah!' She rolled her eyes. 'If you think that, you're not much of a detective. He was too pernickety to have made a mistake with his medicines, you mark my words.'

Dolly had been pouring water from the kettle into a large blue teapot. 'It's true, sir. Every time he saw me, he reminded me that he had to have his jug of water kept full, because drinking water helped thin his blood. And he needed it for his medicine too.'

'Did you notice if he counted his sachets of powder?' I asked as Dolly placed a cup of tea and milk jug in front of me.

'Not that I know of,' Dolly replied, her plain face serious. 'But when they came last time he got himself in a spin about it. He'd knocked over the box of sachets and wanted to know how many he'd taken. There was more screwed up papers than proper ones, and he counted every one of them.'

'That's how he was killed, wasn't it?' Mrs Wiggins said. 'I heard that young copper saying so.'

I took a sip of tea. Dolly went to the larder and came back with a plate of crisp brown doughnuts liberally sprinkled with sugar and oozing with jam.

'Where was the constable when you heard him say that?' I asked.

Mrs Wiggins' eyes slid away. She sniffed. 'Well, he was upstairs in Mr Saunders' room if you must know. If that balcony door's open, I can sometimes hear what's being said through the little window there.' She nodded towards a window set high in the wall; it was a typical kitchen vent, opened and closed by a long brass arm connected to a handle.

'Did you hear anything the morning Mr Saunders was killed?'

'Voices arguin', different ones at different times,' Mrs Wiggins admitted. 'Then something like a thud, just before nine. I was too busy fillin' the breakfast tureens to think of it. But I reckon that's when he was done in.'

'You should have told him earlier,' Dolly chided her gently.

'Aye, well, the young copper asked us, but he's still wet about the ears. I should have been talked to properly, by someone with class, like you, sir. Then, I might have said summat,' she retorted. 'But you know now, so that's as good as you've got from me.'

I sipped my tea, musing for a moment. If that was the time Saunders' body was dragged to the side of the balcony, it made sense. 'Did you hear it too, Dolly?' I asked the maid.

'I didn't sir, even though I was here at the time. I was putting out plates and glasses onto trays to take upstairs. I couldn't hear much because the plates were clattering together as I piled them up,' she replied – which gave her and Cook an alibi too.

'Have you worked for Mr and Mrs Saunders for very long?' I bit into a doughnut, it was delicious. Dolly hastily handed me a napkin as the jam began to squeeze out.

'Not neither of us,' Mrs Wiggins replied. 'We've worked together for years, haven't we, Dolly. Ever since I lost Mr Wiggins.' She looked to the maid, who nodded solemnly. 'I saw an ad in the local paper, and the pay was good, so we went to see Mrs Saunders, and we agreed to take the positions. It didn't take long to find out why no-one stayed with them – they're not gentry, they're a bunch o' thieves is what they are. We only stayed 'cause Lady Clementine asked us to, but we'll be gone as soon as we're allowed out of here.'

None of that surprised me, Ackroyd had already said much the same. I finished another doughnut and wiped sugar from my hands with the linen napkin. 'Did you speak to Mrs Palgrave last evening, or see anyone speaking to her just before she went to bed?'

'We washed up after dinner, then listened to the wireless, didn't we?' Dolly turned towards the cook, her plain face breaking into a smile. 'I love the wireless, it's almost as good as the moving pictures.'

'Aye, and it's a bit of time to ourselves,' Mrs Wiggins added. 'Mr Ackroyd even came down to listen, but that was just because he wanted to get away from all them upstairs.'

I finished my tea and stood up. 'Thank you, ladies. You've been very helpful. And thank you for the excellent doughnuts.' I offered another grin, and left.

# CHAPTER 22

Swift was back in the 'incident room'.

'Find anything?' I asked.

He was writing notes in neat lines. 'She had a ticket to Monte Carlo on the Train Bleu, leaving tomorrow morning.'

'Which confirms she intended going with Devlin Saunders.'

'Yes, although she's now on a one-way trip to join him in the morgue.' He spoke dryly, barely having glanced up from his notebook.

I sat down in the nearest chair and told him what Palgrave had told me about his youthful affair with Gabriel, and how he was terrified Marcus Marriott would kill him for it.

Swift put his pencil down. 'It sounds completely over-exaggerated. Everything I've heard makes him more and more guilty. I think he's just trying to divert attention away from himself.'

'Actually, it's even more damning,' I continued. 'Dolores

blackmailed Palgrave into taking out a loan he couldn't possibly repay. Cedric Smedley made sure the loan was sufficient to win the bidding for Devlin Saunders' shares. Once Palgrave won, he had to hand the shares over to Dolores as part of the divorce settlement.' I tried to summarise it, although it was making my head spin. 'I think the plan was for her to give the shares back to Saunders and the whole "retirement auction" was nothing but a ploy to grab Palgrave's estate when he inherited it.'

He looked bemused. 'You've learned a lot about finance all of a sudden.'

'I've had to.' Actually, I'd been discussing the vagaries of how money worked with Persi. It wasn't the most exciting of pillow talk, but it had made things clearer. 'Anyway, what do you think?'

He considered it. 'Saunders has always tried to extract every penny he could from his victims. It's elaborate but not implausible.'

'And I imagine Dolores would have been well rewarded,' I added.

'By becoming Saunders' wife?'

'Possibly...' Something else occurred to me. 'What if she intended keeping the shares?'

'By double crossing Saunders? That would have been dangerous. Perhaps she did kill him after all.' He thought about it, a frown between dark brows. 'Margaret Saunders said Dolores wanted to run the company.'

'And Dolores slapped Marcus Marriott across the face when he taunted her about doing just that,' I said. 'It might explain why she agreed to the share auction rather than simply waiting until Alfred inherited his father's estate.'

'Yes, because she could have simply blackmailed it out of him.' Swift raised a hand to his chin.

'Actually, there's one thing that might support Alfred's innocence,' I said.

'What?' he asked.

'He's far too stupid to have worked out what was going on.'

That made him grin. 'If stupidity was a valid defence the prisons would be empty.'

'True, but there's no actual evidence against him, either,' I reminded him. 'And we can't make another arrest without it.'

'Yes.' He sighed, then mused over the revelations. 'Their plan was utterly ruthless...What if Marriott or Cardhew learned of it?'

That caused me to pause. 'Judging by their reactions, I'd say there was no sign they had,' I decided.

'Let me write this down,' he said then started laborious note taking. I waited until he'd finished before launching into the details of my chat with Mrs Wiggins and Dolly in the kitchen.

'So, they both have alibis. Did you believe them?' He stopped writing to sharpen his pencil.

'I did, and they said Ackroyd joined them last evening.'

'That wouldn't have stopped him slipping papers under Dolores' door.'

'No, nor anyone. We need to speak to Tremayne again, he's an absolute enigma,' I said.

'I've sent for him. He should be here shortly...' He turned to a fresh page in his notebook. 'If the cook was right in hearing a thump from the balcony just before nine, Lady Clementine is out of the picture.'

'I agree, and don't forget that Ackroyd let her out of the front door, so he's off the hook too.'

'Yes, but the maid didn't hear the thump, so the cook may have been lying, or she could have mistaken the time.'

'Swift, will you stop being so damned pedantic,' I objected.

He looked aggrieved. 'I'm just trying to be thorough, Lennox.' He made another note.

'Why are you using a pencil?'

'Because I don't want to carry ink around with me,' he replied. 'Actually, Angus found the bottle in my pocket and splashed it everywhere.'

'Ah,' I muttered, then wondered where he'd splashed it.

A knock sounded at the door.

'Come in,' Swift called.

It was Ackroyd. Tremayne was behind him.

Ackroyd moved aside and announced in nasal tones, 'Sir Edwin Tremayne, sirs.'

The lawyer stalked in. 'I know who I am, thank you.'

'Indeed, sir, but—' Ackroyd began.

'As do they.' Tremayne nodded in our direction.

'I am aware, sir, but—'

'Off you go now.' Tremayne dismissed him.

Ackroyd went, closing the door behind him with a huffy sniff.

'Another death, gentlemen.' Tremayne came to sit oppo-site us. He held the ebony walking stick and rested both hands on it. 'Was it murder?'

'It was,' Swift replied in subdued manner.

'I understand you have arrested Marcus Marriott,' Tremayne continued.

'He's being held at the local station,' Swift confirmed.

Tremayne eyed him. 'Could he have been responsible for Mrs Palgrave's death?'

'Yes,' I said, before Swift could answer. 'If he was work-ing with someone else. His wife, for instance.'

The temperature in the room suddenly seemed to drop a few degrees.

'Gabriel Marriott is the daughter of the late Admiral Paisley,' Tremayne declared. 'He was a particularly close friend. We both advised Gabriel against marrying Marcus Marriott. She chose not to listen.'

'That doesn't mean she isn't involved,' I said quietly.

Tremayne took a breath and let it out slowly. 'She had a cloistered upbringing, she is naive…'

'The last time we spoke, you implied Marcus Marriott could have been behind the murders,' Swift stated, his confidence returning. 'Was it a genuine conviction on your part, or merely bias?'

Tremayne hesitated. 'Something of both, I suppose.'

I turned the subject. 'Dolores was planning to run away with Devlin Saunders, and she was blackmailing Palgrave into borrowing to bid for the shares. Smedley was provid-ing sufficient funds to ensure Palgrave won.'

His eyes flicked to mine. 'And she would have delivered the shares back to Devlin Saunders,' he concluded, proving he understood how they operated. 'Well, a leopard doesn't change its spots; he always wanted what everyone else had. Rather a neat trick, you must admit.'

'It was despicable,' I said.

He glanced at me, then continued, 'What was Dolores blackmailing Alfred over?'

I told him.

'Alfred Palgrave and Gabriel? Good Lord.' He sounded genuinely surprised. 'I was completely unaware of it.'

'That's hardly unexpected in the circumstances,' I remarked dryly.

He frowned. 'I'm gratified to hear you have unravelled their latest trickery. I would be more gratified if you had managed to avoid any further deaths.'

A flush rose in Swift's cheeks. 'We've only just uncovered their "trickery", and it's probably the cause of the murders, considering all three of the schemers are now dead.'

Tremayne glowered at that and I sought to divert him. 'We've learned Devlin Saunders' body was moved just before nine, which clears Lady Clementine of any involvement.'

He looked grateful for that snippet, and his high-handed manner ebbed. 'Good, I will inform her ladyship of the fact.' He hesitated. 'Is there anything I may assist you with?'

'You can wipe off my debt,' I said.

He regarded me gravely. 'I'm afraid that is impossible,

Major Lennox. The company purchased your debt, it cannot be written off...' He saw my brows draw together. 'I can instruct them to decrease the rate of interest payable.'

'To nothing,' I demanded.

'In the event you uncover the murderer, that may be possible,' he agreed.

I nodded, not being able to think of anything else to say.

'I'd like to ask you to delay the auction of Saunders' shares, please.' Swift made the request.

'Why?' Tremayne demanded, although it should have been obvious.

'Because we want to take more statements this afternoon concerning the death of Dolores Palgrave,' Swift replied. 'And I don't want any more distractions.'

Tremayne narrowed his eyes, then nodded. 'Very well, I will rearrange the bidding for tomorrow morning at half past nine precisely. Although I will not permit that it be delayed again. There are rules to which we must abide.'

'Thank you.' Swift made a note.

Tremayne made to rise, leaning on the ebony stick.

'Just a moment, please, Sir Edwin.' I stayed him. 'Can I ask what you know about the death of Lady Clementine's last husband, Reginald.' I was about to add that he was also Margaret's father, but realised he'd have known that.

'Reginald Knox was a bounder and a wastrel.' Tremayne sat back in his chair, his face cold and hard. 'His whole life was a lie. He was never wealthy, he strung along unsuspecting fools and vulnerable women who fell for his vacuous charms.'

'You knew Lady Clementine at the time?' I asked.

'I did. I'd been at school with her first husband, Sir Anthony Latham. His family owned the Royal Buckingham.' He saw our surprise. 'It was utterly respectable at the time. A small private bank handling loans and savings to a select list of wealthy clients. The major element of the family business was dealing in spices, which Anthony had been running the office in Zanzibar when he died. He had been the heir to it all; without him, it rapidly began to fail.'

'Lady Clementine didn't inherit the Royal Buckingham?' Swift interrupted.

'No it was still held by the Latham family, but they were elderly.' Tremayne settled to his story, his hands clasped on the handle of the ebony stick. 'Saunders realised the Royal Buckingham was ripe for plucking and targeted Margaret as a consequence. He had already established himself in the loan business and acquired the majority shareholding by inveigling himself onto the board. Cedric Smedley was brought in, and between them they took over and built it into a major finance company.' He glanced at us from under thick brows. 'They were utterly ruthless. I offered my services to protect Clementine, and to some extent, Margaret.'

'You're close to Lady Clementine,' I stated.

He shot me a piercing regard. 'Why would I not be, she is an estimable lady.'

'Are you married?' Swift asked the question.

'I am.' His face clouded. 'My wife suffered a debilitating accident many years ago. She is cared for by a group of nurses at our home. She can do little for herself.'

That shut us both up for a moment.

'Lady Clementine said her late husband was killed by a man-eating lion. Which she shot.' I attempted to lighten the atmosphere.

It didn't work. Tremayne remained stony-faced.

'And that she'd known me in the court of King Louis quatorze,' Swift added, watching the lawyer closely.

'She has something of an imagination,' he admitted.

'Apparently she first met me when I was a Roman centurion,' I added, recalling my first meeting with her. 'She said she only kept the most exalted company.'

'Would a centurion be considered exalted company?' Tremayne almost smiled.

'Depends which parties we were invited to.' I grinned.

Swift returned to more serious questioning. 'We don't believe Margaret Saunders' father was actually eaten by a lion.'

'No, he died in Kenya, by a single shot to the head.' Tremayne stood up. 'I bid you good day, gentlemen,' he said stiffly and walked out leaving the minor bombshell hanging in the air.

'Well, the lion certainly didn't shoot him,' I remarked.

Swift leaned back in his chair, sunshine streaming in through the windows behind him.

'Let's try to stick to the facts, shall we, and try to join the pieces together.' He tapped the pencil on the table. 'Smedley lent Alfred Palgrave twenty-one thousand pounds, but only eleven thousand to Marcus Marriott.'

'How do you know that?'

'There was a note in Smedley's wallet. It said MM 11 max. I wasn't sure what it meant, I asked Marriott, and he eventually confirmed it.'

'Oh...' I suppose I must have been elsewhere at the time.

'We don't know how much Sebastian Cardhew was borrowing.' Swift continued tapping his pencil; it was becoming annoying.

'We can soon find out.' I went to tug on the bell pull.

Ackroyd arrived almost on the instant. 'You rang, sir?'

'Tell Cardhew to come here, would you?' I asked him.

'Yes, sir.' He sounded as though it were wearisome. He went off, nose in the air.

I gazed at the balcony, thinking how inviting it looked. Swift sharpened his pencil, the tip had broken off.

Cardhew stalked in. 'Now what do you want?'

'How much was Smedley offering to lend you?' I demanded.

'I'm not going to...' he spluttered, then gave up. 'Well, I suppose it's all academic anyway. It was fifteen thousand, if you must know. He said it was more than enough to outbid the others.'

'Did he now,' I remarked.

'Was he charging for his "advice"?' Swift watched Cardhew, the man was flushed and ill at ease.

'A thousand pounds,' Cardhew muttered. 'He said it was "sensitive information" and confidential, but I could absolutely rely on it.'

'He lied,' I said.

Cardhew flashed a look of outrage at me.

'Had he paid the funds into your account?' Swift demanded.

'No, he gave me his word, and said it was good enough. He said we'd settle up once the bidding was over.' He fidgeted in his seat. He'd left the red blazer off and was dressed in a floral waistcoat over a crisp white shirt and another ridiculous cravat about his pudgy neck – this one in sky blue. 'Has anyone else told you how much money they have?'

'No,' Swift lied.

'The auction will be held tomorrow at nine thirty,' I told him.

'Hum.' He huffed. 'Well, now that Lady Clementine holds the shares I suppose we won't have to pay as much, so it's not all a disaster.'

He really was a detestable little weasel. 'Get out,' I snarled.

That made him jump. 'I'm going to report you! There are people dying all over the place and all you've done is lock us up and be nasty to us. I've got friends in high places. I've got influence. I'm not just anybody...'

'Out.' I stood up and glared at him.

He stared and then scuttled out as fast as his feet could take him.

'Lennox,' Swift said.

'What?'

'I think we should go and have lunch.'

# CHAPTER 23

'Egg and watercress sandwiches, today,' Persi announced from the table in the garden.

I walked over to where she was setting plates and dishes onto the tablecloth and caught her by the waist, kissing her neck as she stepped back into my arms. 'Do you know how to make doughnuts?' I murmured.

She laughed. 'Is that your idea of whispering sweet nothings in my ears?'

'Doughnuts aren't sweet nothings, they're good solid fare.'

'It's a jolly good thing you're so tall, or you'd grow fat on all these goodies.'

'Does that mean you won't make any?'

'I can ask Cook,' she promised, her face solemn. 'We can make them together this afternoon when Tommy comes home from school. He and Angus love helping in the kitchen.'

I gave her another kiss then sat down to let her finish laying the table.

'There are rumours of romance in the village,' she said as she placed knives and forks.

'Dr Fletcher and Lady Clementine?' I guessed.

She laughed. 'You're not quite as oblivious as you pretend. Yes, they were seen at the Wheatsheaf together.'

'Is there anything in it?'

'Happy companionship, I'd think. From what I hear Cyril Fletcher is very popular among the ladies, but he doesn't seem the sort to settle down.'

I grinned. 'I'd have said the same, and besides Lady Clementine has plenty of admirers vying for her attention.'

'Such as Greggs.' She smiled.

'And Tremayne,' I added.

'Uncle Len'x, Uncle Len'x!' Angus came running to me from the house. 'We went lake today an' given duckies bread.' He climbed on my knee and tried to tell me about his morning in his limited vocabulary.

Florence and Swift weren't far behind, and neither were the two dogs. Nicky seemed back in form and dashed about our feet, although he didn't try to nip anyone. That lesson appeared to have been learned.

Lunch commenced amid a great deal of chatter about home matters. It ended the same way, too, although we did manage to eat a fair meal between times, and shared a delicious jug of Pimms. Brendan arrived pushing a wheelbarrow and soon attracted a cargo of small child, two dogs, and a rotund black cat, which he carefully steered towards the orchard.

'What is happening to Marcus Marriott?' Florence asked once Angus was out of earshot.

'We haven't released him yet,' Swift answered, looking more relaxed with a glass in his hand.

'Could he have killed Dolores?' Persi asked. 'Everyone said she was poisoned.'

'What sort of poison was it?' Florence added.

'Cook said it was asinine.' Persi sipped her second glass of Pimms.

'Asinine?' Swift frowned.

'I think she meant arsine,' Persi said and then giggled.

'Apparently someone heard half the story, and it became garbled.' Florence smiled.

I laughed but it was a reminder to be more careful what we said, particularly near open windows.

'It probably was arsine, produced by burning rat poison,' Swift confirmed.

'What effect did it have?' Persi finished her drink; I poured her another.

Swift went into laborious detail about the paper, gas, the appearance of the body, and even quoted the poem from his notebook.

'It's awful doggerel,' I commented.

'Yes, and we're not sure why the accusation was made,' Swift replied.

'Unless Margaret killed her,' I suggested.

'Why? Because she thought Dolores was a "Jezebel"?' Persi leaned forward eagerly.

'Not just that,' I said, and took some time to explain

the rigged bidding for Saunders' shares and the fact that Dolores had also planned to catch Le Train Bleu to Monte Carlo with Devlin Saunders.

Swift then told them his suspicions about Alfred Palgrave because all three victims had plotted together to steal his inheritance.

Regardless of the appalling murders, they still felt sympathy for Palgrave, whereas there was none whatsoever for Margaret.

'Will you release Marriott in time for the auction?' Florence asked as we turned to our remaining list of suspects.

'Probably.' Swift was non-committal.

'I'm surprised Sir Edwin is allowing it to go ahead,' Persi said as she finished her drink.

Swift shook his head. 'He must, it would breach the covenant otherwise.'

'But surely the auction is the catalyst that set the murders off.' Concern was clear in Florence's voice.

'All the more reason to let them battle it out,' I remarked dryly.

'The proceeds will go to Lady Clementine. I hope she receives oodles of money and spends it on having a wonderful time without those appalling parasites,' Persi said quite forcefully.

We all turned to her with mild surprise.

'Well...' She shrugged. 'They've attached themselves to her like leeches. It's utterly contemptible. She can't even call her own house her home. They jolly well deserve everything that's happened to them.'

I decided I should restrict lunchtime Pimms to one glass each from now on.

'Sir.' Greggs arrived. 'Scotland Yard would like to speak to Inspector Swift. Inspector Billings is on the telephone.'

Swift leapt to his feet. 'Excellent, I tried calling him earlier but he wasn't there.' He went striding across the lawn.

'And Dr Fletcher has just arrived, sir. Shall I make another jug of Pimms?'

'No, thank you, old chap,' I replied. 'I think tea will suffice.'

'Very well, sir.' He plodded off, looking rather warm in the sunshine. I expect he hadn't "cast a clout" as it was not yet the end of May.

'And a merry afternoon to you all.' Cyril Fletcher arrived in a flurry of good humour. 'M'lady...' He paused to make a flourishing bow to Florence, then to Persi. 'M'lady.'

They gave him warm smiles; he was ever a favourite among the women.

'Cyril,' I greeted him as he sat down on a spare chair.

'Lennox, my boy. I've just returned from depositing the latest body to the dreaming spires.'

'Not literally, I hope,' I replied with a grin.

'Haha, no actually it was the Oxford morgue. But I don't wish to bring a morbid topic to the table, nor to such lovely ladies.'

'Oh, dead bodies are my speciality.' Persi leaned on the table and regarded him hazily.

'Indeed, and we really must exchange notes sometime, Lady Persi,' Fletcher carried on.

'You can just call me Persi.' She waved a nonchalant hand.

Florence rose to her feet. 'Actually I think I'd better go in search of Angus. He can be a handful.'

'I'll come too.' Persi stood up and smoothed her pretty frock down. 'A walk might clear my head.' She bent to kiss me, then turned to Fletcher. 'And you can tell us all about everything in the incident room later, Cyril.'

'You mean my library,' I reminded her. For some reason she found this amusing and went off laughing.

'The pathologist agreed that it was very likely arsenic.' Fletcher eyed the empty Pimms jug.

'Ingested or inhaled?' I replied.

'Difficult to say until they've opened her up, and I had no desire to stick around for that.' His smile faded and he turned serious. 'But given the circumstances I'd say she probably inhaled it as a gas.'

'Anything unusual about the body?' I asked.

'Not a thing, apart from the effects of the poison. We tested the powder on her hands, there was arsenic mixed with the print from the paper.' He glanced at me, now entirely professional; his moustache neatly trimmed, as were his brows, he was immaculately turned out as ever. 'I took a small sample of burned page and viewed it under a microscope. The arsenic powder was embedded into the paper, it must have been soaked in a solution of rat poison.'

I nodded. 'Like a shallow bath, or basin?'

'Exactly.' He raised a wry lip. 'It was carefully planned and executed.'

'And the killer deliberately kept the pages back to kill Dolores with.'

'Cold-blooded,' he said.

'Cold-blooded, indeed,' I agreed. 'Although the killer couldn't be certain she would burn the paper.'

'No, that puzzled me too,' he replied.

Swift returned with a light step. He greeted Fletcher with a grin and sat down to tell us of his telephone call. 'Billings was pretty caustic over the latest death,' he said. 'But pleased we'd unravelled the financial scheme. He's had checks run on all their banks. Cedric Smedley recently withdrew twenty-one thousand pounds from his own personal account.'

'Which was the sum he forwarded to Palgrave for his loan,' I remarked.

Greggs arrived with the tea and fussed about, pouring a cup for everyone. He probably wanted to hear what was being said, and no doubt he'd listened to Swift's conversation on the telephone too.

'I can't imagine having that amount of money in the bank.' I shook my head. It was more than enough to buy my house.

'Ah, well that's not all,' Swift continued in a mood that was almost jolly. 'The loan to Palgrave may have been supplied from Smedley's bank, but the funds had been transferred into his account only the week before.'

'Where from?' I asked.

'The Royal Buckingham Financial Services' account.' He smiled grimly. 'Saunders lent it to Smedley, who lent it to Palgrave, who would then pay it to Saunders when he won the bidding. The only real outcome of the transactions was that it put Palgrave into debt to the tune of twenty-one thousand pounds.'

'Which was secured on his inheritance,' I stated, my frown deepening.

'Precisely,' Swift agreed. 'It's quite clear what they were up to: they intended trapping Palgrave and fleecing him of everything.'

'They won't be much mourned,' Fletcher remarked.

'I'm just surprised no-one's killed them off before now,' I muttered darkly.

I sat in silence as Fletcher rendered an account to Swift about the initial findings on Dolores' body and the arsenic-infused paper.

'It was all planned...' He sounded angry. 'Completely calculated from beginning to end.'

'Who's to say it's ended,' I remarked.

'There was something else I meant to tell you,' Fletcher said. 'The dagger you found hidden in the ground at Ashton Hall. It wasn't the one which killed Saunders.'

That made us both stare.

'What!' Swift exclaimed. 'But there was blood on the underside of the hilt.'

'Are you sure it was blood?' Fletcher asked.

Swift looked nonplussed for a moment, then admitted, 'No, we have no means of testing it.'

Fletcher nodded. 'I spoke to the pathologist before I left – actually, he was rather surprised to see me with another customer. *"The third in a matter of days and every death quite different,"* he remarked.' A grin spread beneath Fletcher's moustache. 'Interesting deaths are a welcome diversion in the narrow confines of the path lab, don't you know!'

We didn't share the fascination. Well, I didn't anyway.

'The pathologist was reporting on Devlin Saunders' post mortem, I assume?' Swift said as he pulled his notebook from his jacket pocket.

'He was,' Fletcher agreed. 'He had made a closer examination of the heart – well, he'd removed it, actually – and showed me the cut formed by the original weapon. It was quite clear the initial wound had been made by a much finer blade; triangular, almost needle-like and extraordinarily sharp. It had pierced the heart, whereas the arrowhead was too blunt and merely rested against it.'

'Hell.' Swift swore under his breath.

'Hell indeed,' Fletcher agreed. 'And I'm sorry not to have been the harbinger of better news.' He stood up. 'Now if you'll excuse me, I haven't had lunch yet and I'm deuced hungry,' he declared and went off with a merry wave.

# CHAPTER 24

'We'll have to release Marriott,' I said as we followed the path to the front of the house.

'I know,' Swift admitted, walking with his hands in his pockets. 'Billings has insisted, and he said we'd better not arrest anyone else unless we have cast-iron evidence against them.'

That didn't surprise me. I'd half expected Billings to throw us off the case altogether. I suppose Swift's apparently buoyant mood was because he'd shared the same fears and they hadn't yet come to pass.

'We're no further forward, are we?' Swift suddenly sounded dejected. 'No incontrovertible evidence, no witnesses, no proper alibis, and everyone has a motive.'

'But we have a shorter suspect list, now,' I said. 'And if it carries on like this, we can just arrest the last one still alive.'

He looked at me. 'That's not amusing, Lennox.'

I grinned. He climbed in the car while I cranked her up.

'Lennox, wait,' Swift objected as I drove past the police station. 'I thought we were going to release Marriott.'

'You can telephone Fossett. He can do it,' I said over the noise of the engine. 'There's something more important I want to take a look at.'

'What?' he asked as we drove through the gates. Quite a crowd were waiting but we merely nodded politely and refused to answer any questions.

'I'll show you.' I stopped the car and went to rap on the knocker of Ashton Hall.

Ackroyd opened the door. He seemed to be in even more of a peevish mood than ever.

'Sirs, I simply cannot go on. You must allow me to leave, and indeed the kitchen staff should be permitted the same. We are innocents caught in a maelstrom of murder. Anyone could be next and none of us have done anything to deserve such a fate.'

I swore he must have been rehearsing this. 'Nonsense, nobody has any reason to kill you. Go and find Mrs Marriott, would you.'

'But she may not be in the house,' he instantly objected.

'Why don't you know where she is?' Swift demanded. 'No-one is to leave.'

This brought another fit of huffiness from the butler. 'Am I now a prison guard, sir? To keep the household under lock and key? It is simply not possible—'

'Just go and have a look, would you,' I ordered.

That put a stop to the histrionics. He stiffened his back and flared his nostrils with suppressed indignation. 'Very well, sir. I will endeavour to do my duty.' He stalked off, nose in the air.

We waited until he'd gone, then I went over to the umbrella stand in the corner. There were a number of canes among the furled umbrellas, and I pulled out the most likely – a glossy Malacca walking stick with a heavy black handle.

Swift watched, realisation dawning in his eyes.

'A sword stick,' he guessed, then swore under his breath.

The handle released when I gave it a sharp tug, and the blade slid from the hidden sheath with a faint metallic hiss.

'Hidden in plain sight,' Swift said as we both stared at the deadly length of honed steel.

I raised it for a better view. The blade was triangular to provide strength and rigidity, the tip needle-sharp.

'This fits the bill,' I said, dabbing a finger on the point – and almost drew blood.

'We'll have to give it to Cyril Fletcher to compare against Saunders' wound,' Swift decided.

'There aren't many triangular blades.' I pushed the sword stick back into the cane and handed it to him.

'True,' he agreed. 'And you should have worn gloves, Lennox.'

He was right, but on that principle we'd just end up wearing them all the damn time. 'Do you have any gloves with you?'

'Well, no…'

'This killer's too clever to be caught by fingerprints,' I said.

'Fine,' he muttered, then picked out another cane. 'We should test each of them.'

We picked up the walking sticks one at a time to find they were all merely what they appeared to be. No other held a blade.

'Right, incident room!' Swift decided, and headed upstairs with the Malacca cane in hand.

He placed it on the table in Saunders' bedroom. We'd no sooner sat down than he jumped up again. 'I'd better ring Fossett.'

'Fine.' I picked up the cane for a more leisurely inspection. Expensive as it was handsome, it had been crafted by an expert at least a century ago. Sword sticks had been all the fashion in older times, when robbers lurked in unlit alleyways waiting for unsuspecting gentleman to stroll by. I couldn't see a maker's name and was about to slide the blade out when Ackroyd entered with Gabriel Marriott in tow. I dropped the cane out of sight as they approached.

'I have escorted Mrs Marriott as requested, sir,' Ackroyd intoned and then immediately backed out, closing the door behind him.

'Would you please sit down,' I said and waved a hand at the chair opposite. I was quite surprised to see her; I'd thought she would have been with her husband, despite orders to the contrary.

She slid onto a chair, watching me warily. Shadows ringed her eyes; she seemed tired and her clothes and hair were even duller than usual. 'I have nothing to say to you. And I had nothing to do with Dolores' death.'

'Do you have any idea why she was murdered?' My tone was harsh.

'I suppose she must have upset whoever is carrying out these dreadful acts.'

'Are you worried that you may be at risk?' I was trying to rattle her, although I felt uncomfortable in doing so.

'No, why should I be?' She sounded puzzled. 'Dolores has always been manipulative, so were Devlin and Cedric. I think they had probably gone too far.'

'In what way?' I asked her.

'Devlin's retirement, putting his shares up for bidding and Cedric offering loans. They were trying to extort money from their fellow directors. They shouldn't have done it, it just caused them all to turn on each other.' She pushed a strand of brown hair behind her small ear. Her movements were abrupt. There was a lack of grace about her, although behind the drab facade, there was something undefinable.

'Was your husband angry about it?'

She nodded then dropped her gaze. 'Of course he was. He is the most able of them all, without him in charge the company will founder. They all know it, but Devlin let his own stupid greed get in the way. If Sebastian wins, he will strip every penny he can from the company and simply squander it.'

I closed my eyes for a split second, thinking of my home being forcibly sold just to finance the hedonistic lifestyle of someone like Sebastian Cardhew. I shook the rage off and continued. 'And what if Alfred Palgrave won?'

Her eyes flicked to mine again, and then away. 'He's

totally unsuited to manage the company. Marcus said Dolores had been bullying Alfred, demanding he bid for the shares. It was nonsensical.'

'Why do you think Dolores was bullying Alfred to bid?' I watched her face.

'I don't know, I have as little to do with them as possible.'

'You had a relationship with Alfred when you were younger,' I stated.

Her eyes flew open. 'No.' She stood up suddenly.

'Sit down,' I barked at her.

She froze, and then sat back into the chair. 'Don't say anything,' she hissed. 'Marcus doesn't know. He would be deeply hurt.'

'Alfred Palgrave was prepared to relinquish everything to Dolores because she threatened to disclose that you and he were once lovers.'

Colour drained from her face as she realised how Dolores had manipulated Alfred. 'I didn't know. How could I? I only came here because Marcus said it was terribly important. I loathe what they do. I loathe it,' she said with vehemence.

I contemplated explaining Saunders' elaborate plan to her, but decided against. She'd only tell her husband and who knows where that would lead.

'Dolores was going to divorce Alfred. She wanted the shares as settlement.' I chose my words carefully.

'Why on earth did she want the shares?' She looked astonished.

'We think she wanted to run the company herself.'

'But Devlin would never have allowed her...' She looked confused. 'I really don't understand this.'

'What happened between you and Alfred?' I pressured her. There was a secret – I was certain she was hiding something and so was Alfred.

'It was wrong...' I heard the tremor in her voice. She took a breath to calm herself, then looked me in the eye. 'You think he killed Dolores, don't you? You think he murdered them all?'

Well, she certainly wasn't stupid, she'd guessed that right. 'Gabriel, the situation looks very bleak for him.'

She paused in thought, a faint frown on a broad brow. Her skin was flawless, her eyes held a warmth behind the wariness. If she didn't dress so dowdily...

'I can see why you think Alfred may be behind it, but he's not. He isn't the type, he's not brave enough.' Her voice fell. 'He's a coward, actually. He can't help it. He's kind and vulnerable, but he would run sooner than fight. I have forgiven him for what he did...' She broke off, putting her hand over her mouth.

I waited as she fought to compose herself. 'What did he do, Gabriel?' I spoke quietly, feeling guilty at causing her such obvious anguish.

'A baby...I was with child.' She tried to hold back the tears. 'I told him. He was terrified of my father, and how his own family would react. I was only seventeen, he wasn't much older. He ran away to London and I didn't know where he was.' Her body shook and she wrapped her arms across her waist. 'Then I lost it, it was only a few weeks, but

I'd lived in torment every moment of every day…I wanted the baby, but I couldn't tell anyone. And then it…I don't know, there must have been something wrong. I was very ill afterwards. My mother died years before, and father didn't realise.' She rocked slowly in her chair. 'I don't think I can have children now. I told Marcus before we wed, I thought it only fair. It was his dream to have a family, but he accepted that we may not, and he still wanted to marry me. But if he knew the reason, he would be… he would be vengeful. I wouldn't let him hurt Alfred, but I know he would want to.'

I let out a silent sigh. 'Gabriel, please accept my apologies, I am so dreadfully sorry.'

'Don't say anything, please don't repeat this,' she pleaded.

'No, I promise,' I said and meant it.

She stumbled to her feet and ran out as Swift walked in.

'What did you say to her?' He looked back in the direction she'd gone. 'She was in floods of tears, you really should be more circumspect, Lennox.'

I didn't reply. I went onto the balcony for a moment of quiet contemplation.

# CHAPTER 25

'We'll fingerprint the sword stick when Fossett arrives.' Swift had been drawing a picture of the blade in his notebook when I returned to the room. 'And we need to interview everyone who was in the house when Dolores Palgrave was murdered.'

'We've already interviewed them,' I objected. 'We interviewed them when we arrived, and again after Smedley was killed.'

'Yes, but we might gain a different perspective this time.' He began writing. 'The remaining suspects are: Margaret Saunders, Lady Clementine, Alfred Palgrave, Sebastian Cardhew, Gabriel Marriott, Marcus Marriott—'

'Marriott wasn't here last night,' I reminded him.

'I know, but he's still a suspect.' He carried on writing. 'Ackroyd, Mrs Wiggins the cook, Dolly the maid, and Sir Edwin Tremayne.'

'And Tremayne isn't a suspect,' I argued.

'But he was here last night.' He was in full pedantic mode.

'Sirs.' Fossett walked in, slightly red in the face below his police helmet. 'I let Mr Marriott out and made him walk back here with me. He asked if he was under house arrest and I said he was.' He took his helmet off and put it on the table. 'He argued all the way, and I told him 'you can argue all you like, but the law's the law and that's that'. Anyway, he's gone to get washed and changed.' He spotted the Malacca cane. 'Why have you got that walking stick?'

'It was in the umbrella stand. It's the weapon used to kill Devlin Saunders,' I said.

That made his eyes open. 'It never is!'

'Did you bring fingerprint powder?' Swift asked him.

'Yes, sir.' He opened his leather satchel and pulled out the jam jar.

'Check for prints first, then I'll show you how it works,' I told him.

He did as asked while we sat and watched him wield brush and powder. He stared at the prints through a magnifying glass. 'There's yours, Inspector Swift...and yours, Major Lennox. But there ain't nothing more.' He checked against the inky paper with all the prints on it.

'It's been wiped clean,' I said, and then pulled the handle to reveal the sword hidden inside.

Fossett's mouth dropped open. 'I never saw such a thing. And to think it was in the umbrella stand all this time!'

'We haven't confirmed it's definitely the murder weapon,' Swift said. 'But it's very likely.'

'Why did they bury that dagger in the garden then?' Fossett asked.

'To sow confusion, I suppose.' I pushed the sword back into the stick.

'Well, they certainly did that,' Fossett agreed. 'I never seen anything so convoluted, it's like just doin' stuff as they go along.'

'It may be more nuanced than it appeared.' Swift deliberated. 'Gabriel Marriott might have hidden it to protect her husband.'

'But she'd have to know how Devlin Saunders was murdered,' I disagreed.

'Marriott would have told her, they're probably in it together,' Swift countered.

'But if it was Mr Marriott,' Fossett continued, 'how would he have got the papers and that note to Mrs Palgrave when he was locked in the cell?'

'He gave it to Mrs Marriott earlier, obviously,' Swift said. 'And she pushed it under Dolores' door.'

'But it doesn't make any sense, sir,' Fossett said. With which I agreed.

I went to the bell pull to give it a sharp tug.

Ackroyd arrived moments later. 'You rang, sir?'

'Did anyone give you a package for Dolores Palgrave last night?' I asked him.

'They did not, sir,' he intoned.

'Did you see anyone with a package or papers?' Swift demanded.

'I did not, sir. I joined the staff in the kitchen and we listened to a dramatised play on the wireless.'

'Who does this cane belong to?' I nodded at it lying on the table.

'I have no idea, sir, it was among the other items in the umbrella stand when I arrived.' He barely glanced at it.

'Right, thank you,' I said by way of dismissal.

He pursed his lips, gave a sniff and went off again.

'Why d'you think Mrs Palgrave set fire to those papers?' Fossett asked once Ackroyd had gone.

'Guilty conscience.' Swift leaned over his notebook.

'But what had she done?' Fossett asked, his brow creased.

'Blackmailed her husband, had an affair with Devlin Saunders behind his wife's back, manipulated the directors of the company...' Swift began a litany.

He was interrupted by the door slamming open.

'What are you trying to do to me?' Margaret Saunders almost screamed at us.

We all stopped, and stared. Her usual carefully coiffed hair was disarrayed, spiky strands sticking out at angles. Her dress was creased, her eyes almost bulging, and her cheeks flaming.

'Everything has been ruined. My husband dead, my inheritance stolen, my plans destroyed, my guests murdered, and you've even turned Sebastian against me,' she shrieked.

'Madam, this isn't helping,' Swift told her sharply.

'Isn't helping?' she thundered. 'Three people are dead, including that trollop. Who will be next? I can't sleep, I can't eat! You have us locked up here in this awful backwater and there's no escape.' She raised an arm and pointed with a red-tipped finger. 'We're all just cowering in our rooms waiting to be murdered, and you are sitting here doing nothing.'

'Margaret,' a voice called out behind her. Sebastian Cardhew ran into the room. 'What's happened now? Why are you shouting?'

'It's these...these...incompetent brutes.' She was still pointing at us. 'They've ruined it for me, and ruined it for us. Oh, Sebastian.' She suddenly threw herself into his arms.

He looked horrified, then pulled himself together. 'She's right. You have stood back and allowed people to die. This is all your fault,' he shouted over her caterwauling.

'Well, that's a bit rich,' I said, but he wasn't listening.

'You must put a stop to this,' Cardhew continued. 'Or more people may die. Is that what you want?'

'Sebastian, you must protect me.' Margaret clung to the lapels of his red blazer and implored him. 'I am alone in the world now, I cannot trust anyone but you.'

Fossett watched as though mesmerised.

'Margaret, I...' Cardhew forgot about haranguing us as he tried to unlock Margaret's hands.

'And I need your help, Sebastian,' she continued. 'Devlin has hidden all his money from me and I must find it. It's a fortune and all I have in the world.'

That shut him up. You could almost see the pound signs whirring in his eyes. 'Ah yes, yes, of course. It was only the shares that you didn't...*ahem*. Now look, Margaret, you're right. You do need protection. Especially as these incompetents have totally failed to apprehend the monster murdering people in their beds.' He threw a look of disdain in our direction. 'Come, dear, I will take you to your room, and you can explain to me how much money you think Devlin has hidden away. We'll find it together, it can't be that difficult.' He placed a diffident arm around her shoulder as she let go of his jacket and leaned against him.

'Oh, Sebastian, I knew you truly cared for me,' she said in trembling voice.

'Haha, well of course I did, erm…do.' He led her from the room.

'Well, that's just tommyrot, that is,' Fossett fumed after they'd gone. 'Not one of them was murdered in their beds.'

'I think he was speaking metaphorically,' Swift said.

'Incompetent indeed.' Fossett was still aggrieved. 'It'd serve her right if he was the murderer.'

'Or, if she were,' I said.

'Well, we'll show them,' Fossett continued. 'We'll find the culprit and send them off to the hangman,' he declared, then looked at us. 'Who d'you think it is, then?'

'When we know, we'll tell you,' I replied.

'Did Marriott say anything to you?' Swift asked him.

'He did, actually, when it was just the two of us.' Fossett sat down. 'He's an interesting bloke. Did a lot of things during the war. I was too young for most of it, then just as I was called up, they stopped fighting, and that was that.' His eyes flicked away. 'My big brother was killed though. They never found him.'

'Joel Fossett.' I recalled him, a strapping lad with a ready smile and good country sense. We fell silent as memories came unwelcome to mind; the mud and blood, and indescribable horror of the trenches...

'What did Marriott tell you?' Swift broke the quietude.

'He said he'd pushed his men too hard, and he regretted it,' Fossett replied, in thoughtful mood. 'It was after we'd talked for a while, he just come out and said it. Then we got chatting about life and the village. He asked if I'd always lived here...so I told him about Joel, and the farm. He said he'd never had a proper family, and now that he was wed, he wanted to make sure they'd never be poor. His wife's family cut her off, you see. Mrs Marriott, I mean. They didn't like him – not once they heard what company he kept. I think he was very lonely. I talked to my ma about it afterwards. She said he'd probably made himself an outcast but really wanted just to be included, like most folk do, but he hadn't learned how. Once he found his wife he'd seen his chance to have a proper life, with love an' all that.' He looked up. 'My ma's a teacher; teachers know how people think. She's really clever.' He suddenly grinned. 'And she's always telling me off for not talking properly, but I keep sayin' to her, everyone would think I was trying to get above myself if I talked proper all the time.'

We smiled at that, but I felt a pang, too. The binding thread of belonging ran like a steel noose around most communities, and not getting above the rest was probably one of the strongest strands. It helped the weakest, but it held back the brightest and best.

'Did Marriott say anything relevant to the investigation?' Swift was still focused on the case.

'Yes, but I don't know if he realised it.' Fossett opened his own tattered notebook. 'He was injured in his left arm while fighting in the war, and it had stopped his hand working properly. He'd been born left-handed, but he'd had to learn to use his right hand after that.'

Swift stopped writing. 'Could he have used it to screw up Smedley's sachet?'

Fossett grinned. 'I handed him a slip of paper and asked him to give it a twist. He looked at me funny, but did it anyway. It was the twist like the killer made.'

That brought a grim smile to Swift's face. 'We'll make a detective of you yet, Fossett,' he said and wrote the new snippet down.

A rap sounded at the door, followed by Ackroyd. He bore a tray, and was accompanied by Lady Clementine.

'Time for tea!' she declared and walked in as though she owned the place. Which as I recalled, she did.

'Lady Clementine,' Swift began. 'We are conducting an investigation…'

'Does this preclude tea and scones?' She arched her brows.

'No, but we need to conduct interviews…' Tetchiness rose in Swift's voice.

'Well, you can interview me while Ackroyd serves,' she replied and sat down next to Fossett.

Swift muttered something under his breath, then asked her, 'What can you tell us about the events of last evening?'

'Absolutely nothing,' she laughed.

A smile twitched at Ackroyd's thin lips, but he recovered quickly. He offered plates of scones with cream and jam. I accepted one, so did Fossett.

Swift wasn't so easily distracted. 'Lady Clementine, Dolores Palgrave was murdered, and we need to find the killer before anyone else falls victim.'

She took a breath. I expected more lightheaded teasing but she put her hands in her lap and looked contrite. 'Very well. We all had dinner together. Sir Edwin and I had a delightful conversation while the others sat around as if it were their last supper.'

Ackroyd handed out tea.

'Who was there?' Swift asked, as he raised his cup to his lips.

'Everyone, apart from Marcus and Gabriel,' she replied in a grave tone. 'Dolores hardly ate a thing, she smoked through the first course until Edwin asked her to stop. Then she ground her cigarette out into her food, didn't she Ackroyd?' She turned to him.

'I'm afraid she did, m'lady,' the butler replied in the tone of a martyr. 'I had to remove the dish and dispose of the offending item before Cook observed the indignity.'

'Did Dolores Palgrave appear agitated?' Swift continued doggedly.

'Pensive, I would have said, rather than agitated,' Lady Clementine replied. 'She stalked off after she was asked to stop smoking, and I didn't see her again.'

'Did anyone follow her?' Swift wrote each reply down.

'No, they were all rather glum.' She sighed. 'Young people really don't know how to enjoy themselves anymore.'

'It's hardly a surprise in the circumstances,' Swift said.

'Yes, but what do they expect if they carry on in such an appalling manner.' She put her teacup onto its saucer. 'Now, Sir Edwin and I are going for a walk through the woods; we have many memories to recall.' She beamed. 'I do hope you catch this killer soon, I really don't wish to enter my next life until I am finished with this one. Toodle-oo.' She waggled her fingers and left, with Ackroyd following closely behind.

# CHAPTER 26

'She's totally bats,' Fossett remarked before cutting into his scone with a fork.

'Dolores was probably more concerned with the bidding and her planned escape to Monte Carlo,' Swift said.

'What?' I asked.

'Lady Clementine just said Dolores was pensive last evening at dinner,' he reminded me.

'Ah,' I mumbled, between bites of scone, cream and jam.

'Where is this Monte Carlo place, anyway?' Fossett asked.

'Monaco,' Swift replied dourly. 'Sun, sea, and sin, especially gambling.'

'I'd like to try that,' Fossett said.

We both looked at him.

He grinned. 'Well, we don't get much of that around here.'

Swift muttered something about law and order. I finished my scone.

'Right,' I declared. 'I'm going home.'

'What? Why?' Swift frowned.

'Because we need to talk to Persi, and Florence. They've drawn up an incident board, and I think it would be useful.'

'But we haven't interviewed everyone...' Swift began an objection.

'We've heard enough, Swift, and most of it has just added to the confusion,' I countered. 'If we thrash it out with the girls, they might throw some fresh light on things.'

'Sounds like a good idea to me, sir,' Fossett offered.

Swift let out a sigh of exasperation. 'Fine, but if we need any more information we'll come back.'

I refrained from rolling my eyes and led the way out. Fossett carried the Malacca cane under his arm.

'You can come with us in the car, Fossett,' I offered, knowing that he'd walked from the police station and was without his bicycle.

'Oh, sir.' He beamed. 'Shall I crank her up?'

Permission duly given, I started her up and we motored off in serene style.

Frank Wright opened the gate. There were only a handful of people with him. I wasn't sure why – perhaps they'd all gone home for afternoon tea, or were they losing faith in us? I suspected the latter, given the arrest and release of Marriott, the plethora of deaths, and apparent contradictions over the means of murder. There was nothing quite like a bullet to the brain, or a dagger in the heart to make murder clearly identifiable, whereas in reality it was often more subtle – or it was when perpetrated by someone clever, anyway.

Were we being outwitted? I pondered as we drove home. The inhabitants of Ashton Hall were mostly devious, manipulative, and ruthless. It was the manipulative part that bothered me the most. Whoever it was, was orchestrating events and I just couldn't see beyond their smoke and mirrors.

'Oh, I think that's a jolly good idea.' Persi smiled when we explained why we'd returned earlier than expected.

'Angus has just dropped off to sleep,' Florence said. 'So we'll have some quiet time.'

Swift led the way to my library and we gathered around the girls' "incident board".

'Right.' Swift leaned over the table. 'We need to start at the basics, "who, when, where, and why".'

'I'll take notes, sir.' Fossett was keen.

'Swift, if we knew "who" we wouldn't be doing this,' I remarked.

'That's what we're trying to find out, Lennox!' Swift replied tartly. 'We'll work through everything according to procedure and process. It requires sound police—'

'That's what we've been doing,' I countered. 'What we need is an eccentric approach, something to shift our viewpoint.'

'Oh, what an inventive idea.' Florence came to my defence. 'We could begin by discussing their personalities.'

Actually that hadn't been what I had in mind, but Swift immediately leapt on it.

'Excellent.' He opened his notebook. 'Let's start with
Devlin Saunders – what caused him to be so despised that
someone murdered him?'

This produced almost an hour of exchanging opinions,
a couple of disagreements, and general postulating. Fossett joined in; even Greggs had something to say. I leaned
back in my chair and listened. It was conjecture, and quite
entertaining, but not particularly useful. After another
hour they'd dissected the characters of most of the Ashton
Hall inhabitants, and I needed a drink.

'Wine, Greggs,' I ordered. 'A decent burgundy.'

He looked meaningfully at the clock on the mantelpiece. 'At this hour, sir?'

Since I married he had become more and more of a stick
in the mud. I've no idea why. 'Yes, Greggs, at this hour.
Half past four is a perfectly reasonable time for a drink.
We had Pimms at lunch, for heaven's sake.'

'As I am quite aware, sir,' he replied then made a rapid
exit when he noted my expression.

'What about motive?' Persi suggested. 'We think money
is behind it, but it may not be.'

'Hope of gain, or fear of loss,' I said.

'What does that mean?' Florence asked.

'It's Lennox's theory,' Swift replied before I could. 'He
says there are only really two motives for murder.'

'And passion,' I said. 'Which you insisted on adding.' I
directed that at Swift.

'So, three motives,' Persi said. 'Which do they each
have?'

'Marcus Marriott would be hope of gain,' Florence replied.

'Alfred Palgrave would be fear of loss,' Persi added.

'Margaret Saunders would be hope of gain,' Fossett said with a grin.

'As would Sebastian Cardhew.' Swift joined in with good grace.

'I really can't think of a motive for Gabriel Marriott,' Persi said. 'Apart from despising them all, and even that doesn't make sense because her husband is no better than the rest of them.'

'And it doesn't fit the list of motives,' Fossett pointed out.

'That's because the list is deficient,' Swift said, which began another debate. This was brought to a halt by the arrival of Greggs bearing a decanter of rich red Burgundy. Apparently no-one else was ready for a glass, so I asked for a large one.

'What if it was two of them working together?' Persi began, and this involved various theories, many of which were highly unlikely, and others that we'd already considered.

'Assuming Saunders' body actually was moved to the edge of the balcony just before nine in the morning,' I began, 'why don't we use your map to indicate everybody's positions at that time?'

They all thought this a jolly good idea, and the girls moved to their drawing of each floor of Ashton Hall on the roll of wallpaper. Greggs found some chess pieces to represent the inhabitants and helped the girls and Fossett place them in the various parts of the house.

I watched while sipping my wine, which was just the sort of tonic I needed.

'What about the evidence?' I suggested.

'Ah, yes, we should assemble it,' Swift agreed. We still had the arrow, and Fossett had the sword stick. Cyril Fletcher had returned Marriott's dagger earlier in the day, and Swift had the envelope containing some of the pink paper that Dolores had set fire to.

'What about Mr Saunders' will, sir?' Fossett asked.

'Sir Edwin Tremayne has it,' Swift reminded him.

'There's the code to the vault,' Fossett said.

'We have the list of debtors we glued together,' Florence offered and fetched *Who's Who* from the bookcase. 'It took us hours,' she said as she took a thick card from between the pages. It had the look of a jigsaw puzzle made from a paper trail, but the list was quite readable and nobody mentioned my name being on it, although it was clear to see.

I perused the other unfortunates as Swift supervised the girls and Fossett. They laid the items of evidence around the drawing of the floor plan, placed the chess pieces in the rooms, and considered what it may mean. It was almost six o'clock by the time we realised it hadn't shed any new light at all.

'We've fashioned a timeline,' Persi offered. 'It might help pinpoint alibis.'

'Or the lack of them,' I said.

She unveiled another length of wallpaper drawn in various colours with days and times along three stripes. We went over them, and picked over the details of the various statements along with Swift's pages of neatly written notes.

I could see frustration and dismay beginning to build in their faces. Despite our concerted efforts, nothing revelatory had emerged from the exercise.

Tommy came bouncing into the room. 'Hello, sirs. I thought you were up at Ashton Hall,' he chattered. 'I went there first, just to see how you were doin', and they said at the gate that you'd given up and gone home. But that's not true, is it? You'd never give up, 'specially with these murders being right in the village where we all live. You haven't given up, have you, sir?' He swept tousled hair from his face as he asked the question.

'No, we were just working through a summary of the case,' Swift replied.

'It's not getting us anywhere, though,' Fossett admitted, which caused Swift to frown.

'Go and change out of your uniform Tommy,' I ordered.

'Oh, sir…'

'Now,' I demanded.

Tubbs came in as Tommy went out, and jumped up onto the table. He started to pat the chess figures with a black paw; it didn't take a moment for him to push them all over onto their sides.

'Oh no you don't.' Persi picked up the little reprobate to hold in her arms. He purred loudly as I gazed at the chess pieces lying randomly on the floor plan of Ashton Hall.

And then it dawned on me who it was, and why, and how easily deceived we'd all been. It was so very obvious, and yet none of us had spotted it, until now.

'Right, we'll have dinner at the pub,' I declared and stood up.

'Lennox, for heaven's sake...' Swift objected.

'Come on,' I insisted. 'It's Cook's night off, and the King's Head are serving steak pie and mash.'

'But it's the bidding in the morning. Once the auction is over they'll be free to leave,' Swift argued. 'Billings was quite clear, we don't have the authority to detain them any longer.'

'Swift, I know who's behind it,' I said.

That set them all clamouring, but I wasn't prepared to say anything more.

'Lennox, you should tell us the name at the very least.' Swift was insistent.

'Just let me have a change of scenery, and a chance to let the idea ferment. Then I'll tell you,' I promised.

'Greggs, you can come too, and Tommy. We'll walk to the village.'

It took a while for everyone to organise themselves. Angus woke in a niggling mood and had to be carried on Swift's shoulders all the way along the old cart track. Foggy led the way with Tommy skipping alongside.

Fossett stopped at the police station to change into casuals then joined us at a long wooden table overlooking the slow-moving brook. Mallards kept beady eyes open in the hope of a crust, their yellow fluffed ducklings cheeping as they paddled among the shallows. Talk of the actual murderer couldn't be mentioned in front of the youngsters so we passed the meal in comfortable discourse and easy laughter.

The church bell tolled the hour as we left the convivial confines of the pub to stroll through the village. Peace had fallen with the night, the stillness only broken by lowing cattle in distant meadows and the hoot of owls gliding by on silent wings.

The war memorial stood on the corner of the green. Someone had left a handful of wild flowers on the stone step supporting the modest cenotaph. We paused before it to gaze at the names: Fossett, Trimble, Craddock, Tippet, Foster, Briers, Hotchkins, Dix, Lewis. I could still put faces to each one lost in those far-away fields and sent a silent prayer for their souls to the man upstairs. *For those who sacrificed their lives to keep our country safe and to win the war to end all wars, we shall never forget you.*

We followed the track at meandering pace as the chill drew in, and sometime later, when the youngsters had been put to bed, and the fire lit, I told them who had done it, and how they'd so very easily evaded us.

# CHAPTER 27

'There won't be a confession, and there's no conclusive evidence.' Swift was still maundering over the problem next morning.

We'd had breakfast, no-one was allowed to mention a word in front of Tommy, but he had realised something was afoot and pestered us unceasingly to tell him. We didn't, of course.

I drove the Bentley at moderate speed as Swift and I talked.

'We'll catch them off guard,' I said.

'We can't let the killer get away with it, Lennox. If we don't pin them down today, we have to let them go,' Swift repeated for the third time

I nosed the car through the crowd around the gateway into Ashton Hall. Frank Wright pushed the gates open and then ordered everyone back.

'Three down now,' someone shouted. 'There ain't many more to go.'

'You're not going to let them get away with it, are you,

Major Lennox?' A lady spoke out. I think it was Mrs Brick-house, the librarian.

'Best get the blighter soon. Can't be having three murders and none hanged for it,' Mr Craddock called.

'You will uncover them, won't you, Major Lennox? I can't think you'd allow them to escape.' That from Shelley Bays, the baker's wife.

I nodded and waved and then roared the car up the drive to screech to a halt on the gravel in front of the house. There was no reason for the turn of speed, other than to relieve some of the tension knotting through my mind.

Ackroyd opened the door, his nose in the air as usual. 'The household have assembled in the drawing room for the bidding, sir.'

'Right,' I said as we walked past him, heading in the direction of raised voices.

'You will sit down. At once!' Sir Edwin Tremayne's voice rose above the others. 'And be silent.'

We arrived just as a hush descended.

Fossett was already standing near the doors opening onto the terrace. Sun streamed through the glass behind him. His buttons shone, as did his black boots; he seemed to be even more spruced up today than usual, standing straight-backed, hands behind him and helmet placed firmly on his head. He saluted when he saw us, but didn't speak.

Swift raised a finger to summon him. Everyone looked at us, then watched as Fossett crossed the room.

'Sir Edwin made me and Mr Ackroyd move all the

chairs this morning, like they were facing a stage,' he told us sotto voce. 'He said it was for the bidding. I didn't say a word about your plan, sirs.'

'Very good, Fossett,' I said as I glanced at the assembled.

Lady Clementine was sitting alone on a damask sofa. She wore the yellow and peacock blue outfit and waved gaily at us. We nodded politely in return.

Margaret Saunders was seated on a spindly legged settee next to Sebastian Cardhew. The grieving widow had donned black, which seemed incongruous for any number of reasons. Her hair fixed and make-up carefully applied, she resembled a perfectly poised manikin. Cardhew was almost as precisely turned out, still sporting the ridiculous red blazer, his hair slicked, the silk cravat tied with a practised panache, and cream trousers pressed in sharp creases.

Marcus and Gabriel Marriott were on another sofa, both absorbed in a whispered conversation. They hadn't appeared to notice our arrival, or were just studiously ignoring us. He wore a smart city suit, similar, but far more expensive, than Swift's; she wore another drab frock in green.

Alfred Palgrave came in looking flustered. 'Must we do this? I think it awfully inappropriate in the circumstances.'

'What circumstances?' Sebastian Cardhew asked.

'My wife's death,' Palgrave retorted, his cheeks flushing.

'Well, my husband has just died too,' Margaret Saunders threw in.

'Yes, but you don't care.' A tremor caught in Palgrave's voice.

'Oh, please don't pretend Dolores is any loss.' Margaret had regained her confidence. 'She and Devlin would have been on their way to the continent if someone hadn't served them their just desserts.'

'Now, my dear,' Sebastian gently scolded her, which made everyone stare. 'Please don't allow yourself to become agitated.'

'Of course, Sebastian.' She gave him a dazzling smile, her red lipstick smearing the tips of her teeth.

Palgrave dithered in confusion, his hair barely brushed. He'd dressed with apparent haste in a rumpled white shirt and informal flannels. He plonked down on a wing chair nearest Lady Clementine.

'Gentlemen, be seated,' Tremayne ordered us. He'd taken a stance in front of the fireplace.

'We're waiting for Dr Fletcher,' I told him.

'Dr Fletcher is not germane to this meeting.' He'd prepared for the event in formal Victorian lawyer togs: gold chain, elaborate waistcoat, starched dickie, black trousers and tailcoat.

'Yes he is,' I replied.

'Major Lennox, I accept your presence here today because you are investigating these appalling deaths,' Tremayne lectured, 'but I do not see where Dr Fletcher would fit in.'

'We're here to arrest the culprit who has caused the appalling deaths,' I said as though it were an everyday occurrence. 'And Dr Fletcher *is* germane.'

Stunned silence fell for a moment, then questions shot out from all over the room.

'Quiet. We will not answer any questions until we're ready,' Swift shouted. The babble lessened but didn't cease.

'You don't have to make a song and dance out of it,' Marcus Marriott snapped. 'Just tell us who it is.'

'All in good time,' I said then leaned against the wall with arms folded.

Ackroyd entered. He may have been knocking but no-one would have heard. My dog came in with him, followed by Greggs and Cyril Fletcher.

'What ho, Heathcliff.' Fletcher grinned. 'Not late are we?'

Foggy rushed about, his tail wagging madly, and then jumped up to sit with Lady Clementine when she called him a 'darling little doggy'.

I frowned at my butler.

'Alas, sir. Mr Fogg escaped and I was searching for him,' he explained as if this were the first time he'd fabricated the same excuse. 'We discovered him sitting on the front doorstep, and Dr Fletcher suggested that I may be of some use within.'

There was absolutely nothing whatsoever that Greggs could do of use and he knew it. Not that it ever stopped him. I was about to dress him down when Tremayne spoke in icy tones.

'Ackroyd, close the door and stay in front of it. We will have no more interruptions.'

'Very well, sir.' Ackroyd did as told, then took his place with gloved hands lined up with the seams of his trousers. Greggs stood nearby in similar pose, rather marred by wobbling chins and his butlering outfit stretched a little too snug over his paunch. Fletcher came to join Swift and me. I'd explained today's order of battle to him over the telephone before I'd even had breakfast, and he'd promised to come and join the affray. Actually he'd been very keen on the idea.

'This meeting is called to order,' Tremayne began. 'As you are aware, the president and majority shareholder of the Royal Buckingham Financial Services, Mr Devlin Saunders, had taken the decision to retire, and agreed that his shares would be sold to the highest bidder.' Tremayne adopted a lawyerly pose. 'To facilitate this act, and to exhibit good faith, a covenant was signed to that effect, and now, despite his unfortunate demise, that covenant will be enacted.' He turned stiffly towards Lady Clementine. 'The proceeds of the sale will devolve to Lady Clementine, as and when Mr Saunders' will has passed probate.'

'I believe Devlin's will may be contested.' Sebastian Cardhew spoke up. 'And I think we should delay the bidding until the court has made a decision.'

'Who is contesting it?' Marcus Marriott sounded as though he already knew the answer.

'I am,' Margaret Saunders replied archly, and then threw a challenging look at Lady Clementine. 'I am his widow, and his shares are rightfully mine, Clementine. You tricked him into leaving them to you.'

Lady Clementine laughed. 'He thought he was tricking me, actually. Sadly for him, I outlived him.'

'But he would have left them to me, once you were

gone.' Margaret's cool poise suddenly cracked. 'Everything he had should be mine. You've always taken everything away from me, even Papa.'

'Don't be ridiculous, Margaret.' Lady Clementine spoke sharply. 'I never *"took"* your father from you, and I didn't *"take"* any of his money either, because he didn't have any.'

'It *was* his. The moment you married him, everything you had became his. That's the law.' Margaret's face darkened. 'And when he died, it should have been mine.'

'Have you forgotten the circumstances of his death?' Lady Clementine spoke softly but with a hint of steel beneath the words.

'You wouldn't...' Margaret hissed, glaring at her.

Lady Clementine fixed her with a cold stare until Margaret looked away, her face creased in fury.

'There will be no challenge to Devlin Saunders' will.' Tremayne spoke coldly, then fixed his gaze on Sebastian Cardhew. 'Will there?'

'I...I...' Cardhew stuttered, then looked at Margaret who shook her head. 'No, no, I don't think so.'

Fossett's eyes had rounded, as had most others during the unexpected spat. The veiled threat and counter-threat left us with more questions than answers, but Tremayne deftly returned to the proceedings.

'Does each director present agree that they will be bound by the bids they offer today? And that they have the wherewithal to support such bids?' Tremayne demanded.

'Yes, I do.' Marcus Marriott was the first to reply.

'As do I,' Sebastian Cardhew said with determination.

'And I do,' Alfred Palgrave muttered.

'Very well.' Tremayne stood with one hand on his lapel. 'I will accept your opening bid, Marriott.'

'One thousand pounds,' Marriott replied.

'Two thousand,' Cardhew countered.

'Ten thousand,' Alfred Palgrave said loudly.

Heads swivelled to stare at him. Marriott and Cardhew regarded him with open hostility.

'Eleven thousand,' Marriott said, a frown forming between his dark brows.

'Twelve,' Cardhew said.

'Fifteen,' Palgrave shouted. He'd flushed pink but seemed determined. I had no idea why he was bidding; it didn't make sense now that Dolores was dead. Unless he'd been lying to us, of course.

'Eighteen thousand,' Marriott countered, his eyes boring into Palgrave.

Cardhew had turned to Palgrave. 'You...you can't. Why are you doing this? You don't want the company, you were only involved because Dolores forced you.'

'Twenty-one thousand,' Palgrave shouted, ignoring Cardhew entirely.

A flicker of uncertainty crossed Marcus Marriott's face. Gabriel extended her hand to squeeze his. He gave an almost imperceptible nod.

'I bid twenty-one thousand, five hundred pounds,' he said clearly.

'I'm...I...I can't match that,' Cardhew stuttered, sweat breaking on his forehead.

Palgrave grinned but said nothing.

'Are there any more bids?' Tremayne demanded.

No-one spoke. Marriott's gaze had fixed on Palgrave 'Well?' he demanded.

Palgrave shrugged. 'All yours, Marriott, and I hope you think it's worth it.'

Lady Clementine suddenly laughed. 'Dear Alfred, you ran the price up, didn't you?'

Palgrave gave a weary grin. 'Might have done,' he admitted.

She flashed him a beaming smile. 'I knew you had a good heart.'

'We have won, then?' Gabriel Marriott addressed Tremayne.

'Your husband has.' He spoke gravely. 'Although you must lodge the funds into the Corporation's bank account before I can complete the legal transfer.'

'I will telephone my bank,' Marriott said and made to stand.

'Look, I protest.' Cardhew jumped to his feet. 'Palgrave didn't even want the shares, he just forced the bids up. He admitted it.' He pointed a finger at Palgrave, who had leaned back in his chair and crossed his arms.

'You lost, you idiot. Sit down,' Marriott suddenly bellowed, causing everybody to freeze.

Cardhew blinked then sat down abruptly.

'You will all remain seated,' Tremayne ordered. 'Major Lennox and Inspector Swift have a task to complete.' He turned to us. 'I believe that to be your intention?'

'It is,' Swift replied.

'Very well.' Tremayne stalked to the sofa and sat next to Lady Clementine with my dog between them. Foggy was the only one who seemed to be enjoying himself.

Swift moved to the vacated spot in front of the fireplace. 'Three people have been murdered in this house. These murders were conceived, prepared, and executed by a cold-blooded killer and the culprit is in this room.' He raised a hand to signal Fossett towards the door. 'Constable, guard the exit. Nobody is leaving until we have made an arrest.'

# CHAPTER 28

Fossett marched smartly over to where Ackroyd was standing by the door, which made the butler take a few hasty steps aside.

'Ready, sir,' Fossett rapped out.

I had remained leaning against the wall, next to an oval card table where Fossett had placed our few items of evidence.

'Lennox,' Swift said, and came to exchange places without further explanation.

'Bravo, old chap,' Cyril Fletcher called out, which earned him a few frowns and another smile from Lady Clementine.

'Look,' Marriott said, 'would you just arrest whoever it is, and let us get on with our business.'

'Your business is the cause of these deaths and you can damn well wait,' I retorted sharply.

'I'll remind you to mind your language, Major,' Tremayne lectured.

'Yes, sir, my apologies,' I replied, then took a breath and

continued. 'Three dead and it's quite probable the killer hasn't finished yet.'

That caught their attention.

'I haven't done anything.' Margaret Saunders sounded irritated. 'Why should anybody want to kill me?'

'Guilty by association,' I replied.

'Now, that's not true.' Sebastian came to her aid. 'Margaret was merely Devlin's wife, she wasn't part of the business. She never assigned loans to clients—'

'But *you* did.' I threw in the accusation. 'You extorted every penny and more. Just as Saunders and Smedley had.'

'These clients came to us,' Cardhew shot back. 'If they put themselves up to be fleeced that was their own stupid fault. And before you get on your high horse, you just remember that we loaned money to them because the banks wouldn't.'

'My loan is on your list.' I raised my voice. 'Your company bought it and then added an extortionate rate of interest to escalate the debt in order to foreclose. You and the rest are nothing but thieves running a damn racket.'

'You give it to them with both barrels, Heathcliff,' Cyril Fletcher called out. 'Well done, my boy!'

I have to admit, that wasn't exactly the way I had meant things to go, and I had to apologise again for swearing in front of the ladies.

'Lennox, could you just stick to the investigation,' Swift hissed at me.

'Fine,' I muttered and tried to remember what I'd intended to say. 'The arrow did not kill Devlin Saunders.'

Swift took the arrow from the box of evidence and passed it to me. I held it up, but they began arguing before I could speak.

'Utter rot,' Margaret shouted. 'Of course it did, we all saw it sticking out of him.'

'No, it didn't,' Cyril Fletcher rebutted. 'I examined the body, and attended the post mortem. He was stabbed with a long, sharp blade.'

'It wasn't by my dagger,' Marriott stated.

'And neither of us buried it in the garden,' Gabriel said in support.

This came as a surprise to most of them as we hadn't actually let on about the dagger, or the reason for Marriott's arrest.

I handed the arrow back to Swift and he gave me the Malacca Cane.

'No, the dagger,' I whispered. Swift rummaged in the box and handed it over. I held it up, allowing rays of sunshine to catch on the blade. 'There's blood under the hilt.'

'The blood is mine,' Marriott stated as though wearied. 'Its previous owner stabbed me with it.'

'In your left arm?' I guessed, remembering what Fossett had told me.

'Yes.' Marriott's dark eyes fixed on me. 'And I shot him before he could do any more damage.'

'When was this?' I asked.

'During the war, of course,' Marriott retorted. 'The crest on the hilt is Prussian.'

'Perhaps you could explain how my husband was killed,

Major Lennox.' Margaret Saunders spoke with sarcasm in her voice. 'Rather than swapping stupid war stories.'

That earned her a glare from most of the men in the room, apart from Cardhew who looked down at his manicured fingernails.

'Your husband was stabbed with a sword stick, Mrs Saunders.' I went to Swift and swapped the dagger for the Malacca cane. I tugged the handle, slid out the blade and showed it to Cyril Fletcher. 'Is this the right profile?'

He examined it closely, particularly the tip. 'The end is very slightly distorted,' he pointed out. 'Probably bounced off a bone at some time. I'm almost certain it was used to stab Saunders through the heart.'

'Exactly, and once he was dead the arrow was pushed into the wound to disguise the true means of murder. But it was too blunt to penetrate the heart, which is how we knew he'd been killed by a blade.' I held the sword stick up.

'I say, wasn't that in the umbrella stand?' Alfred Palgrave called out.

'It was.' I strolled back to the spot in front of the fireplace. 'How do you know?'

'I was going to use it when I went out walking, but I thought it rather pretentious for a country stroll and decided against,' he replied.

'Did you touch it?' I asked him.

'No, I just saw it. I took an umbrella in the end, and didn't even have to use it because the clouds cleared away,' he replied in apparent innocence.

Margaret Saunders' eyes hadn't left the gleaming blade in my hand. She seemed mesmerised by it. 'The cane was Devlin's.' She shifted her focus to me. 'He didn't bring it here. I know he didn't, he was looking for it in our London house just before we left...I'd forgotten until now.'

'It's your house now, Margaret,' Sebastian reminded her.

She wasn't listening. 'How ironic... He was so proud of it, a proper gentleman's cane, he called it. He liked to be thought a gentleman.' Her eyes switched to mine. 'It serves him right, he was a monster,' she said, then leaned back against the cushions with a grim smile of satisfaction on her lips.

I turned back to face the room. 'Saunders' body was moved to the edge of the balcony with the arrow stuck in his chest to make it appear as if he'd been killed by someone outside the house.'

'Fine. You've established it wasn't my dagger, and you locked me up for nothing,' Marriott stated.

I ignored him. 'Cedric Smedley died of a heart attack. Someone poured a sachet of his medication into his water, causing an overdose. That person was right-handed. Who here is left-handed?' That confused them; none of them moved. I turned to Marriott.

'You were born left-handed, weren't you.' I watched him. 'But you've been forced to use your right hand since you were wounded.'

'Major Lennox,' Tremayne said. 'I would ask you to explain yourself.'

'Fine,' I replied. 'Fossett, would you demonstrate to everybody how Smedley twisted his used sachets? And why it matters,' I asked.

'Righto, sir.' Fossett came forward and I moved to join Swift by the wall. Greggs came to join us.

'Sir, should I arrange refreshments?' my old butler asked.

'No,' Swift replied. 'I don't want any distractions.'

'I wouldn't mind a snifter,' I said.

Greggs raised his brows as though thoroughly shocked. 'It is barely beyond breakfast, sir.'

'Greggs what is all this nonsense about drinking?' I demanded as Fossett demonstrated paper twists to the assembled.

'*Ahem.*' He cleared his throat. 'According to the newspaper, an excess of alcohol can...erm...' His cheeks turned pink. 'Affect the...erm...possibility of fathering...ah... babies.' He mumbled the last word.

I laughed, which made a few heads turn. I lowered my voice. 'Greggs, I suspect more babies have been fathered due to an excess of alcohol, rather than the lack of it.'

He turned huffy. 'As you say, sir.'

I should have been annoyed at his nonsense, but I was actually rather pleased he was keen to see children about the house.

'And that's how he was killed.' Fossett had finished his demonstration, holding up a piece of twisted paper. I moved forward to take his place.

'Smedley was given an overdose of digitalis,' I resumed. 'Palgrave, you mentioned your father took the same medication.'

'Yes, what of it?' he replied warily.

'You knew how dangerous it was, and how easily it could cause an overdose,' I continued.

He watched me but didn't reply.

'You were being blackmailed by your wife,' I said. 'You had every reason to kill her, and every reason to kill Saunders and Smedley.'

'Look, I didn't. I wish I had, but I just couldn't kill anyone,' he answered, his voice wavering.

'You were the target of a trap set up by the three victims, weren't you?'

'Please explain what you are talking about, Major,' Tremayne cut in. He was sitting with Foggy resting his head on his lap, which rather belied his stern lawyerly act.

I sighed, and detailed the ploy to extract Alfred Palgrave's inheritance from him. I was careful about how much, or rather how little, I said about the reason for the blackmail. They sat throughout in stony silence.

'I had no idea what they were doing,' Marriott snapped, evidently furious.

'So you say.' I spoke dryly, then turned to Margaret Saunders. 'You knew your husband was planning to run away with Dolores Palgrave.' I was certain she did and wanted to goad her.

'He wasn't running away.' She rose to the bait. 'He was going for a fling, then he'd have come back. He's done the same thing often enough before. He would never leave his precious company, or his money.'

'Margaret, you knew about the scheme!' Cardhew exclaimed in outrage.

'No, no, just his plans for Monte Carlo,' Margaret assured him. I don't think he believed her, I certainly didn't.

'My God, I'd have killed him myself if I'd known,' Marriott muttered.

'You would not, Marcus,' Gabriel said quietly, then turned to me. 'The auction was a charade, were his plans to retire?'

'Yes,' I replied.

'Then they have reaped their just rewards,' she said calmly.

'Major Lennox,' Tremayne demanded sharply. 'I will remind you that I have a train to catch.'

'Fine.' I took a few steps then turned to face them again. 'Dolores Palgrave died because she was angry.'

'She was always angry,' Alfred said.

'She wanted to run the company, didn't she?' I replied.

'Yes, and she was clever enough,' he agreed.

'I think you mean devious enough,' Margaret said.

'Major Lennox,' Tremayne reminded me.

'Yes, yes,' I said with some exasperation. 'Dolores was infuriated by a note that had been pinned to some sheets of newspaper that someone had left in her room, or pushed under her door,' I stated. 'Swift will read the note out.' I glanced over at him.

He pulled his notebook from his pocket and flicked through it. '*Your greed has found you out, and here's the proof,*' he read aloud. '*Sleep well, Jezebel, for tomorrow brings the noose.*'

'She was a Jezebel,' Gabriel Marriott said loudly enough for everyone to hear. Nobody argued the point.

'But you really should explain how she was killed,' Lady Clementine insisted.

I tried to be brief and ended by telling them the pink pages were from Devlin Saunders' newspaper.

'The arsenic was in the rat poison from the shed,' Fossett called out.

'Exactly, thank you Constable Fossett,' I said.

'And the pathology laboratory has confirmed she did die from inhaling arsine gas,' Cyril Fletcher added, helpfully. 'I called them this morning.'

'Right.' I stopped pacing and faced them.

'What if she hadn't set the paper alight?' Alfred Palgrave asked.

'I doubt she would have died,' I replied.

'How was the rat poison fixed into the paper?' Tremayne asked.

'It was mixed with water in a shallow bath, and the paper was left to soak it up. Once dried, the pages were ironed flat,' I explained 'Weren't they?' I said, and looked the culprit straight in the eyes.

# CHAPTER 29

He didn't flinch.

'I wouldn't know,' he said.

'Yes, you would.' I lowered my voice.

Swift held up the list the girls had glued back together. I pointed to it. 'Your name's on this list of debtors.'

'I think you'll find it isn't.'

'Not "Ackroyd", I mean your real name. We informed Scotland Yard this morning, they are searching for your real identity now. They'll find out who you are.' I advanced on him.

He laughed.

The room was as still as a summer's day before a storm.

I swung around. 'Lady Clementine, you lied.'

'When?' she replied.

'Frequently,' I rejoined. 'But most specifically you lied when you said Ackroyd opened the front door to let you out the morning of Saunders' murder.'

'I may have forgotten the details. I am an old lady, after all.' She shrugged, entirely without remorse.

'Who could move around this house easily?' I asked the rhetorical question. 'Who is able to search through everyone's belongings? Who knows the movements of the staff. Who wears gloves at all times? Who else, but you?' I turned back to face him.

'That doesn't prove a damn thing,' he drawled. Gone was the posturing, the peeved tone, the false outrage. He looked me in the eye, oozing confidence, a light curve to his lips as though it were somehow really quite amusing.

'I thought your constable said it was a right-handed man?' Palgrave said. 'He's left-handed. I noticed when he poured the tea.'

'Another ruse to throw us off the scent,' I replied.

'It can't be Ackroyd,' Margaret Saunders suddenly burst out in disbelief. 'He's a servant.'

'Exactly,' I said. 'He knew where Smedley kept his powders, and how and why he was so particular about water in his carafe. He had access to the iron to press the paper. He had keys to every room.' This is what I'd realised when Tubbs had knocked over all the chess pieces on the girls' incident board. It had to be someone who could access everywhere and move about unremarked. 'Who else was better placed to do all that, other than a servant.'

Ackroyd grinned. 'And a good one, don't you think?' His accent was as cut-glass as mine. He seemed be enjoying himself, almost showboating.

'I thought you were excellent,' Lady Clementine said in support.

'Clementine, did you know!' Tremayne was incredulous.

'No, no, Edwin, how could I?' She waved a hand. 'But he had a little "je ne sais quoi". I felt that we may have met before in some distant past.'

I had to bite back a grin. 'Who are you really, Ackroyd?' I asked again. I saw Fossett from the corner of my eye advancing on him, handcuffs at the ready.

'I'm not saying a word,' Ackroyd, or whoever he was, replied calmly. He was close to the door; I knew he was ready to run.

Marriott leapt to his feet. 'Stay where you are.' He pulled a gun from a hidden shoulder holster and pointed it.

That broke the trance-like atmosphere, and everybody stood up and started shouting.

'Shoot him, shoot him.' Cardhew pointed at Ackroyd.

'Hurry, he'll kill us all, hurry,' Margaret cried out in support.

'No, you can't just shoot an unarmed man,' Palgrave objected. 'Gabriel, stop him.'

Cyril Fletcher had grabbed the Malacca cane and was wielding it like a club.

'Oh, sir,' Greggs called out, then rushed to Lady Clementine and Foggy, to stand with his arms outstretched in protection.

Swift grabbed Ackroyd by the shoulders. 'You're under arrest. Turn around.'

Fossett dashed up and tried to apply the cuffs. Ackroyd suddenly ducked and twisted, knocking Swift against the door. Marriott stepped forward, gun at the ready. Fossett snatched Ackroyd's arm; he wrested it away and threw a punch. Fossett ducked but was wrong-footed. I pushed through the milling crowd, shoved Ackroyd backwards and pinned him against the wall.

'Handcuffs,' I yelled at Fossett who rushed forward with Swift, and they managed to lock the handcuffs onto his wrists.

'Marriott put that gun away.' Tremayne strode to his side.

Marriott did as told while we wrestled Ackroyd over to the nearest chair.

'Now you sit down and stay there,' Fossett ordered. The lad was red in the face with his helmet knocked askew.

Ackroyd leaned back in the chair, his hair falling over his brow. He looked at me and gave a low laugh. 'Bravo, old boy. I didn't think you had it in you.'

'Don't you move.' Fletcher came over, still holding the Malacca cane aloft. I took it from him and put it back on the table. Someone jostled against it. There were far too many people in the room.

'Right, clear the room,' I shouted. It had the effect of stopping them in their tracks, but they didn't actually move.

'You'll hang for this,' Cardhew shouted at Ackroyd.

'You are an utter fool,' Lady Clementine told him. 'For heaven's sake, go away.'

'Clementine, I will not allow you to speak to Sebastian in that manner...' Margaret turned to berate her step-mother.

'Margaret.' Lady Clementine turned to her. 'Please, just leave my house and do not return. I really have had enough.'

'What?' Margaret stared. 'What do you mean?'

'I have done as much as I can for you, Margaret, but I think it is time you led your life independently of me.'

'Are you telling me to go?' Margaret instantly bristled.

'Yes, and if you should ever attempt to return I shall have the gates locked.' Lady Clementine spoke with determination. 'And I shall ask Sir Edwin to take legal action against you.'

'You aren't thinking clearly, Clementine. I'm your family. I'm all you have.' Margaret wasn't going quietly.

'No, Margaret. I am all *you* have. I have tried to be a mother to you, but I will not shoulder the burden any longer. You are finally free of that appalling man you chose to marry, now you can go and make a decent life for yourself, and leave me alone,' Lady Clementine said in steely tone.

'Come, Margaret.' Sebastian Cardhew slid his arm under hers. 'We'll take the next train home. We have work to do in London. We must find all those funds Devlin left behind.'

'But I can't leave her, Daddy said everything would be mine one day. I just have to wait…' Margaret appeared to be almost dazed.

'Margaret, you really don't want to remain in this tedious backwater. Come along now.' He was insistent and she finally allowed him to lead her away.

Swift had taken a seat next to Ackroyd and had begun to read the formal terms of arrest. Fossett stood on guard, glaring fiercely at the prisoner.

Greggs sidled up, holding Foggy in his arms. 'Sir, may I return to the Manor? Lady Clementine has assured me she is quite safe.'

'Yes, off you go, and tell m'ladies what happened, would you? I'll be home as soon as we're finished here.'

'Very well, sir,' he said and tottered off.

Cyril Fletcher was staring at Ackroyd, who didn't seem at all concerned at his predicament or Swift's attempted interrogation.

'I'm absolutely astonished, Heathcliff. I'd never have imagined it was him. What gave the game away, eh?'

'My cat, actually,' I told him, then grinned. 'I'll explain later, Cyril. Would you call the police in Oxford, please? We need a secure cell for the prisoner. He's too damn clever to be held at the local station.'

'Well if you insist, but I really would like to hear what's what.' He followed Greggs out of the room, shaking his head.

Tremayne and Marriott were deep in conversation. Gabriel went to join them and they left together without a backward glance.

'Lady Clementine,' I called to her as she headed to the door. 'We will need to talk to you later.'

'Any time, my dear Heathcliff, I'm not going anywhere.' She walked out with a determined step.

'Can I be of help?' Alfred Palgrave came over; he was the last of them.

'Go into the corridor and close the door behind you. Don't let anyone in until the police arrive,' I told him.

'Very well,' he agreed and went to carry out orders. He seemed to have regained some colour, and his confidence with it. I suppose that came from the fact he hadn't won the bidding and the loan would be voided when he returned the money.

I turned to Ackroyd. 'Who are you?' I demanded again.

'He won't tell us, sir,' Fossett said.

'You have no actual proof against me, do you, old boy?' Ackroyd grinned. 'You'll never make this stick.'

'Why did you do it?' I demanded.

He fixed his gaze on me, sharp intelligence glinting in his eyes. 'Why would you think?'

'Either you suffered at their hands, or someone close to you did,' I guessed.

'Were you working with Lady Clementine?' Swift demanded.

'I've already told you.' Ackroyd frowned. 'I wasn't working with anyone.'

'But you're obviously not a butler,' I said. 'So what were you doing here?'

'I am a butler; I took the job after I fell on hard times.'

'But not under your true name,' Swift stated.

Ackroyd smiled again.

'You killed three people,' Fossett accused him. 'That's murder, that is.'

'I killed many more during the war,' Ackroyd replied. 'Nobody mentioned murder then.'

'Who did you serve with?' I sat down on another chair to face him.

'Rifle Brigade, 8th battalion. We were shot at quite a lot.'

I nodded. The rifle brigade were frontline and took huge losses. The green jackets always went in first and had a reputation for fearlessness.

'And after the war?' I asked quietly.

He glanced away. 'My brother was killed in battle, he was the heir. I was reported lost. My mother became...' He pushed his hair back from his forehead. 'She became confused and kept wandering off. I think she was searching for us. My father lost sight of her one day and they found her in the lake. He went to pieces after that. The place was let to go to rack and ruin. He ran up debts, those debts were purchased...' His lips turned down. 'He hanged himself. I came home, rather battered but alive, and they were all gone. There was nothing left, aside from their graves in the churchyard. The estate had been foreclosed, broken up and sold.' He glanced up at us. 'So I thought I'd better get a job, and voila, here you find me.'

Nobody spoke for a moment.

'It doesn't matter if they deserved it, they'll still get you,' Fossett told him with sympathy in his voice

'*They seek him here, they seek him there, those blighters seek him everywhere,*' Ackroyd misquoted from *The Scarlet Pimpernel*, then laughed. 'They haven't got me yet.'

'At least that rhymes,' I said. 'The one you wrote for Dolores was dreadful.'

He acted affronted. 'I thought it quite apt, actually.'

'So you admit it?' Swift threw in.

'Good Lord, no. I'm merely playing along with your game,' he replied.

'It's not a game, and you'll hang for murder,' Swift retorted.

'How are you going to convict me?' he drawled.

'You brought the sword stick with you from Devlin Saunders' house in London,' Swift stated. 'That was an error. You said it was here when you arrived, which was untrue. Margaret Saunders knew her husband didn't bring it. Nobody else could have done.'

'Nonsense, anyone could have brought it.' He laughed it off.

'But if Margaret swears you did, what do you think will be the outcome?' I rejoined.

His laughter died on his lips. 'You mean she'll lie from simple spite?'

'Her, or one of the others. You can't trust any of them, and there's a reward of two thousand pounds up for grabs,' I reminded him.

'Well, I'll just have to have faith in the jury being trusted and true, won't I.' He shrugged, although I could see uncertainty growing in his eyes.

I should have pressed him harder, forced a confession out of him, but I didn't have the heart. I might have done the same in his shoes, although I doubt I'd have been able to act the butler.

Swift stood up, obviously intending to take up where I'd

left off, but loud voices and stern orders were heard from the hallway, followed by the tramping of boots.

The door opened.

'Police. You've caught a murderer?' A uniformed inspector addressed us. A bevy of men were crowded behind him.

'We have,' Swift declared. 'We are holding him under arrest for the murders of three people in this house.'

'Right, we'd best take him to the station then. Come on, lads.'

# EPILOGUE

*Braeburn Castle, Braeburn. May 10th 1923*
*Lennox,*

*We have arrived home after a long train ride. Angus has now added steam engine noises to his repertoire. Florence is well and thoroughly enjoyed our time in Ashton Steeple. Please pass our thanks to Persi, Greggs, Tommy and Cook.*

*Nicky caused chaos; he stole a lamb chop from a diner and buried it under a gentleman's top hat. They were very kind about the trespass, but I think he should stay at home until he's better behaved.*

*I assume you heard Ackroyd escaped. There was a telegram waiting for me when we arrived at the castle.*

*I've no idea how the police escort failed to spot the pretence. Feigning sickness was so obviously a contrivance, and he did it close to a busy railway station — that should have been more than enough to alert them to his intentions.*

*Needless to say, Billings is furious and has ordered a full investigation.*

*The Yard have identified him as Sidney Clayton Wood-roffe. He was a second lieutenant in the 8th battalion Rifle Brigade and came from Lewes in Sussex. His story fits with the* *one he told us at Ashton Hall. He was decorated for valour, <u>and</u> had a batman called Victor Ackroyd, who was killed in a German air raid on their HQ.*

*Oxford have offered a reward for information on his whereabouts, but there's been no reported sighting of him.*

*Talking of rewards, I'm afraid I doubt Margaret Saunders will pay up unless he's caught.*

*I hope that isn't a dreadful blow to you, given your circumstances. I do recall Sir Edwin Tremayne saying he may be able to arrange for the interest on your debt to be written down.*

*I will keep you abreast of the situation regarding Ackroyd, or rather Sidney Woodroffe.*

*With most sincere regards,*
*Swift.*

I put the letter with the others on my desk. Sunlight filtered through the windows, birds sang in the garden, and all had become peaceful in my quiet corner of the world. Tubbs came to sit in the basket amid the pile of bills; he purred away to himself, his eyes closing as he nodded off to sleep.

I blotted the nib of my pen and began writing.

*The Manor, Ashton Steeple, Oxfordshire. May 12th 1923*
*Swift,*

*News of a more positive nature; Marcus Marriott has dissolved the Royal Buckingham Financial Services company and forgiven ALL debts, including mine.*

*Lady Clementine came with Marriott and Gabriel the day*

314

*after you left. Apparently Gabriel had persuaded Marriott some time ago that he should close the company the moment he had the chance. He has now signed a binding agreement with Tremayne for this to be done once the legal necessities have been completed.*

*In recognition of this extraordinarily generous act, Lady Clementine has waived any payment from Marriott for the shares.*

*I don't need to tell you that the closure of the Royal Buckingham has brought enormous relief to us. We opened a bottle of champagne with them to toast their generosity. Once Marriott relaxes he's an interesting chap, and Gabriel is really very sweet.*

*Life here, and in the village, is returning to the usual rural rhythm. Excitement has died down over the murders at Ashton Hall. There is much speculation as to the whereabouts of Ackroyd, or rather, Sidney Woodroffe. The common belief is that he's escaped to foreign parts. Although they continue to 'seek him here, and seek him there'.*

*Lady Clementine is a colourful addition to our small community and still has all the older chaps vying for her attention, including Cyril Fletcher, and Greggs, of course.*

*Persi has decided we should begin work on the roof as it has been leaking. Fossett has offered the use of the police ladder — when it's not being used to rescue cats from trees. I have ordered slates and copper nails, and Brendan has volunteered to help, although neither of us has a head for heights.*

*Sincerely,*

*Lennox.*

'Sir, sir!' Tommy came dashing in. 'A telegram! It just came, the postboy brought it and Mr Fogg chased him all the way to the end of the drive. I keep telling him he wouldn't hurt a fly but he doesn't listen.'

'The post boy or the dog?' I held my hand out for the telegram.

'Neither of 'em, sir.' Tommy laughed. 'What's it say? Have they caught Mr Ackroyd, 'cause I don't think they should. Lady Clementine said he was a proper war hero...'

'Yes, thank you, Tommy.' I interrupted the flow and slit open the envelope to pull out the telegram. It was unusual that it should be sealed.

*Lennox. STOP. Court has passed sentence on Birdcage Murders culprit. STOP. Reward can now be paid. STOP. You and Swift are entitled to it all. STOP. I have sent news directly to him. STOP. DCI Billings. Scotland Yard. STOP.*

I read it twice, and then once again.

'What does it say, sir?' Tommy was almost hopping on the spot in front of my desk.

'It says we can afford to employ a roofer to fix the roof,' I replied, then closed my eyes for a moment to thank the man upstairs for the good fortune that was ours. 'Will you ask m'lady to come here, Tommy,' I said. 'And tell Greggs to mix a jug of Pimms.'

'But it's only four o'clock, sir,' he reminded me.

'I don't care what time it is, Tommy.'

'Right you are, sir.' He didn't go. 'Did I tell you about the newspaper we're doing at school, sir? It was my idea and Mrs Summerour has agreed to print the very first edition.'

I sighed. 'Fine, I hope it isn't full of murder and death.'

'No, sir, well, not entirely, but the front page is really good. I wrote it myself and do you know what the head-line is?'

'No,' I replied thinking I'd have to ring for Greggs myself. 'What is it?'

'The butler did it!' he said, and then skipped off merrily in the direction of the kitchen.

I do hope you have enjoyed this book. If you'd like to leave a review, I'd be very grateful, but please don't be tempted to give any hint of who the culprit is. I have had reviews where the culprit has actually been named and it's really upsetting for everyone. Sorry, if I'm sounding school marm'ish, and I'm sure you wouldn't dream of doing such a thing.

Would you like to take a look at the Heathcliff Lennox website? As a member of the Readers Club, you'll receive the FREE audio short story, 'Heathcliff Lennox – France 1918' and access to the 'World of Lennox' page, where you can view portraits of Lennox, Swift, Greggs, Foggy, Tubbs, Persi and Tommy Jenkins. There are also 'inspirations' for the books, plus occasional newsletters with updates and free giveaways.

You can find the Heathcliff Lennox Readers Club, and more, at karenmenuhin.com

You can also follow me on Amazon for immediate updates on new releases.

* * *

Here's the full **Heathcliff Lennox** series list. All the ebooks are on Amazon. Print books can be found on Amazon and online through your favourite book stores.

Book 1: Murder at Melrose Court

Book 2: The Black Cat Murders
Book 3: The Curse of Braeburn Castle
Book 4: Death in Damascus
Book 5: The Monks Hood Murders
Book 6: The Tomb of the Chatelaine
Book 7: The Mystery of Montague Morgan
Book 8: The Birdcage Murders
Book 9: A Wreath of Red Roses
Book 10: Murder at Ashton Steeple
Book 11: To be announced! Hopefully ready for Christmas 2023, I will let you know soonest.

And there are Audio versions read by Sam Dewhurst-Phillips, who is superb. He 'acts' all the voices – it's just as if listening to a radio play. These can be found on Amazon, Audible and Apple Books.

You may like to try the **Miss Busby** series. So far there is only one book, but more are in the pipeline.

Miss Busby Investigates: Murder at Little Minton

## A little about Karen Baugh Menuhin

1920s, Cozy crime, Traditional Detectives, Downton Abbey – I love them! Along with my family, my dog and my cat.

At 60 I decided to write, I don't know why but suddenly the stories came pouring out, along with the characters. Eccentric Uncles, stalwart butlers, idiosyncratic servants, machinating Countesses, and the hapless Major Heathcliff Lennox. A whole world built itself upon the page and I just followed along.

Now, some years later I have reached number 1 in USA and sold over a million books. It's been a huge surprise, and goes to show that it's never to late to try something new.

I grew up in the military, often on RAF bases but preferring to be in the countryside when we could. I adore whodunnits, art and history of any description.

I have two amazing sons – Jonathan and Sam Baugh, and his wife, Wendy, and five grandchildren, Charlie, Joshua, Isabella-Rose, Scarlett and Hugo.

I am married to Krov, my wonderful husband, who is a retired film maker and eldest son of the violinist, Lord Yehudi Menuhin. We live in the Cotswolds.

For more information you can contact me via my email address, karenmenuhinauthor@littledogpublishing.com

Karen Baugh Menuhin is a member of The Crime Writers Association, The Author's Guild, The Alliance of Independent Authors and The Society of Authors.

Printed in Great Britain
by Amazon